The Wedding Lies

ALSO BY JADE LEE WRIGHT

The Baby Group
The Wedding Lies

THE WEDDING LIES

JADE LEE WRIGHT

JOFFE BOOKS

Joffe Books, London
www.joffebooks.com

First published in Great Britain in 2026

This book is a work of fiction. Names, characters, businesses, organisations, places and events are either the product of the author's imagination or are used fictitiously. Any resemblance to actual persons, living or dead, events or locales is entirely coincidental. The spelling used is British English except where fidelity to the author's rendering of accent or dialect supersedes this. The right of Jade Lee Wright to be identified as author of this work has been asserted in accordance with the Copyright, Designs and Patents Act 1988.

Cover art by Nick Castle

ISBN: 978-1-80573-470-3

To the boys who stole my heart, Felix and Chester

PROLOGUE

Charlotte Walker staggers down a cobbled pathway beneath an inky sky. The alcohol drains from her veins with every step, her senses sharpening as she sobers. Heavy footsteps thud behind her, forcing her to pick up her pace. If she can just get to the cathedral on Stag Hill, she'll be safe. Someone will help her.

She fights the urge to stop for as long as she can, but exhaustion soon makes her legs give way. Clutching onto the iron fencing trailing up the hill, she gasps for breath. The air stings as it enters her lungs, winter demanding penance for what she's done.

Standing in the mist, bathed in the glow of the moonlight, she looks around, drawing in the cool night air. She thinks she's lost him, for now. Shoulders sagging like a wilting carnation, tendrils of her breath drift away from her. Nothing, not even a lone fox or an owl disturbs the stillness.

Allowing hope to surface, she thinks of her boyfriend down in the town centre, searching for her. She wishes she'd stayed there, by the River Wey, waiting. But her patience had stretched thin, and she'd started walking.

She can't be sure when he'd started following her. She'd been too consumed in her drunken haze to care. If only she'd noticed before leaving the warmth of the pubs and the laughter of people inside behind.

Her phone lets out a shrill tone, shattering the silence. With trembling fingers, she tries to mute it, but it falls from her hands. The screen splinters as it lands on the ground. She's about to bend to pick it up when he speaks. Two words that turn her cold.

'Found you.'

She runs, a primitive act, abandoning her phone as she sprints further up the hill.

Frost glistens on the bricks of the cathedral as she makes her way to the base of the stone steps. An irrefutable sense of dread washes over her as she hammers on the door, pulling at the handle, but it's locked.

Boots hit stone, and as she snaps her head in the direction of the sound, a hand wraps around her mouth, muffling her screams. The last thing she sees before her world goes black is his cold, ghoulish smile.

And just like that, on a frostbitten January night in Guildford, Charlotte Walker vanishes.

You are cordially invited to the

Wedding

of

Ivy Cohen
and
Stephen James

Saturday, January 17th 2026
at four o'clock
Shadowmoor Lodge, Surrey Hills

Reception to follow

CHAPTER 1

Ivy
One Week Before the Wedding

I pluck a suitcase from the pile of luggage littering the airport floor. It's lighter than I remember, but I'm too busy fighting my way through the swarm of angry passengers in Terminal Four to check.

Spotting Stephen outside the men's bathroom, I absent-mindedly graze my thumb over my engagement ring. Biting my lip, I take a moment to appreciate him. Even under the harsh glow of the fluorescent lights, he looks good. Dark wisps of hair frame his face. Those arresting, deep-set blue eyes find me amongst the crowd, making my heart somersault. I grin, tugging the suitcase along behind me as I stride towards him. Whistling, he looks me up and down, making my ears grow hot.

'Good to go?' he asks, grabbing the suitcase. He dumps it on top of the other bags already loaded on the trolley.

'Yep. Sorry, that broken carousel's a nightmare,' I say, dabbing beads of sweat from my forehead. 'Let's just get married!' My heart thumps eagerly as I smooth down my merino wool jumper.

'We have to see if my mum approves of you first,' he teases, lightly tapping my backside as we make our way through the crowded terminal.

'Ha!' I give him a playful shove, but as I look away, my smile falls. 'Is this outfit okay?'

'You asked me that three times before we left home,' he says, grabbing me around the waist and pulling me in. 'She'll love you, Ivy.'

He bends to kiss me. 'Besides, your ass looks great in those . . . what're they called?'

'Jeggings,' I laugh, touching a tangle of blonde curls fallen from my fishtail braid. 'I'm just nervous.'

'What for?' He tucks the strand of hair behind my ear.

'It's just a lot, isn't it? Meeting all your family right before we get married. What if they *don't* like me?'

'They'll like you because you make me happy,' he says.

'That's so cliché.' I grin, shaking my head at him, but inside I'm beaming. I don't think I'll ever get over just how lucky I am to have found Stephen.

Swiping right had been easy enough. I'd been nursing a hangover in bed, a cup of coffee in hand when I'd downloaded the dating app two years ago. I'd done it out of boredom, my usual C25K run postponed after a night in with a bit too much prosecco. The guy I'd been seeing had ghosted me, and I'd been licking my wounds, needing the validation that I was, in fact, desirable. Stephen had been the first person I'd matched with, and from the moment we started chatting I knew he was different, not just because of his British charm either.

He'd recently moved from England, alone with no family or friends, on the hunt for a fresh start — and so I'd taken him under my wing. Helped him get a job in photography, which worked well whenever I needed someone to make a portfolio for a new fashion line I was busy with. We complemented each other. If anything, we've gone from strength to strength in our relationship over these last two years.

'C'mon, you. Let's get out of here,' he says, steering me out of Heathrow Airport and towards the taxi rank.

Sleet lashes down outside, and as we join the queue for a taxi, I pull my scarf up to my chin.

'Isn't this supposed to be England?' I choke, grimacing as a gust of wind bites at my cheeks. 'It feels like we're in Antarctica.'

'This isn't South Africa. Wherever we go in Europe, it'll be freezing for you,' he chuckles. 'Brace yourself for our honeymoon.'

Rolling my eyes, I smile at the thought of our château in Bordeaux on the Garonne River. I've been dreaming of it for weeks, envisioning the quiet evenings snuggled up partially clothed after marvellous sex, sipping on a French Merlot. As a taxi pulls up in front of us, I blink away the thought.

'Where to?' the driver asks, his tired eyes staring at the stream of traffic in front of him.

'Hey, mate. Can you take us to Surrey Hills, Shadowmoor Lodge?' Stephen asks, opening the door for me as the driver nods.

I clamber in, out of the cold, while Stephen hoists the bags into the boot.

'Where you both from?' the driver asks, glaring at me in the rearview mirror.

'South Africa,' I say, offering him a genial smile. 'I mean, he's not. Stephen's from here originally.'

'Holiday?'

'Yes, I guess so. We're getting married!' I say.

Stephen wedges himself into the car beside me, his lips cold as he presses them to mine.

'Married! Wow.' The driver gives us a gold-toothed smirk. 'My advice? Don't do it!' he cackles.

'Thanks,' I mutter, forcing a tight smile.

We pull into the gridlocked traffic, and I glance at Stephen, who squeezes my knee, holding my gaze until I tilt my head to his shoulder.

A story of a local woman blares through the speakers as we head down the M25.

'Thirty-one-year-old Charlotte Walker was last seen at a riverside pub in Guildford,' the radio presenter says. 'Her friends all went home, but she'd stayed behind, waiting for her boyfriend to pick her up. He never found her, or so he's saying.'

'Can you believe it?' I shudder. 'She's my age.'

'Awful,' Stephen says, pulling me close.

'Here,' the driver huffs, tossing a rolled-up newspaper at us.

Unspooling the paper, I grip the pages, staring at a photograph of a woman with dark skin and black corkscrew curls accentuating her features. She looks so full of life, with a big smile and eyes that sparkle.

'She's beautiful,' I whisper.

Stephen grunts in response, the way he always does whenever I make a comment about another woman's appearance. Never looks, barely bats an eyelid. He's always said I'm the only woman he notices, but it's hard to believe. I know I'm not ugly, but I wouldn't say I'm particularly beautiful. Not compared to some of the women we pass on the streets, women I know are far prettier than I am. Still, Stephen will never acknowledge them. It's one of the many things I adore about him.

The news ends, and the radio presenter starts wittering away to a guest on the show, the missing woman already forgotten. Turning my attention away from the article, I gaze out to the motorway. As much as I try, I can't seem to get the missing woman out of my thoughts.

'Do you think they'll find her?' I ask after a while.

'It's been a week already. It's not looking good,' Stephen says, still studying the paper, but I ignore him.

* * *

Thunder cracks, rattling the skeletal trees as the taxi inches down a rutted dirt road. Kneading my knuckles into my tightening chest, my heart accelerates. Deep in the bowels of the countryside, we have entered a hinterland, and I can see no easy way out. Branches scratch at the car window, as if they're trying to get to me, pull me into their embrace.

A fallow deer ventures from the bracken, stopping at the sight of the taxi. A buck follows, lowering his antlers as a warning not to get too close. Grumbling, the driver idles, waiting for their next move.

'Look!' I breathe, feeling calmer by their presence.

'Don't get too excited,' Stephen laughs. 'We hunt them. It's the season for hunting that doe right now.'

My jaw drops. 'We?'

'My family. Every year.'

How had I not known this about him? I look into those cobalt-blue eyes, trying to picture him shooting an animal, but I can't. This is the man who refuses to go to an animal rescue centre because, if he does, he'll leave with every single creature in there.

He'd driven over a baboon once. It had darted out into the road while we were on a road trip through South Africa, singing along to 'Danger! High Voltage' by Electric Six. That song has never been the same since. Stephen hadn't been able to face getting out of the car to look. I'd had to do it. I never had told him that the baboon had a baby gripped into the fur of its belly, that there was no saving them. I'd lied. Told him I'd seen it run off into the density of the forest, in shock but alive. The relief on his face had been worth it.

'And you're included in this hunting?' I ask, slowly, almost mechanically.

'When I'm here.' He shrugs.

His words thread through me as I stare out at the deer. 'Didn't know you could shoot.' I didn't know he had it in him either, but I don't say that.

'Oh, I can't. I have a terrible aim.'

His joke falls flat. I try to mask a shiver with a wan smile, but I'm poleaxed. I've never liked guns.

'This the place?' the driver asks hesitantly, interrupting my thoughts.

'The one and only,' Stephen says as the car pulls up to a clearing in the woods.

I squint up at a cabin nestled beneath a canopy of dead leaves, looking out to a frosty lake. It's one of seven cabins dotted around the grounds, and bigger than I expected it to be. Bigger than my own home, despite my crippling mortgage. It's two storeys, with a pitched A-framed roof and a central window hiding behind the branches of towering trees. Icicles drip from the sill, water landing on the veranda with gentle pitter-pattering taps. A cloud of smoke billows from the stone chimney and the moss-covered roof sags, as though the cabin itself is weighed down, sad.

'Mum's given us the best one. She calls it the honeymoon cottage,' he says, opening the car door.

If this is considered the best, I wonder what the other cabins are like. Maybe it's better in summer, when the trees are lush, and wildflowers scatter the ground. Maybe it will look different at sunrise, when a kaleidoscope of warm reds, deep purples and gold shimmer through the trees.

Stepping out onto the frost-tipped grass, I feel it crunch beneath my boots. I blow into my hands, the cold air a shock to my system. A gust of wind carrying the stink of fertiliser and something else, something rotten, hits me. My eyes swivel to Stephen, who covers his mouth with his hand.

'Ah. The smell of the countryside!' he says, his voice muffled beneath his fingers.

I hold my breath, a pigeon whistling past my head. It lands on a rusted lantern hanging from a tree standing sentry as bamboo windchimes clatter in the breeze.

A voice startles me, making me spin on my heels.

'So, you're the infamous Ivy.' Stephen had taken a long time to do the initial introductions. He'd wanted to make sure we were serious I guess, but we've connected in recent months over the upcoming wedding, so his mum is instantly recognisable now under her umbrella, her weathered face familiar from our video calls. 'Nice to finally meet you.'

'Lovely to meet you, Ingrid.' I try not to squirm as my face is crushed to Ingrid's bosom.

While Stephen hauls our luggage from the car, Ingrid ushers me into the warmth of the cabin. It's redolent with a deep, hearty aroma of caramelised onions, roasting garlic and beef, earthy and strong.

'Follow me. I'll show you to your room,' Ingrid says, ambling down the hallway.

The lacquered wood walls are adorned with vintage photo frames. I spot Stephen, frozen in time within them. I want to come back and revisit these pictures later, to acquaint myself with the younger version of my fiancé. The him before me. The beard is missing, along with that deep divot between his eyebrows I've come to love. South Africa, it seems, has hardened him.

The wooden floorboards groan beneath an old patchwork rug as I follow. There's a flicker of light from a distant room and a low rumble of voices, but we head in the opposite direction.

The bedroom door creaks as Ingrid pushes it open, revealing a four-poster bed and a mounted stag head looming over it. Its branched, gnarled antlers an impressive crown of bone. As we move into the room, I feel those glassy black eyes follow me.

'Let me look at you,' Ingrid says, holding me at arm's length. Her bony fingers are ice cold, sharp nails pressing into my skin.

'Gosh,' Ingrid whispers, eyes travelling my body up and down. 'Strange.'

My forehead creases, a cold shiver creeping down my spine. 'I'm sorry?'

Ingrid's eyes widen, broken blood vessels weaving like a fine lace across the whites of her eyes. 'Nothing. Nothing at all,' she says, shaking her head furiously. Her eyes stay glued to mine. 'I'll let you get settled in.'

Standing motionless, I watch as Ingrid shuffles out, clicking the door shut. Eventually, when I'm sure she isn't coming back, I breathe out, gazing around the room. It's musty, dust coating every available surface. The trees outside cast willowy shadows along the floorboards, their branches tap, tap, tapping at the windowpanes. I look out, to a gaggle of children in thickly padded snowsuits, dashing around between the ancient tree trunks. A peel of frivolous laughter drifts through the woods and up into the cabin. At seeing the children, so guileless, so completely carefree, my lips spread ear to ear. I feel the shimmer in my eyes as I watch them, unable to control my emotions, the ache in my heart that makes my chest expand.

Turning away, I survey the rest of the wood-toned room. The quilted bedsheets and arched dark wood mirror, desilvered, covered in dust. The bathroom with white quartz countertops and jarring lighting that seems to highlight my every imperfection. I'm busy running a fingertip along the antique bedframe when the door bursts open.

'Jesus,' I sigh, my pulse quick.

'Nice place, right?' Stephen says, hurling the bags into the room.

Bobbing my head, my smile doesn't quite meet my eyes.

'What's wrong?' he asks, the grin slipping from his face.

'Nothing. Nothing at all,' I say, aware I'm repeating my future mother-in-law's words. 'It's great.'

'Well, c'mon then, get unpacked,' he says. 'I want to test out the shower with you!'

I grin, warming as Stephen rolls my suitcase towards me.

Kneeling down, I release the clips and look inside.

'Stephen,' I say after a beat. 'This isn't my stuff.'

CHAPTER 2

I flip the case closed, inspecting it. It's almost identical to mine, bar a few scuffs here and there. I groan inwardly.

'I must've picked up the wrong one,' I sigh, running a hand through my hair.

Stephen laughs. 'Only you'd have such awful luck,' he says, flopping blithely down onto the bed. Angling his phone camera at me, he takes a picture.

'My wedding dress is in that suitcase!' I snap, twisting away from him, my eyes wet.

'Sorry, I just wanted to update the family WhatsApp group. Let them know. But, no signal,' he says, suppressing his laughter and holding up his phone.

I'm scowling in the image, hunched over the suitcase in the fading light of day. It's left unsent in his group chat.

'Stephen, please delete that,' I say. 'I look miserable.'

The cabin groans around us, juddering as the howling wind picks up its pace.

'Relax, no one's going to see it. We're too far from any cell towers for anything to go through.' He beckons me over to the bed. 'You don't get any service out here in the woods. It's too remote.'

Tilting my head to the lightbulbs hanging from an art deco branch above me, I try to blink back the tears in my eyes.

'It's part of the charm of this place,' Stephen is saying, but I'm only half listening. 'People come here to disconnect. Ride the horses. Hunt. Canoe. Enjoy the wildlife and riverside walks.' He looks at me and shrugs. 'Escape.'

'There's horses here?' I sniff, brightening slightly.

He nods, patting the empty space on the bed beside him.

'I'm sorry,' I breathe, dragging myself towards him. 'I'm just really stressed about the wedding, and losing the dress right now is the last thing I needed.'

'We'll get it back,' he says. 'Look, don't panic. Please? I'll call the airport. They'll find it for you. I'm sure the person with your case wants their stuff back just as much.'

A knock at the door pulls our eyes from the suitcase. Stephen leaps from the bed, throwing open the door. Ingrid stands at the threshold, peering in at us.

'Sorry to disturb. Dinner's ready in about ten minutes,' she says. 'Proper English Sunday roast.'

My heart drops. 'I was hoping to get an early night,' I say. 'It was a long flight.'

'But I made a big welcome dinner.' Ingrid's pupils flare, a shadow passing over her face.

'Oh, okay. Thank you,' I say meekly, watching as her eyes light up.

'That's lovely, Mum. Sorry, Ivy's had a bit of a disaster, she picked up the wrong suitcase at the airport.'

Ingrid gasps, stepping into the room. I return to the floor, flipping the case open again, as if miraculously my things will now appear inside. Ingrid crouches down beside me.

'Oh, no! I'm sorry. Do you need anything?' she asks.

I shake my head. 'I'm fine, thanks.'

'Don't be silly, you've had a long flight. Let me find you something a bit . . . comfier . . . to wear?' Ingrid's eyes hover over my clothing.

Surely the jumper isn't something she'd disapprove of. I'd made sure to select something refined, classy even. Is it the jeggings? Are they too tight? Or my heels — admittedly not the most sensible footwear for a cabin in the woods but I'd wanted to look nice. I wanted to look like the kind of girl you're proud to take home to your family.

'Thanks, Mum,' Stephen says. 'That'd be great.'

My cheeks flame furiously, but Ingrid scuttles from the room before I have a chance to object.

'I'm fine in what I'm wearing,' I mumble, disappointed that I'm being made to change from the outfit I'd spent hours choosing.

'She's just trying to help, my love. You've been wearing that for—' He pauses, checks his watch. 'Over sixteen hours now.'

I sigh again. Sixteen hours. No wonder I'm exhausted. Spent. All I want to do is dig out my paisley cotton pyjama set and get an early night, not be forced in close proximity with Stephen's family. Especially not after losing my luggage. I'm not in the mood.

'Can we call the airport now, before dinner? I'm really worried about my wedding dress.' I lift myself up from the floor, making my way over to him.

'Of course,' he says, tugging his phone out of his pocket. 'Oh, no.'

'What?'

'There's no signal,' he reminds me.

'Stephen!' I cry. 'I *need* to find it. We're getting married this week! I don't care about the rest of the stuff, but I need my wedding dress.' My heart thrums violently in my chest.

'I know. I know, darling,' he breathes, stilling me by the shoulders. 'Look, worst comes to worst, I'll just borrow a car. Drive back to the airport in the morning and find it.'

'Really?' I ask, my muscles relaxing under his grip.

He dips his head. 'Really.'

'Knock, knock,' Ingrid says, bustling in with a garish dress in her arms.

She lays it out on the bed, and I fight to keep the smile on my face. It's nothing I'd ever wear, but if I refuse, I'll come across as ungrateful.

'Thank you,' I force myself to say.

'You get yourself ready.' Ingrid grins, taking Stephen by the hand. 'We'll be downstairs in the lounge. Most meals and drinks will be here, I'm afraid. The other cabins will be taken up by the children, so this one offers us adults a bit of respite.' She winks.

'Is it big enough for everyone?' Stephen laughs, and I was thinking the very same thing. The James family is big. Will all of the adults fit in this cabin?

'We'll make it work, darling,' she says. 'The kids will be eating separately, earlier for their bedtime routines too. Besides, this cabin is the one with the extendable dining table, remember?' She's dragging Stephen from the room as she speaks.

When I'm alone, I stare down at the dress, all ruffles and a high neckline that makes me queasy.

Stripping my clothing reluctantly from my body, I burrow into the ruches until my head finds an opening to slip through. I do up as many buttons as I can before I can't reach any more, then stand back and look at my reflection in the floor-length mirror.

'Oh, God,' I mutter, picking at pieces of itchy material. I can't help it. Eight years of studying fashion design part-time has made me particular about the clothes I wear. This dress is significantly less comfortable than my own clothing. I can't help but think Ingrid's chosen the vilest thing she could find in her wardrobe.

I consider myself in the mirror. If I had my sewing kit with me, I'd make some adjustments or at least attach a waistbelt from my suitcase. Something to revamp this dismal dress. But right now, there's nothing I can do to save this ensemble.

Hesitantly, I head out of the bedroom and down the hall, donned in my future mother-in-law's clothes.

* * *

Pausing outside the lounge, I listen to the droning voices coming from inside.

'She's definitely different,' Ingrid says.

'Different how?' A voice I don't recognise chimes in.

'Well,' Ingrid says, lowering her voice. 'She's not his usual type. *At all.*'

The last few words come out in a hiss. I push myself up against the wall, closing my eyes. What do they mean, not his usual type? I realise then that I've never actually seen what Stephen's exes look like. He'd wiped his social media pages of any traces of them when they'd parted ways. It was easier to move on that way, he'd said. Pretend they'd never existed. It never bothered me. Until now.

I chew at my bottom lip. My knee-jerk reaction is to retreat back to the bedroom while I still can. I'm about to do just that when Stephen rounds the corner.

'There you are!' He grins, two wine glasses in his hands. 'Come on, everyone's in here.'

Begrudgingly, I follow. Ingrid and another woman straighten as Stephen leads me into the room. They're sitting beside a crackling fireplace, logs turning to ash. More heads turn in my direction from all corners of the room. They're like a pride of lions, this intense family all congregated in a room barely big enough for everyone. I swallow, breathe and smile.

'That's better.' Ingrid offers a smarmy smile, looking me up and down. 'I'm so glad the dress fits.'

'Thanks for lending it to me,' I say, trying not to scratch at my skin.

Ingrid places a hand on the small of my back. 'Let me introduce you to everyone,' she says.

I inhale, taking a large sip of the ruby-coloured wine. It's one of the nicest malbecs I think I've ever had. Intense. A mixture of pepper and blackcurrant. 'Sure,' I say, licking my lips.

I'm paraded around the room, meeting family members from aunts and uncles, first cousins, second cousins, even a grandfather. There's a barrage of questions. How am I? How was the flight? What do I do?

I start thinking about getting up in front of everyone to make a speech. Save myself from having to answer the same questions again and again. But I persevere until I've circled the room.

The most common question, and the reason everyone is gathered here, is if I'm ready for the wedding. Is there anything they can do to help? Everyone seems genuinely charged with anticipation for the big day.

I'm very aware the room is dominated by men. Women are few and far between, their skin glowing from the flames.

'Wow, big family!' I breathe, names already slipping from my memory. I haven't been paying attention, although I know I should. My lost suitcase gnaws at me. The anxiety over my missing wedding dress building.

'Yes, Stephen tells me your own is relatively small?' Ingrid says, steering me back towards the fireplace.

I shake my head, taking a large gulp of wine. 'Not small. Just not close.' I try to reply as truthfully yet succinctly as possible, while trying to put a stop to the topic. Talking about my family is goading. It brings out a darkness in me I'd rather not show.

Subtly, I bow out of the chat, finding Stephen across the room. He's immersed in a conversation with one of his cousins. A timid man in his thirties with fetid armpits and glasses magnifying his beady eyes. Eyes that had roved shamelessly down to my breasts when I'd been introduced.

Shuffling towards Stephen as discreetly as I can, I slip into their conversation.

'Sorry to hear your girlfriend can't make it,' Stephen says. 'I was looking forward to meeting her.'

'Wouldn't hold your breath, we broke up,' his cousin, whose name I can't recall, snivels.

'I'm so sorry, what happened?' I interject, finding my in.

Both men look up at me as though they've only just noticed my presence. I smile at them shyly, wondering if I've interrupted something. There's a flicker of annoyance in his cousin's eyes.

'Well, Ivy, she was a lying bitch. That's what happened.'

'Ben,' Stephen says with a wince, glancing at me.

I stay rooted to the spot, unsure what to say. Luckily, I don't have to say anything. Debbie, an aunt dripping in burnished gold jewellery, sidles up beside me.

'Will some of your family be making it to the wedding?' she asks. Her plump lips break apart, and I can't decide if her smile is friendly or not.

I stare into Debbie's shimmering eyes, flames dancing inside them. 'No.'

'Oh, you poor thing,' she says, touching my shoulder. The tawdry rings weighing down her fingers are cool against my neck.

Ingrid glides over, a crystal flute glass in hand. Her dark red lipstick is painted around the rim, and in the firelight, I can't help but think it looks like blood.

'It's okay, I have friends coming,' I say, looking from Ingrid to Debbie. 'They're the only family I need.'

Ingrid's expression remains unreadable. She motions for everyone to make their way to the dining room.

'Let me help you bring out the food,' I offer, but Ingrid shakes her head.

'You're a guest!' she scoffs. 'Take a seat.'

I can't help but feel like Ingrid's starting to give me a wide berth as I watch her hurry to the kitchen.

* * *

'So, Ivy. Stephen tells me you used to be married?' Ingrid says, bringing a forkful of beef to her lips.

'Engaged, Mum,' Stephen says, sharply.

'Engaged,' she parrots, cold eyes piercing mine, her lips curving up just slightly.

I nod, my head swimming from the wine. 'I was engaged, yes.' I really don't want to elaborate. Why should I? Tonight is about Stephen and me. This week is about us. I shouldn't need to relive the trajectory of my past. Not now, or ever.

When no one speaks, I take a deep intake of breath. They're going to make me talk about it.

'He ran off with my maid of honour,' I say, dolefully. 'Got her pregnant.'

'A week before the wedding,' Stephen adds, dunking a Yorkshire pudding into a thick sea of gravy.

A silence falls over the table. Cutlery forgotten, they all stare at me.

'I don't understand,' Ingrid says with a shake of her head. She's smiling, whether out of disbelief or vindictiveness I can't tell.

'I never understood it either,' I say, trying to sound lighthearted, but failing miserably. I take another sip of wine, willing the night to be over.

It's been easier over the years to talk about it, to seem nonchalant about what was the worst time of my life. I've shielded myself from the memories. Before, they'd penetrate into my very core, debilitate me. I've learned to protect myself.

Ingrid's hand is over her mouth. 'Your maid of honour?' she asks, for clarity, it seems.

I pierce a steamed carrot on my fork, sink my teeth into it and nod.

'They had a baby?' Ingrid asks, fingernails digging into the tabletop. 'Go on,' she pries.

I could be wrong, but her eyes seem to have grown hungry. Finishing a mouthful of food, I clear my throat in the otherwise silent room.

'Shiloh, yes. Beautiful little thing,' I say as Stephen finds my knee beneath the table. 'I can't be mad at them when it was clearly meant to be. They had a baby, and I think they're still together today.' I shrug. It's a line I've told myself so often I can almost start to believe it.

'Very diplomatic of you,' Ingrid observes, pursing her lips. It doesn't sound like a compliment.

Glancing up at her, our gazes fasten onto one another across the table. I can't help but feel like Ingrid's mood has shifted. She seems to be judging me, calculating my every word. It's disquieting, as intolerable as the dress I've been made to wear. But, I think, it could just be the wine getting to my head. Stephen always tells me wine seems to put me on edge, make me paranoid.

'And this all happened days before you were supposed to get married?' Natalia, one of Stephen's cousins, gawps. Her burgundy hair is cut in a stacked bob just grazing her shoulders. She's staring at me behind gold wire glasses, shaped like pentagons.

'Yes,' I say. Now, when I speak about Sean and Nesta, I feel nothing. I've trained myself to be that way. That isn't who I am anymore. I'm not the grieving fiancée, lost and confused. Angry. I've grown stronger. Moved on. Now, I have Stephen.

'Doesn't it make you anxious, being days away from this wedding?' Natalia asks, lustrous brown eyes searching mine.

I don't want to tell them that the last few days have been the most triggering, most anxiety-inducing days I've had in years. It is scary. I'm very aware that everything could be ripped away from me at any moment. It's all I've been thinking about, but I won't admit that. Not to them. Not even to myself.

'Should it?' I ask drily, cracking a smile. Looking around the table, I'm met with a loaded silence.

CHAPTER 3

'I really don't think your mum likes me, Stephen,' I say, sinking into bed beside him. I can't stop Ingrid's words from rattling around in my brain. *Not his usual type.*

I keep thinking of the way she'd held me and uttered the word '*strange*'. What had she meant? And why did she seem to turn on me the second I'd walked inside the cabin?

'You're just tired. It's been a long day.' He sighs, leaning over to plant a kiss on my cheekbone. 'Don't be silly.'

I'm trying not to be, but surely it's not all in my head. Something Stephen had said before we arrived is bothering me too. *We have to see if my mum approves of you first.* His mum doesn't approve of me. That much is obvious.

Pulling the butter-yellow duvet over myself, I glance up at the taxidermy above my head while Stephen turns the pages of a weathered Harlan Coben paperback.

Dinner had gone alright, for the most part. Better than I'd expected it to given Ingrid's hostility. Other than being peppered with questions from his family, I'd come away from the night relatively unscathed. It's the subtle quips from Ingrid irking me. So elusive no one else seemed to notice them, certainly not Stephen.

* * *

Six Days Before the Wedding

After a night of broken sleep, I reluctantly pull myself from the bed. Stephen's side is already empty, cold. I hope he's gone to the kitchen to make coffee.

Without my robe, I snatch his crumpled jumper off the floor, burrowing into its warmth. It's so cold my breath dances in front of me as I pad over to the window. Drawing back the curtains, I admire the ice patterns filling the window, swirling like ferns across the glass, then crack the window open slightly. The fresh morning air bites at my forearms.

'Better hurry, we need to get there before first light,' I hear someone say.

'Gonna snow all day. We have time, girls will still be out.' I'm sure that's Ben talking, the creepy cousin who keeps staring at my chest.

'I better say bye to Ivy before we go,' Stephen says.

'Oh, don't worry, darling, I'll let her know when she's up. You boys go have fun. Happy stalking.' Ingrid's voice is so close, it's startling.

My forehead creases at a series of metallic clunks. Rifles being hoisted up on shoulders. I back away from the window, feeling nauseous all of a sudden.

'Bring home some meat!' Ingrid calls after them.

* * *

Standing beneath the shower head, I lather shampoo into my hair. The hot water cascades down my body, and I tilt my head up to the steady stream. By the time I wrap a towel around myself, early morning pearlescent light is creeping in through a crack in the curtains.

Pulling on one of Stephen's jumpers, I venture down the hallway, my hair drip drying on my shoulders. The aroma of coffee beans, freshly ground, lures me into the kitchen. Stephen's left an old ceramic mug with chipped edges out on the countertop for me, the way he always does. One teaspoon of sugar is already sprinkled at the bottom. Next to it, there's a note scribbled on a scrap of paper.

Morning my future wife,
Heading out with the lads for a hunt.
Make yourself at home. I'll be back in a few hours.
Love you,
S.

I sigh, grabbing the pot of coffee. Stephen promised he'd find my suitcase first thing today. Without it, I can't relax. I check my phone, and even though there's still no signal I try calling the airport anyway. The call disconnects before it even rings.

Taking the first sip of bitter, strong coffee, I jump as Ingrid bustles in.

I blink in surprise at Ingrid inviting herself inside unannounced. Automatically, I straighten, knocking my knees together. I wish I'd chosen one of Stephen's baggier jumpers, but I didn't. I'm in something slim fit and it clings to my bare legs.

'Morning,' I say, offering a smile showing all of my teeth, hoping it detracts from how little I'm wearing.

Ingrid acknowledges me with a brusque look, dropping a pile of cardboard boxes down on the countertop. The thud is impressive. 'Hello, dear,' she says, her energy frenzied. She shakes her hands out, short of breath.

'What're those?' I eye the boxes.

'Wooden place cards,' Ingrid says, rifling through one of the drawers until she finds a pair of kitchen scissors. 'For the wedding.'

She punctures the Sellotape, gliding the blade swiftly across the packaging. My stomach leaps as I watch her pull out a piece of old driftwood with a name engraved in it.

'They're stunning!' I breathe, stepping closer.

'Yes,' Ingrid muses, inspecting her set of absurdly long, apricot-coloured fingernails.

Peering into the box, I see that almost one hundred pieces of driftwood lie inside. I catch glimpses of various names in a pretty, swirling font. 'Ingrid, I can't thank you enough.' There's a subtle inflection of surprise in my voice. I mean it, though. I am thankful. When Ingrid had insisted on planning our wedding, I'd been terrified. But, I think, looking down at the wooden place cards, she's doing an incredible job.

'Want some coffee?' I ask, the scepticism I harbour for Ingrid starting to shift just slightly. I start hunting through the cupboards for another mug when Ingrid steps in front of me, tugging open a cupboard above the toaster.

She plucks a mug from the shelf. 'I know my way around here,' she reminds me, her tone acrimonious as she reaches for the coffee pot.

When Ingrid's coffee is poured, I help her unwrap each individual piece of driftwood. My fingers graze over the names, many of which I don't know. Once again, I'm amazed by the enormity of Stephen's family. They take up the majority of the wedding party.

When I find the place cards with the names of my bridesmaids etched into the surface, I grin. There's no maid of honour this time, just three of my best girlfriends. Kayleigh, Georgie and Rosie. Three women who know me better than I even know myself.

'When do they get here?' Ingrid asks, tilting her head in the direction of the place cards.

'Friday evening,' I say. 'Day before the wedding.'

'Ah yes, now I remember. And the four of you will be staying here?'

I drop my chin. 'Yeah, they'll stay here with me. Stephen arranged another cabin for him and his groomsmen on Friday night, I think?'

'That's right.'

We work in silence, sorting the place cards into piles. Our seating plan is a little unorthodox, I know. Without my immediate family coming, my table includes my bridesmaids instead.

'They'll have flown all this way,' I reason when Ingrid wrinkles her nose in obvious disapproval.

'It's your wedding,' Ingrid says woodenly. 'Now get dressed, we need to take these over to the barn.'

After I'm dressed, back in the merino wool jumper and jeggings from yesterday, I follow Ingrid to the weather-beaten barn, its roof smothered in settling snow. The rotting door opens with a yank, disturbing roosting owls as the wood splinters. I step inside, taking it all in. Twelve large, round tables scatter the area, already draped in white gauze table runners. The exposed beams are cloaked in ivory tulle, with fairy lights strung up in every direction. It's very boho chic — and I kind of love it.

'Don't panic, we'll be putting some heaters in here on the day,' Ingrid assures me, her warm breath lingering in the air. 'Now, I have a little surprise for you.' She bends, her hands disappearing into one of the boxes stacked at the side of the barn.

'Oh my gosh,' I gasp as Ingrid lifts up a vintage sewing machine. It's wrapped in a sheer bow.

'Your centrepieces.' Ingrid smiles, setting it down and plucking another machine from the boxes.

Guilt washes over me. Maybe I've been wrong about Ingrid. These sewing machines are all vintage Singers. I don't even want to imagine what it must have cost to source twelve of them.

'This is so thoughtful of you,' I say. I'm blown away, tears stinging my eyes.

'It's all in the detail, isn't it? You're a fashion designer. I thought these would highlight that,' Ingrid says sagely, waving a hand, as if she hasn't done anything important.

We start arranging the place cards on tables, and as we do, my excitement bubbles. It's all coming together. My wedding, the one I thought I'd never have, is taking shape.

When we're done, we stand back to admire our work.

'Thank you, Ingrid,' I say, because even in such a dilapidated barn, I can't deny it's beautiful. It's better than I could have imagined.

'There's more arriving throughout the week,' Ingrid says, moving a sewing machine around on one of the tables. She fiddles with the bow.

'Ingrid?' someone calls.

Both of us blanch, snapping our heads up.

A gaggle of women barge into the barn, their eyes landing on Ingrid.

'Hurry up. Wedding cake's not going to bake itself.'

I smile at the women. The only person I remember is Natalia, who looks shell-shocked. The other aunts and cousins, who seem to have multiplied overnight, smile back at me.

'It looks amazing in here!' Natalia gushes, her effervescence infectious. 'Ivy, this is Freya. Stephen's sister.' Natalia pushes a striking-looking woman in her twenties towards me.

My mouth parts, my mind fizzing. Stephen has never mentioned a sister, just six burly brothers I'd met last night.

'Hello, Ivy,' Freya says curtly, hazel eyes regarding the barn. She's looking anywhere but at me. 'Sorry I missed you at dinner yesterday. Delayed flight.'

I think about stepping forward, giving her a hug, but decide against it. She doesn't seem like the hugging type. She has Ingrid's mannerisms. Abrupt, frosty. As I look at her, I think that she is winter. As cold and frigid as the season we're in. The sunbeam she's standing in does little to thaw her.

'It's great to meet you,' I say eventually, grappling for something else to say, but I come short.

Freya doesn't respond. Instead, she hooks an arm through Ingrid's. 'Bit dirty, no?' she says, nodding at an old set of light-up marquee letters spelling the word LOVE.

I turn my attention to the sign. It's riddled in grime and spider's webs, and even though this is Freya's family barn, I feel a rush of shame. Like somehow it all isn't good enough for anyone, like I'm being judged. Wrapping my arms around myself, I attempt a smile.

'We need you in the kitchen, Mum,' Freya says, examining my smile but not returning it. She's already steering Ingrid away, leaving me standing very still, unsure of what to do.

'Sorry about her,' Natalia whispers as the women saunter out of the barn. 'Takes her a while to warm up.'

'Have I done something to upset them?' As I say it, I wish I could take it back.

'Them?'

'Freya,' I mumble. 'And Ingrid.'

'They're hard nuts to crack, but don't worry. They will.' Natalia puts a meaty hand on my shoulder. 'Crack, I mean. And honestly, consider yourself lucky Freya's staying out of your way.'

My interest piques. 'What d'you mean?'

'She's always been pretty protective of Stephen,' Natalia says. 'Tends to drive away anyone he dates.'

I frown, something inside of me churning. 'Weird. You'd think as his sister she'd want him to be happy.'

'Let's just say those two have always had a bit of a weird relationship,' she says, starting to walk back towards the entrance of the barn.

'Wait, please.' I reach out and grab her arm.

She twists to face me. 'You'll quickly see not everyone is a huge fan of Freya,' she whispers. 'Especially not the other brothers. They grew up resenting her. Stephen was the only one who ever really gave her the time of day.'

My heart grows for Stephen, the empath. Always caring more about others than himself.

'But why didn't they like her?' I can't help but ask.

Natalia sighs, takes my hands. 'Ingrid adopted her after she realised adoption was the only way she was going to get what she really wanted. A girl.'

'Oh . . .' My voice trails off.

'Stephen adored her, protected her. They had a special bond.'

'Had,' I repeat slowly.

She drops my hands and shrugs. 'Yeah, something happened. I don't know what, really, but when Stephen started bringing girls home, she suffered a lot from jealousy. Couldn't handle him distancing himself from her.'

Goosebumps scatter my arms and a cold shiver creeps up my spine.

We head back outside, where winter's white is blinding. Everything frozen. It reminds me of being inside a snow globe with the flurry starting to come down.

'Hope it stays like this for the wedding on Saturday,' Natalia says. 'Imagine the photos!'

I can imagine it. It's all I've been doing for weeks. Imagining. Hoping nothing goes wrong. Waiting. That's been the excruciating part. Waiting for my wedding day to finally arrive. I hadn't allowed myself to believe it would, not at first. Until I'd boarded that London flight, I'd been sure something would get in the way. A cancelled flight. A car crash on the way to the airport. Anything. Something. Everything. I catastrophised. Couldn't picture the day I'd get to the retreat where our wedding was going to be hosted. Even as the plane touched down and skidded along the runway, I was sceptical. How could I not be? It's a part of my psyche forever broken.

'You don't have it easy. I wouldn't want to come into this family the way you have,' Natalia says, snapping me from my reverie. 'Doesn't even seem like you have a say in anything to do with your own wedding, bless you!'

I look at her, perplexed. I have had a say, haven't I? I recall many evenings on video calls with Ingrid, telling her about the wedding I'd always envisioned. Granted, it was never in a barn, in winter, in England. I'd dreamed of a big summer wedding at one of South Africa's vineyards sprawling the wine route in the Western Cape, but Stephen had begged me to consider something closer to his family.

'This is pretty much the polar opposite of everything I wanted,' I say under my breath, looking around.

'What was that?' Natalia asks, beaming at me.

'Nothing. Just thinking out loud,' I say, shaking my head as I realise. Ingrid has commandeered the entire wedding.

* * *

On the way back to the main cabin, we pass the stables. Four thoroughbred horses kitted in thick coats and blankets whinny at the sight of us, tossing their heads.

'Ingrid loves her horses. These guys race in the Derby and Royal Ascot every year.'

Pretending to look impressed, I lean against the stables. 'God, I'd love to ride again,' I sigh.

'Why don't you ask Ingrid?' Natalia asks. 'The horses would love a good run around, I'm sure.'

'Oh, I don't know. It's been so long.' I laugh nervously as one of the horses moves towards me.

I let the horse close the gap between us, looking up into his big, curious eyes. Slowly, I extend a hand, placing it on the bridge of his greying nose. He flares his nostrils, studying me with his ears flicked forward. His warmth is comforting, his steady silence calming.

'He likes you,' Natalia says, reaching over and brushing his black forelock to the side. 'This is Shadow.'

'Shadow of Shadowmoor Lodge,' I whisper as he pushes his muzzle into the palm of my hand.

'Come on, it's freezing out here,' Natalia says, rubbing her hands together.

Reluctantly, I step away and traipse after her.

* * *

Five pairs of eyes swing in my direction as I enter the kitchen.

'Natalia.' Freya smiles briefly, then lets it fall. 'Ivy.'

'Natalia, glad you're here,' Ingrid says, looking up from a sea of ingredients in front of her. 'Spiced apple or chocolate orange?'

'Chocolate orange, every time!' Natalia grins.

'Excellent choice,' Ingrid says, selecting a bottle of orange extract and beating it into a mixing bowl of other ingredients. 'We've just finished baking some trial cakes for the wedding. Couldn't come to a consensus on the flavour,' she tells everyone.

My attention drifts to a tiered cake standing proudly in front of Freya. I realise then that no one has asked for my opinion on anything. Not the venue or the décor in the barn, not even the cake. I watch Ingrid start frosting the cake with a creamy glaze. Freya's standing beside her, filling icing into a piping bag.

I want to step forward, give my opinion on some things, but I hold back. Giving Ingrid a reason to be standoffish with me is the last thing I want, and so I opt for getting out of her way as quickly as possible.

'Ingrid, would you mind if I took one of your horses out? Shadow, maybe?' I ask.

Ingrid looks up, tilting her head. 'You ride?'

I'm not sure whether to be offended by her surprise.

'There's a lot you don't know about me,' I say, making sure not to break eye contact.

'Is that so?' Ingrid's brow raises slightly. 'Well, my horses are incredibly special to me. Shadow's retired. He'd love a ride, Ivy.' The smallest of smiles plays on her lips.

I grin, feeling like I may have finally broken through some sort of barrier with her. Maybe this will earn her respect, or maybe even approval. 'Thank you!' I say, spinning on my heels to leave.

'There's helmets, waterproof trousers and paddock boots in the tack shed,' Ingrid calls after me. 'Dig around. You might find some that fit you.'

I incline my head, looking from Ingrid to Natalia, who appears to have lost interest. She's homing in on the cake, eyeing it hungrily. I turn to go, but Ingrid stops me in my tracks.

'Wait,' she sighs. 'You'll need thermals, too. It's freezing out there.' She drops a spatula into her mixing bowl. 'I'll just be a moment.'

With Ingrid next door picking up some thermals, Stephen's aunt, Debbie, tries explaining how to get to the bridleway. 'You can't miss it. You just take a left at the well,' she says.

I try to listen, try to take in the directions I'm given, a right here, a left there. But the truth is I desperately want to get lost, like the rest of my things. I watch Natalia's eyes crinkle happily as she bites into the cake, crumbs falling from the corners of her mouth. I know I should stay, get to know these women more. They are my future family after all. But all I want to do is venture off into the woods and feel free. If only for a few hours.

* * *

As the crisp air works its way into my lungs, my jaw unclenches. My shoulders loosen, and my lips curl up as I wind my way through a muddle of countryside lanes. Allowing my body to sway along with the motion of the horse, I start to take in my surroundings. Snowdrops push their heads up, beginning to flower as I ride along a riverbank. I have to duck beneath a trail of ivy, already weighed down with clusters of frostbitten berries.

It feels good to be outside, to be alone for a while. I've never been particularly good around big groups of people, much preferring to spend an evening in with a takeout than at a busy restaurant. People drain me, and just having this time to myself makes it feel like I'm recharging my batteries. I'll need it before heading back to face the masses today.

I'm caught in a copper shower beneath the sycamore trees when I see the woman from the news, the one I'd seen in the newspaper article on the taxi ride to Shadowmoor Lodge. I'm convinced it's her, sitting in the passenger seat of a car, a little black Peugeot caked in dirt. *Restrained* might be a better description, I think, as I see the driver holding his arm across the woman's chest, keeping her still. The car is inching by and from my vantage point up on horseback, it's obvious something is very wrong. The woman's eyes are huge, brimming with tears.

Shifting my gaze to the driver, an old man with a moustache, salt and pepper hair and dark eyes, I watch him as he speaks. Whatever he says, it makes the woman's lips set in a thin, trembling line. Then the car speeds up, startling Shadow.

My stomach flips as the horse rears up in alarm. Fighting to calm the animal, I do my best to read the licence plate before the car disappears from sight. I need to get back to the cabin, and fast. Already I'm struggling to remember if the first two numbers of the licence plate were 02 or 05. My mind is racing.

Thundering back to the cabin, the horse's muscles ripple as I try to remember the details. The licence plate number and the make of the vehicle, a Peugeot 107, I think. The black puffer jacket the driver was wearing. Small details, but as a self-confessed Netflix true crime junkie, I know that to the police the smallest thing could be significant.

The clack of hooves echoes as I steer the horse back to the stables. Dismounting, I unbuckle the girth and slide the saddle off with shaking hands. I'm carrying the tack back to the shed when I stop dead. There, up ahead, is the same car with the same licence plate. I blink in surprise as I notice a man in the same puffer jacket disappear behind the tack shed. My mind races. The girl has to be here, with him.

The bit and bridle slip from my arms, and I drop everything else down with it. Leaving the tack on the ground, I charge to the cabin and grab the newspaper I'd kept from the taxi ride. Before getting the police involved, I have to be sure I've just found the missing girl.

Thumbing through the pages, I study the photograph, and as I do I start to become even more convinced that it's her. They share the same defining features. Wiry, coiled hair, full lips and brown eyes set just far enough apart to make her stand out.

My mouth dries as I reread a section of the article:

> *Last seen wearing an orange turtleneck, black leggings and a St Christopher necklace, Charlotte Walker disappeared from a pub in Guildford on the 3rd of January 2026.*

Falling to the floor in the bedroom, I peel up the suitcase lid. Rifling through the contents, my fingernails dig into the knitted fabric of an orange turtleneck. I push it aside. Surely it's a coincidence. But it's not. As soon as the necklace chain entwines with my fingers my heart stops. Whoever this suitcase belongs to, they're in possession of the items the missing girl had last been seen wearing.

How had I got it? My mind flicks back to when we'd arrived. There had been a stack of other suitcases by the front door, but I hadn't thought much about them. Other family members were arriving throughout the day, and I *had* heard other voices in the cabin as I'd been led up to the bedroom. They must've stopped here first before heading to their own cabins — and somehow Stephen must have accidentally switched my suitcase with someone else's. Someone who knows exactly what happened to Charlotte Walker.

CHAPTER 4

I'm desperate for Stephen to get in. I feel like I'm going crazy. I need him to talk me down, to tell me I'm being ridiculous. I need his logic, his calm.

When I hear the guys emerging from the trees like a swarm of excitable bees, I peer out of the window. They're carting back the limp body of a deer on a sled, its head lolling to one side. I'm about to head out to greet him when I see Freya striding towards him.

As she gets closer, Stephen folds his arms across his chest. I watch their interaction and body language closely. Considering they were once so close, I'm shocked by how unforthcoming he seems to be with her.

'What happened between you two?' I whisper, touching the windowpane.

Stephen's eyes dart up to our cabin and I spring back, hoping he hasn't seen me staring. I don't want to be *that* person.

After a few seconds, I chance another look. They're still talking, but Stephen is pushing the deer from the sled. It lands with a sickening thump at Freya's feet.

I can't hear what they're saying but watch as he withdraws a knife and sticks it into the abdomen. The deer opens up in a bloody red smile, the blade slicing all the way up to the sternum. I grimace as he reaches around the diaphragm, pulling out internal organs that steam in the icy air. Just before I turn away, Martin and Ben take the deer by its legs, throwing it onto its front. Scarlet splatters the earth, and I run to the bathroom, throwing myself around the toilet bowl.

* * *

'Hello, you!' Stephen says, sauntering into the bedroom.

His tweed shooting briefs are splattered with mud, a rifle is slung over his shoulder. Bile rises in my throat as he shrugs off the gun and leans it against the log-panelled wall. I slam the suitcase I'm sure holds vital clues into Charlotte Walker's disappearance closed, staring up at him, wild-eyed.

'Woah. Everything alright?' he asks, pulling me to my feet.

My legs feel heavy, and I find I can't actually move them. My eyes keep flicking to the gun. I notice his hands, stained red, and quickly drop them.

'You're mad at me,' he says when I don't respond. 'Please don't be. I was just catching up with my family.'

'I'm not mad,' I say slowly, robotically, my brain in overdrive. I can't concentrate. Can't focus. Charlotte Walker's face is at the forefront of my mind. I have her things. How is that even possible?

'Good. Everyone's meeting in the lounge for drinks in half an hour. I think some more family have arrived,' he says, ripping off his shirt.

Gregarious as ever. I hate that he can't see something is bothering me. Something more than just me wanting to have some one-on-one time with him. Something much more. But there is that dependency there too, and I wonder if it's selfish of me to be wanting that one-on-one time with him with everything else going on. I watch him unbuckle his belt, his jeans falling to his feet. His social habits are something I've always found hard to get used to as an introvert myself. But I've been trying to understand that this is the first time he's seen his family for a couple of years. It's why he wanted us to stay here instead of a hotel. *'Why travel all this way if we aren't going to get as much time with them as possible?'* he'd asked when we'd been discussing accommodation before we'd left. I wish I'd kept hold of that obstinate nature I'd once prided myself on. Headstrong, I'd called it, but Stephen had gradually softened me. Now though, the very last thing I feel like doing is meeting his family in the lounge for drinks. My stomach twists as I take a sidelong glance at the gun, a distraction, making my head hurt.

Standing in front of me, his toned, sculpted body on show, he sighs. 'Is it the gun? Want me to get rid of it?'

I nod, squeezing my eyes shut, but is it? Between Charlotte Walker and the gun, I can't seem to catch my breath. The last time I'd seen a gun was in South Africa, when a man had stuck his arm through my open car window and pointed it at my head. I'd had to do everything he'd asked or face lethal consequences. I can still feel the cold metal pressed against my temple. I can still see his finger, resting on the trigger. One flinch and I'd have been blown to bits right there on the motorway.

'I'm sorry, I didn't think.' Stephen shakes his head, grabbing the barrel of the gun.

It's out of the room in seconds, and while he finds somewhere else to put it, I wander around the room. I reach my arm out in every direction, my phone held high in my quivering hand, but there's no signal to be found.

'Come on, come on,' I hiss. I have to call the police. I have to get help. The longer Stephen leaves me alone to think about it all, the more I spiral.

'Are you still searching for a signal?' Stephen laughs as he pushes the bedroom door back open. 'You're wasting your time.'

I freeze, my arm still outstretched. 'Stephen, I-I . . .' I stammer. I don't know what to say. I'm not even sure I should say anything even if I could. *The missing girl is here.* The words are on my tongue, but something stops me from saying anything. Instead, I shake, uncontrollably.

'Baby, please calm down,' he says, lowering my arm and stroking it. 'The gun's gone. I was an idiot for bringing it in here. I'm sorry.'

Despite his words, I continue to tremble. His calloused fingers run through my hair, his thumb grazing my temple.

'I'm here,' he whispers, his voice warm, honey drizzling in my ears. 'I'm here.'

His words soothe me, and I liquefy in his arms.

'I know I said I'd sort your suitcase out. I will. I'm sorry, I just really wanted to spend some time with the boys. I needed it.' His eyes penetrate mine, reminding me of what he's sacrificed to move across the world to be with me. 'I could've moved back home and been closer to my family a long time ago, but I chose to stay here and be with you,' he'd told me a number of times during heated arguments. It's the one thing I can openly say I don't like about him, the way he sometimes resents me, as if I'm keeping him in South Africa against his will when, truthfully, he moved there before he'd even met me.

When we'd met, he'd told me he'd needed to escape, so using it against me whenever we fight is a low blow I don't appreciate. But perfection doesn't exist, and so it's easy to let the subtle digs in the heat of the moment go, because he never means it.

'I need to talk to you actually,' he says, his voice turning to a hushed whisper.

'You do?' I ask as he takes my hands, gripping onto them tightly.

'I'm sorry I left you alone with my mother today. I know she can be . . . a lot,' he says quickly. 'And there's a reason for that.'

He looks over my shoulder, as if trying to make sure we're alone despite the door being closed.

Whatever he's about to tell me seems serious. His eyes are frantic, darting all around the room. It's startling and I'm not sure how to respond because I have something serious to talk to him about too. I need to tell him what I found today. I need to tell him about Charlotte Walker, here, on this property. Alive. For now.

I open my mouth, about to respond when the bedroom door opens.

'Hello, you two.' Ingrid smiles, leaning on the door as it sways. Red wine coats her lips, creeping up the corners of her mouth. 'Coming for drinks?'

'Yes,' Stephen says, pulling on his jeans. 'Mum, do you mind giving us a second?'

'Everything alright?' Ingrid asks.

'Everything's fine. Do you mind? I just need a moment with my wife,' he says, smiling.

'Fiancée,' Ingrid reminds him, her voice clipped. 'And yes, yes I do mind. There's family here who want to see you and meet the bride!' The way she says the word bride, it's as though she's talking about a cockroach. One that needs to be squashed.

'Come on, Ivy, we don't need to wait for Stephen,' she sniffs. 'He can join us later.'

I'm pulled from the room before I have a chance to protest, mute from shock. But even as I'm guided down the hallway, I touch the phone in my pocket, willing it to find just one bar of signal.

* * *

'Wait,' Stephen calls, his feet heavy as they thump down the stairs.

Ingrid swivels with me still in the crook of her arm.

'I'm here,' he says, taking my hand. 'We can go together.' He stares his mother down.

'Wonderful.' Ingrid's tone is an octave too high. Releasing me to him, she marches to the lounge.

'Stephen, please. I need to talk to you,' I whisper, hoping Ingrid can't hear me.

'I need to talk to you too,' he murmurs back, but he doesn't stop.

As we're about to round the corner, Ingrid twists. Her smile creases her face. 'Darling, I've got a surprise for you,' she says, her painted lips trembling. 'Dad's here.'

I watch Stephen's body slowly collapse. Cave in on itself. It's done in slow motion, the way his knees buckle. I'm laden, fighting to keep my balance.

'What?' His hand grips mine tightly, and I feel my knuckles crack.

'He's here, darling,' Ingrid says. 'He's here.'

I know what this means to him. I know his dad has been sick. Until now his attendance at our wedding has been a big question mark. We weren't sure if the doctors would let him fly over from Spain in his condition. He'd also always been a bit of an enigma to me. He wasn't good with technology, so we'd never video called. Just the odd phone call here or there, when he'd felt well enough. But the conversation had always been dominated by Stephen, trying to have as much time with his dad as he could, even if it was from afar.

Entering a room filled with Stephen's family, I watch my fiancé freeze at the sight of his dad. He's sitting with his back towards us in an armchair by a blazing fire.

Taking a tentative step forward, Stephen's hand grips mine a little tighter. I want to let go, to let him have this moment with his dad alone. It's the first time they'll have seen each other in two years, maybe more. I'm also not certain I'll make a good first impression. Not right now. Not when my mind is swirling with questions about this girl I need to figure out how to help.

'Dad,' Stephen croaks, reaching out and touching his father on the shoulder. 'You made it.'

The old man turns in his seat, and I quickly lower my eyes to the floorboards. I don't want to intrude on this moment. I want Stephen to share it with his dad before I get introduced.

'I wouldn't miss your wedding for the world,' his dad rasps. 'Wanted to surprise you as soon as I got the fit-to-fly letter.'

Dropping my hand, Stephen walks around the armchair and into his father's embrace. They clap each other on their backs, and as Stephen burrows his head into his dad's neck, I see the little boy he must have once been.

'Thank you,' Stephen sobs, his shoulders heaving. 'This means so much to me.'

'Don't be silly, boy. It's good to be back here, and good to get away from Mallorca for a while. Too bloody hot and sunny for me.' He coughs, clears his throat. 'Besides, your mum always moans about visiting the retreat alone, so this'll shut her up a while.' He grins.

* * *

They're still holding each other as I slowly peer up through my lashes. My jaw drops. The first thing I notice is his moustache, and then the black puffer jacket.

'It's him,' I mutter, so quietly no one seems to hear me.

CHAPTER 5

'Ivy, come meet my old man. Marcel,' Stephen says, extending his hand.

I have no choice but to move towards it. When I lace my fingers through his, I realise I'm shaking.

'Ivy,' Marcel wheezes. Cold blue eyes so similar to Stephen's stare me down.

If he can recognise me from earlier, when I was up on horseback, I can't tell. His face is deadpan. There's no friendly smile welcoming me into his arms, but there's nothing else there either. No hostility or sense of familiarity, no air of caution. But still my skin crawls as he limps closer, planting a wet kiss on my cheek. Trying to compose myself, I straighten, offering the best smile I can muster, but it's no use.

Ingrid gives me a quizzical look. 'Ivy, you look as though you're in shock, love.'

'Bless her, she's nervous!' Natalia says, wafting over. 'First time meeting everyone. Imagine how you'd feel. It's *a lot* of people.'

'I-I'm fine,' I stammer, but I glance at Natalia with quiet appreciation before turning my attention back to Marcel. It's him. I'm sure of it.

'Did you manage to find your wedding dress?' Debbie asks as she approaches. A strong musky aroma follows her and her gold bracelets jangle as they move up and down her wrists.

'No, she went out riding horses all day instead.' Freya smirks alongside her, completing the circle formed around the fireplace.

'You went riding?' Stephen eyes me curiously. 'Why didn't you say?'

'Uh-oh. Trouble in paradise?' Ingrid laughs, and she looks around the group, hungry for their reactions.

'Everything's fine,' I manage to say. 'I don't drive. If I did, I'd have gone to the airport myself to find my suitcase. I just wanted to de-stress. I took Shadow out for a ride.'

'You don't drive? Why ever not?' Ingrid asks, alarmed. 'Surely that's very limiting for you.'

I run my tongue over my front teeth, flaring my nostrils. The heat from the flames is suddenly all-consuming. I fight the urge to fan my hands in front of my face.

'Mum,' Stephen says. A warning. I can hear it in his voice.

'What, darling? I just can't imagine being in your mid-thirties and not being able to drive,' Ingrid says loftily, throwing an amused look around the group, looking for their agreement.

'I can,' I snap. 'Drive, I mean. I just—'

'She was hijacked in South Africa,' Stephen interrupts.

I don't stop him. I can't. I just let him continue. On top of being mute I'm now frozen too.

'She can drive,' he says, placing a hand on my shoulder. 'She just doesn't want to right now.'

Natalia nods in understanding. 'Hijacked? I can't even imagine.'

'That doesn't matter right now. Ivy, you went riding while we were out hunting,' Stephen says, his breathing heavy. 'Why didn't you stop her?' His eyes glisten as he looks around the circle.

'Could've been bad,' Marcel says, battling to lower himself back down into the armchair. The women flock around him to help.

I'm not sure how to respond. My blood runs cold as I realise I could have been mistaken for a deer out there today. A gun could easily have been pointed in my direction. Again. Someone could have shot me and Shadow. I shudder at the thought.

Still trembling, I look from Ingrid to Freya. Neither of them meet my eyes.

'We told her where to go,' Freya says, folding her arms across her chest.

'They did,' I say quickly, remembering Debbie explaining how to get to the bridleway. I hadn't followed their instructions, and now I can't believe the danger I put myself in. 'They gave me directions.'

Stephen grinds his teeth. 'I need another drink,' he says, stalking away.

An awkward silence follows. Looking around the group, I wonder why they hadn't warned me about the hunting. They hadn't even brought it up. Ingrid wouldn't have wanted any harm to come to Shadow, I try to rationalise, even if he is retired.

My phone vibrates in my pocket, sending my nerves spinning. Signal! I'm so relieved that the international charges that may be incurred don't even bother me. Taking my phone out right here, right now would be too obvious, so I force myself to keep composed. I wait until Ingrid and Debbie start another conversation, something about tablecloth hires being outlandishly expensive.

'Honestly, just order them from Amazon or find some second-hand on Facebook marketplace,' Freya says. 'They're just going to get covered in food anyway.'

'Freya!' Ingrid gasps.

As she starts going off on a tangent about how she doesn't want to be seen as someone who can't afford nice tablecloths, I seize the chance to slink away.

'It's lovely meeting you,' I squeak, touching Marcel's arm before scurrying out of the room.

Finding my way to the guest bathroom, I slam the door behind me and twist the lock. I sit on the toilet, staring at the glowing

LED candles on the barn stool positioned by the sink with rolled-up hand towels and an aromatherapy diffuser. It gives the room a lavender scent that should calm me, but it doesn't. Trying to steady my breathing, I pull my phone out of my pocket and tap at the screen. I'm ready to call the police. I have to. Stephen may hate me for this, in fact, I'm sure he will. He'll be devastated. But a girl's life is at stake, and I need to do something.

My fingers touch the screen again, but it's completely flat. Massaging my temple, I bite the inside of my cheek until I draw blood. Did I get so many messages that my battery drained? I sigh, knowing I need to get back to the bedroom and get my phone on charge.

There's a knock on the door, followed by Stephen's voice.

'Babe. Everything alright?'

'Everything's fine,' I choke out. 'Wait there. I'll just be a minute.'

Getting unsteadily to my feet, I stare at my reflection in the bathroom mirror. There are dark rings beneath my eyes, something I'd usually cover up with concealer, but without my suitcase, I've had to go without any makeup. I feel exposed, vulnerable, and I don't like it. But the shadows framing my face only grow as I try to figure out what to do. I have a choice to make. I can either pull Stephen into the bathroom right now and tell him everything, or keep everything from him.

Pushing myself away from the basin, I open the door and peer out. Stephen's waiting on the other side.

'Hey,' I murmur as he steps towards me.

'I can't believe he's here,' he whispers, shaking his head. 'My old man. He made it.'

I watch his puffy eyes fill with tears and think about the nights I'd cradled him in my arms whenever the doctors told us Marcel had only weeks to live. He'd always beaten the odds. He'd always got better. Somehow. Experimental drugs, good doctors, luck. He always bounced back, but each time we got a call to say things weren't looking good, it made Stephen fall apart. I could never really understand it; all I knew was that he kept telling me nothing could prepare you for losing the people you love. I've never had that problem. My family are still alive, I think, but I haven't had contact with them in years. It was a gradual process. I'd always made the effort, called on a Sunday to check in, listened to the latest drama unfolding in my parents' lives. It was Stephen who made me realise my parents never even messaged me to ask how I was, let alone phoned me. Every bit of communication was always instigated by me. It had stung, realising my parents actually really didn't care. But I have Stephen now, so I know I'll be okay.

He takes my hands in his now, and they feel warm, comforting. I don't know what it feels like to have a dad you care this deeply about, and my heart breaks at the thought of telling Stephen what I know. What I *think* I know.

Squeezing his fingers, I make myself smile. I can't tell him. Not yet. If I'm wrong, he may never forgive me. I'd be accusing his dad of abduction, possibly murder. Stephen would hate me if I'm wrong. He'd call off the wedding. No. If I'm going to rope him into this, I need more clarity on things.

'Shall we go back in? You've got a lot of catching up to do with him,' I say, already pulling him down the hallway.

* * *

My eyes burn into Marcel's back as I sip my wine. I can't look away as I grapple with my thoughts. I haven't seen Stephen this happy since the night I'd said yes when he'd got down on one knee. The guilt is insurmountable. How am I supposed to take this happiness away from him? I wish my bridesmaids were here. I need to talk to someone. My friends would know what to do, but it's still days before they all arrive, and unless I get my phone working, I have no way of contacting them.

I need to get back to the bedroom and put my phone on charge. I need to talk to my girls, because I don't know who I can trust here. Natalia? She's still part of the family. As much as I like her, I'm not sure if putting full trust in her is a good idea.

Deciding to feign illness, I tell Stephen I need to go to bed early.

'I'll come with you,' he says, stroking the hair that has fallen along my shoulder blades. 'You do look pale.'

'No, you should stay up with your family. Especially your dad,' I say, trying to reassure him.

'It's about time I called it a night myself,' Marcel grumbles, staggering to his feet. 'Put these old bones to bed.'

There's a ripple of laughter in response as everyone hovers around the fireplace.

'I guess we can't all stay here if these two are off to bed,' Ingrid says. 'This is their cabin, after all.'

I flood with relief. As soon as everyone's vacated, I can be alone with my thoughts and figure out what to do. One by one, I kiss family members on both cheeks and say goodnight.

The minutes tick by, but eventually, we're standing alone next to the dying embers in the fireplace. Stephen wraps his arms around me, resting his forehead against mine.

'Alone at last,' he sighs, his hands venturing down to the small of my back.

'I am actually feeling a bit sick,' I say, hating myself as I step away from his touch.

'Go get into bed then, I'll bring you up a glass of water.' He smiles. 'I just need to lock up.'

I nod and back away from him. On my way to the cedarwood staircase, I stop. My fingertips touch the cold glass window, slick with condensation. Outside, shining torches dance in every direction as Stephen's family make their way back to their cabins. A faint whinny from the horses echoes through the night. I'm still watching the lights disappear when an arm hooks me around the stomach.

I gasp, twisting around, and thump Stephen in the chest with my fists. 'Don't do that!'

'You're jumpy!' he laughs, holding his hands up.

I grab the cotton fabric of his shirt and bury myself into him.

'Woah, you okay?' he asks.

'Tired,' I say, and it's not a lie. 'Stephen, what were you trying to tell me earlier about your mum?'

'Oh. Right. Ivy,' he says, sighing. 'My mum. She's different. She can get a little . . . obsessive.'

'Obsessive?' I frown.

'About whoever I date.'

I can't help but laugh. Like mother, like daughter? I think back to what Natalia had said about Freya, about how she's always been protective and driven girlfriends away. Then I think, it wouldn't be a wedding without a bit of family drama, would it?

'Stephen, we aren't just dating. We're getting married. This week!'

'I know, and to be honest I think that's why she's been a bit weird,' he says. 'This is all new territory for her.'

'All of your brothers are married,' I point out. I don't let him know that Natalia has filled in some of the gaps. I want to hear things from his point of view.

'Yeah. But I'm the youngest. The baby.' He gives me his cheeky, lopsided smile he knows I love. 'Just take her with a pinch of salt, please?'

I nod, my eyes heavy. It stings as I blink, sleep silently begging me to surrender. Stephen leads me up to the bedroom, and he chucks the throw cushions to the floor as I enter the bathroom.

While I brush my teeth, I watch him turn on the shower.

'Fancy joining?' He grins, dropping his clothes to the thick bathmat.

'Not tonight,' I say, spitting into the sink.

His face doesn't fall, but he doesn't smile as he makes eye contact with me in the mirror. I cup my hands and splash water onto my face, blindly locating a towel to pat myself dry. By the time I emerge from the Egyptian cotton, Stephen's already pulling open the shower door. Deciding to let him brood, I slip out of the bathroom.

I wait for the shriek of the geyser. When hot water starts flowing from the showerhead I jam the charger into my phone. Foot tapping restlessly against the floor, I wait for my phone to boot up.

I'm busy typing in my passcode when a rap of knuckles against the bedroom door makes me jump.

'One moment,' I call, punching in the six-digit code. My phone unlocks, and a handful of messages from various apps jump up on the screen. There's one bar of signal. I stare at it, my hands shaking as another knock sounds. I still. Stephen locked up before he came upstairs. It's supposed to be just the two of us in the cabin.

'Hello?' I call hesitantly, unmoving from the bed with my phone in my hands. My eyes dart from the door down to the phone. That one bar of signal is still there.

When no one responds, I lower the phone down to the bedside table. Slowly, I rise from the bed and edge towards the door. Another sharp knock hits against the wood, hard.

'Stephen!' I shout, a tremble in my voice. Whether he can hear me over the shower or not, I can't tell. But the knocking continues.

'Fuck it,' I breathe, wrenching open the door. As I look out onto the landing I swallow back a scream.

CHAPTER 6

'Hello, Ivy,' Marcel says. 'I think you have something that belongs to me.'

I tremble at the sight of him, at that cold predatory smile. As he holds up his phone, I squint at the open WhatsApp chat, at the photograph Stephen had taken of me with the wrong suitcase. It must have gone through to the group chat when we'd found a signal earlier. Drawing in a deep breath, my eyes travel up to meet his as he wheels a suitcase in front of him. My suitcase. My eyes widen; my worst fears confirmed. An uncomfortable silence yawns around us.

'So, where's mine?' he asks, his moustache twitching. The more I look at him, the more I see the man from the car when I was up on horseback.

'Of course, sorry,' I say, turning back into the bedroom. My mind whirs. Does he know I've seen what's inside the case? Does he know I know who those clothes belong to?

Calling the police will break Stephen's heart, make him hate me. That's the only thing I'm sure about. Our wedding will be cancelled. I bite at my nails as I drag my feet over to the case.

'Brought over some of Freya's clothes with me,' Marcel calls after me, still standing out on the landing. 'In case you were wondering.'

I pause, my hand on the handle of the hardshell Samsonite. His explanation is plausible, yes. But he doesn't know that I've seen the news. That I saw the young woman in his car. These clothes match the description of the clothes Charlotte Walker was last seen wearing. Everything down to the necklace. That can't just be a coincidence, surely? My one advantage is that he isn't aware of how much I know, and I intend on keeping it that way.

Reluctantly, I hand over the suitcase.

'Thanks,' he says. 'You sleep well, Ivy.' Backing away, his eyes never once leave mine.

I click the bedroom door shut and rush back over to the bedside table. My trembling fingers work to unlock the phone, and I pull up the keypad, punching in the number for the police. My thumb hovers over the call button, but as it does, Stephen emerges from the bathroom, steam billowing around him.

'Hey,' he says, rubbing his hair dry. 'How're you feeling?'

'Sick,' I answer, and I'm not lying.

He walks up to me, the towel wrapped around his waist. 'Give me this,' he says, holding the palm of his hand out for my phone.

Faltering, I glance down at the screen, at that one bar of signal that had been there just moments before. It's gone, faded away.

'You need to rest. Can't have you unwell for the wedding, can we?' he says, placing my phone face down on the bedside table. His hand fumbles beneath the lampshade, then everything goes dark.

* * *

Five Days Before the Wedding

I pull my wedding dress out of the suitcase. Unzipping the garment bag, I sigh with relief as the soft Chantilly lace falls between my fingers. This should be the last thing on my mind but just knowing my dress is safe puts me at ease. In one way, at least. In another, my trepidation soars. All night all I was able to think about was that Charlotte is out there, somewhere. Somewhere in the cold. Or is she being kept in one of the other cabins? I haven't been invited into most of them yet. Everyone seems to congregate around our cabin. Is Charlotte inside one of them, being held against her will?

How am I going to find this missing girl, help get her away from Stephen's dad and still get married in five days' time? I was always sure something would go wrong, put a spanner in the works. I was waiting for it. But I could never have predicted this. Stephen's dad, such a vital part of his life, is . . . what exactly? An abductor? A murderer? I don't know. I'm not sure I want to know. But if I do nothing and ignore what I saw, I wouldn't be able to live with myself. So, as much as it hurts, I know I need to do something.

I slip the dress back into the bag, concealing it again before hanging it in the dark oak wardrobe. Will I get to wear it? My mind taunts me. Reminders of my previous dress, for my previous wedding, eat away at me. I can't handle another wedding dress left to gather dust on a hanger. I can't. This is supposed to be it. Finally. This is finally my time. My day.

My nails dig into my scalp, a nervous habit. All morning I've been checking my phone, but that one bar of signal has never returned. I need to get back to the lounge. I need to send a message to my girlfriends. An SOS. A warning, maybe.

Stephen kicks open the bedroom door, carrying in two coffees. I quickly close the doors to the cupboard, kissing him appreciatively as he places the coffee down beside me.

'Thank you.' I smile, taking a sip, the coffee scalding my tongue.

'What's on the agenda today, then? Now we don't need to worry about your suitcase, we have a whole day to play with,' he says, crouching down in front of me and planting a kiss on my knee.

'I thought you could take me for a walk,' I say. 'A tour of the grounds. It'd be nice to get a feel for the place. Figure out where we can take wedding photos, maybe.'

It's a suggestion that rolls off the tongue. Of course I want to know where to take the photographer on Saturday to capture the best wedding pictures. It's an easy excuse. Perfect. He doesn't need to know I'm looking for Charlotte Walker, searching for any possible place she may be hidden. What happens if I end up finding her is another story, one I'll figure out when I get there.

'Great idea,' he says. 'Wrap up warm, it's absolutely freezing out there.'

I dig in my suitcase, retrieving a khaki sweater I'd knitted in a plush, heavy fabric. Pulling it on over my head, I pair it with some fleece lined thermal tights I'd had to buy for the trip. Even as I do up my ankle boots, my feet snug and warm wrapped up in the woollen lining, I'm sure I'm still going to be cold outside.

Looking out at the snowy day, I wonder how people endure unforgiving, inclement weather like this for months at a time. It's beautiful, yes, and different, but after growing up somewhere sub-tropical I'm not sure I can ever get used to this. This chill that goes right through to my bones.

Before we leave the room, I unhook my phone, now fully charged, and tuck it into my slate blue shoulder bag. There hasn't been a chance to check it yet, to call the police. I want to, but I need to choose the right moment. A niggling feeling is telling me to be careful, to not rouse suspicion. Not even in Stephen.

'It's early, but what about a Baileys hot chocolate for the walk?' he asks, wrapping a scarf around his neck.

'Why not? We are on holiday,' I say, trying to seem relaxed. Trying to be fun, like I would be if I hadn't seen Charlotte Walker yesterday. Under normal circumstances I'd be wanting to start every morning leading up to our wedding with a mimosa in bed. That's who I usually am. The Why Not girl. It's something I know Stephen has always loved about me, so it's hard to keep up the façade, especially around him.

He simmers the milk and pours it into two travel mugs, mixing in the hot chocolate powder. He adds the liqueur, squirts in whipped cream and sprinkles cocoa shavings over the top.

'This is a winter staple in England.' He grins, handing me one of the mugs. 'Well, this and mulled wine. But I thought you'd appreciate this more.'

'Very decadent!' I manage, wrapping my fingers around the stainless steel.

'Right, let's go. I need to be back around lunchtime. Promised Mum I'd help saw some logs to use as coasters for the wedding, going to try to make some plate holders too,' he says. 'I think we have a family games night tonight, by the way.'

'That'll be nice,' I say, wishing I could believe it. But the truth is that Ingrid, Freya and Marcel have made me feel beyond uncomfortable. Scared, even. It's far from the happy family gathering I'd envisioned, but the biggest part of me is still hell-bent on trying to make the most of it, for Stephen's sake.

Lacing a gloved hand through Stephen's, we head out into the frosty morning. It's nice having a quiet start to the day, without his family swanning around. I'm not sure where we are. Looking out into the fog, I can't see any sign of life in any of the other cabins. Not a soul in sight. Something about it unsettles me.

'So, this is the tree where my childhood dog, Miss Ellie, is buried,' Stephen says, guiding me towards a large oak tree. 'We'd always find her out here in the summer. My brothers and I would swing from this branch, and she'd lie in the shade, watching over us. She was literally Nana from *Peter Pan*.' His laugh is warm as he's reminded of memories from his past.

I've always loved hearing stories from his childhood. But I'm beginning to notice all of them have always been about him and his brothers. He's never mentioned Freya, not once in all of his recollections. I want to ask him about it, but it feels like I'll be overstepping if I do. So instead, I silently ruminate on it.

My eyes travel the length of the weathered, braided rope holding up a rotten seat. Instinctively, my hand clasps onto my womb. Stephen notices, and sighs.

'Still nothing?' he asks, gently.

I shake my head. 'Not yet. No period, but the last test I took was negative.'

'It might just be the stress of the wedding,' he says, leading me away from the swing.

Exhaling, I nod. I know that. I know it's probably the stress of the wedding. Or we mistimed things again. The app hadn't been accurate, maybe. I'm tired of the excuses, though. When are we going to accept that we just aren't going to have a baby? I know it can take some time, and we haven't even been trying for a year yet, so I know I'm being impatient. Jumping to the worst conclusion. But how can I not?

'You never know. Maybe you're pregnant right now. How amazing would that be?' He grins, his breath dancing around us.

I close my eyes, wishing he wouldn't say that. That hope we once clung to has become old. For me, anyway. I guess for most people, trying for over a year isn't really all that long. I know people try for a lot longer before needing to get help. I keep telling myself I'm being impatient, to keep believing in that tiny shimmer of hope. It's always there, even when I'm convinced it isn't.

We'd done everything perfectly this month, again. I'd tracked my ovulation. I'd found my peak period, pulled him into the bedroom the second he got home. I'd hiked my legs up on the headboard afterwards and waited fifteen minutes. Everything we've done should equate to a baby. Should. But every month, it's another teasingly late period. Another disappointingly negative pregnancy test. One line. Never two.

Wait. There had been a second line, once. But it had turned out to be an evaporation line, and that had been the cruellest ruse of all. Especially as with each passing month, I feel the jolt of that ticking clock and the immense pressure I'm being swept up in.

Sometimes I look in the mirror and I can hardly recognise myself. When had those wrinkles around my eyes formed? I've always wanted to be a young mum. And women have started having families later and later these days, focusing instead on building their careers. Which is exactly what I've done. But I could have sworn a year ago the makeup, the Estée Lauder foundation I blended into my face, hadn't crept into the crevices on my forehead, making them more apparent the way it does now.

Now, every time I take a selfie unless there's a glaringly obvious filter, I absolutely hate how old I look. Old and barren, like one of those Tudor wives to Henry VIII. But even Catherine of Aragon gave him a daughter eventually.

'You packed some tests with you, right?' he asks, and I nod my head, thinking of the packets of Clearblue tests tucked away in my suitcase. I'd splashed out this month, purchased the triple-check early ones, the ones that tell you how far along you are.

'Then let's take another when we get back today,' he says.

'I need to test first thing in the morning, Stephen. Especially this early on. It's when the hormones are the strongest or something,' I say, suddenly wishing I'd taken a test today but at the same time, glad I haven't. I don't know if I can handle another negative result right now.

'Fine. Tomorrow morning.' He squeezes my hand. 'It's a date.'

I know the sooner I take the test he'll stop that slightly judgemental look he gives me when I have a glass of wine. He'll never stop me, but he doesn't like it. I'd stopped drinking completely in the beginning, too afraid to harm the baby in any way. *The baby.* Assuming one would just appear in my womb. But it hadn't worked that way. I know that's one of the reasons he's been upset I'd gone out horse riding, too. Just in case. That mentality, the 'just in case', the cautiousness, has run its course for me though. I can't stop living my life completely, even if it is just a glass of wine here or there. Because when another month brings no baby, I've honestly started to wonder what the point of it all is. I hate that I feel that way, and it's something I keep hidden away in myself. It's not something I could tell Stephen. His hope is still very much burning bright, and every time we try to conceive, he's sated for another two to three weeks while we wait.

* * *

We continue walking, and I take a sip of Baileys hot chocolate. The liqueur grounds me, I think. I'm able to lock away the fears of infertility into a chamber of my brain and throw away the key.

'This is the wishing well.' Stephen grins, his hands patting the stone of a well further up the grounds.

'I saw this yesterday,' I say. 'While I was out riding. Debbie told me to take a left here to stay on the trail.' I grow cold as I peer down into the dark abyss. If Charlotte Walker is down there, chances are no one will ever know. I shiver, hoping I'm wrong. Willing Charlotte to be somewhere else. Anywhere else.

'She what?' Stephen jerks his head in my direction. His fists clench, his nostrils flaring.

'Debbie told me where to go, to get to the bridleway,' I say, stunned by his response.

'She told you to go left?' he asks, pupils dilating.

'Um . . . I think so?' I say, suddenly questioning myself. I try to recall the conversation I'd had in the kitchen, but my mind is blank. 'Does it matter?' I ask with a laugh.

'Ivy, did they tell you to come this way or not?' Stephen asks, standing in front of me. His breathing is heavy, his chest heaving.

'I think so, I can't really remember,' I stammer. 'But I turned around and went the other way. It looked nicer and I wanted to explore.'

'Jesus. Ivy. If you'd gone this way, you'd have gone right into the firing line of our hunting. You could've been shot.'

CHAPTER 7

I swallow down the severity of the situation. Stephen doesn't wait for me as he marches back to the cabins, his boots cracking frozen puddles on the ground. I have to sprint to keep up with him, gulping back the air tinged with the aroma of woodsmoke and fir trees.

'Stephen, please. Don't!' I cry as he hammers on the door to a cabin with an upstairs balcony in the treetops. A robin flies frantically away, fluttering off into the soft sunlight casting long shadows around us.

'Mum!' he roars, and I don't think I've ever seen him quite this angry. It terrifies me, the way he's raking his hand through his hair. The balcony creaks, a movement catching my attention.

Ingrid rises from a wicker teardrop chair and looks over the wooden railing.

'Oh, hello you two,' she calls, giving us a queenly wave. Oblivious to Stephen's outrage. 'I'll be right down.'

While we wait, Stephen's ragged breathing lulls, swirling around him before vanishing.

'Please don't cause a scene,' I beg, shifting my weight from foot to foot.

The cabin door opens, and Ingrid sails out in a cream sweater dress, belted around her waist. It's the first time I've noticed just how bony and gaunt she is. The second she spots Stephen's blazing eyes, her smile fades.

'What's happened?' She looks between us.

'Did you or did you not tell Ivy to go left down by the well when she went horse riding?' Stephen asks through gritted teeth.

'Left? No! Of course not.' Ingrid places a hand to her chest, an edgy laugh rattling out of her. 'I didn't even give the girl directions.'

I don't like the way she says, *the girl.* It makes me bristle. But she's right.

'She didn't, Stephen,' I say, nodding at Ingrid. 'She wasn't even in the room when Debbie told me where to go.'

'Debbie told you where to go?' Ingrid lets out another bark of laughter.

'Why's that funny?' I ask, before I can stop myself.

'Debbie's never been here before. She doesn't know these grounds. I'm surprised you didn't end up in Tadworth or Ockley with her directions!'

Stephen takes a step back, squeezing his eyes shut. 'How can your own sister not have been here before? She only lives down the road,' he spits.

'Despite what you might think, darling, we aren't that close,' Ingrid says, her words clipped. 'You wouldn't know, you've been *away* in a different country for so long.'

I can't help but pick up the bitterness in Ingrid's comment. 'Can we just forget about it?' I mumble. 'It was obviously a misunderstanding.'

Stephen holds a finger up, shushing me. I stare at the frozen ground, growing increasingly uncomfortable by the exchange as Stephen and Ingrid continue to bicker.

'She could have died,' Stephen hisses, his hands flapping wildly around. 'Why would you have even let her go riding while we were hunting?'

'The important thing is nothing happened,' Ingrid says. 'Thank goodness for that.'

I can't detect any relief in her voice.

'Now, if you don't mind, I need to start making preparations for games night tonight.' Ingrid spins on her heels and walks back up the stairs to her cabin.

Before she opens the door, she pauses, looking back at us. 'I know it's your wedding and you're a bit high-strung, but please. Both of you. Don't take it out on me.' Her eyes glisten with hurt, and it kills me to see, especially after everything Ingrid's done for us. For me. I think of those vintage sewing machines and the effort she went to.

The door closes, leaving Stephen and I out in the clearing, alone. For a moment, I don't know what to say. It's eerily quiet with nothing but dead leaves rustling around on the frozen earth.

'Great,' I whisper, dipping my head to my chest. 'If she didn't already hate me, accusing her of trying to murder me has definitely done it.' With every interaction, I feel like I'm taking a step back in my relationship with my future mother-in-law.

'I need to speak to Debbie,' Stephen says, his fists still clenched.

'No. It was a mistake, my love,' I say. I take his hands, gently unfurling them. 'Debbie must've just been trying to help. She didn't know that's where you guys go hunting.'

'If something had happened to you . . .' His voice trails off, his body going limp.

'But it didn't, like your mum said. I'm fine. That's what matters, right?'

He bows, pressing his forehead against mine. I feel the fight deflate from him as I stroke his back. I wait until his breathing rhythm returns to normal, then pull away and look at him. His hands are shaking.

'I'm fine,' I whisper, overwhelmed by the extent of his love for me.

He chokes back a sob, bobbing his head furiously.

'Hey. It's okay,' I soothe. 'Why don't you go back to our cabin, make us some tea. It'll help with the shock. I'll be right there; I just want to talk to your mum quickly. Apologise.'

'No,' he snaps, suddenly tense again.

I give him a questioning look as a cold breeze works its way through to my bones.

'I'll talk to her myself later. Come with me,' he says, pulling me away from Ingrid's cabin.

* * *

Instead of returning to the cabin, we continue to walk the grounds. Our Baileys hot chocolate, now lukewarm, forgotten. I want to get back to the tack shed, if anything to pack away the gear I'd abandoned when I'd seen Stephen's dad after driving with Charlotte Walker in the passenger seat. I need to look inside it, figure out if that's where Charlotte is, but we seem to be heading in the opposite direction.

We're trekking through one of the many overgrown trails, stepping over moss-covered logs and faint animal prints embedded in the frost when we stumble across an open firepit.

I feel it instantly, a heaviness weighing me down, an oppressiveness. Blackened stones circle the remains of charred wood. A clinking and a clattering make me turn towards the trees, where handmade decorations hang from pendulous branches. Pendants, shards of glass and draperies of fabric. Nausea rolls up from my stomach into my throat. I can't be certain, but it looks like someone has been here recently.

'What is this?' I breathe, unable to draw my eyes away.

'The campfire. In summer we'd come out here at night, pitch tents, roast marshmallows,' he says. 'Tell ghost stories.' He winks at me, his bad mood lifting, but it doesn't make me feel any better.

'Do you still use it?' I ask as ash stirs in the wind.

'Mum does. Bonfires, I think.'

'Bonfires?'

'Yeah. To get rid of the things she doesn't want or need anymore.' He shrugs.

'Like what?' I ask, shivering.

'Garden waste, mainly. There's a lot of it here, in the woods. You might've noticed,' he laughs. 'This is the only clearing it's safe to have a bonfire without the risk of setting the rest of the woods on fire.'

I step closer, my boots kicking at branches that crumble to powder from my touch. Reaching out, my fingers connect with a piece of ripped material dangling from a tree. It's faded, mottled with mould. I'm still investigating, looking at the other scraps of fabric that don't seem quite as weatherworn when he tugs me, hard.

'Come on, let's go. We should be getting ready for games night.' He pulls me by the arm, but I stay rooted to the spot, still looking around.

'Oh my God, is that a bone?' My eyes become saucers as I stare down at something resembling a femur bone by my feet.

'We have barbecues out here sometimes, too. For the meat we hunt. Deer, partridges, rabbit,' he says, cagey, tugging at my sleeve. 'Please. Let's go.'

He can't seem to get away fast enough, and I have no choice but to follow him.

* * *

Back at the cabin, I can't shake the nausea settling in the pit of my stomach. My imagination is running wild with possibilities of where Charlotte might be, and what all of this might mean. While Stephen busies himself in the kitchen, making apple cinnamon pastries and milky tea, I'm in the bathroom, dry retching. The powdery scent of sugar is too much for me.

When the queasiness subsides, I do some quick maths on my fingers. When I land on the answer I've been working out, I suck in a deep breath. I'm ten days late. I've never been this late before. For the second time today, my hands drift to my stomach. Staring at myself, sallow and shell-shocked in the bathroom mirror, I exhale. As much as I try to stop it, hope blooms in my chest. Could this be it?

Before I've had a chance to fully let the moment sink in, the nausea returns, and I throw myself back over the toilet bowl. If this is purely my reaction to the stress I'm feeling right now, the world is crueller than I thought.

Stephen comes in, a china teacup shaking precariously in its saucer. He places it down by the sink, stooping down to my level.

'You still feeling rough from last night?' he asks, holding my hair back.

I nod, wiping at my mouth.

'Sure you don't want to do a test now?' he asks.

Nerves flutter inside me. We look at the box of pregnancy tests on the side of the sink, and Stephen squeezes my hand. 'Go on.' He nudges me.

'Wait in the bedroom for me?' I smile nervously at him. He nods, retreating slowly.

'Stephen,' I call. 'What if it's negative again?'

His eyes soften, his mouth forming a kind but wary smile. 'Then we keep trying.'

As soon as I'm alone, I slide one of the tests out of the box and brace myself. There's a quiver in my hands when I finally unwrap the test and remove the cap.

Please, I beg inwardly as I part my knees and slide the test between my thighs. It's a stark contrast to my past. To when I'd pleaded for the test to be negative, after my hijacking. Sometimes I'm scared I wished away pregnancy so much back then that it somehow turned me infertile. And it feels like I've paid for it ever since.

As soon as it's done, I carefully replace the cap on the test and wait. When enough time has passed, I pick up the stick, squinting. I've already trained my heart not to gallop, but still, there it is. A second line. Faint. Tiny. Hardly visible, really.

I don't believe it, not at first. I grab my phone and put on the torch, shining it right into the result window. I'm so scared to allow myself to believe it, that at first, I truly feel nothing but confusion.

Studying the test again, I allow myself a smile. Small at first. But it grows under the whir of the bathroom's extractor fan. The smallest second line is there. It's undeniable.

I don't even register what I'm doing when I fling open the bathroom door, charging towards Stephen's side of the bed.

'Stephen!' I cry, throwing myself over my fiancé. 'Stephen. Congratulations. You're going to be a dad!'

Bewildered, he sits up in bed. 'What?'

'You're going to be a dad!' I say again, brandishing the pregnancy stick under his nose. 'There's a second line. Look.'

There's a quintessential mixture of elation and scepticism in his eyes. He takes the test from me and screws up his eyes. He remains silent for a while, and I scrunch up fistfuls of the bedsheets in my hands while he studies the test.

'I don't see it,' he says eventually, his words imbued with frustration. He gives me a heavy look.

'No. It's there,' I say steadfastly. 'See.' I grab my phone from the bedside table and shine the torch light over the test. I watch him look again.

'Ivy—'

'You can see it, right?'

He exhales, slowly. 'Kind of,' he says, but he shakes his head.

Irritation bubbles inside me. He either sees it or he doesn't. I don't know what '*kind of*' means. My exhilaration dwindles as I put the test down between us.

I know he's only trying to protect me. I watched him get broken down month by month with each negative test, with each tear shed. He's held me close and never given up, always keeping true to his word to always be there for me. No matter what. 'We'll just try again next month,' he's always said, unwavering in his optimism. Now, with a clear positive test result, I guess I can understand why he isn't wanting to fully believe it.

'Maybe give it a few days, retest then if you're still late,' he says, running his thumb along my jawline.

I nod. I'll do that, for him. But deep inside I know I don't need to, because I know. I know. I know. I'm pregnant.

Finally.

'You okay?' he asks, pulling a face, a grimace. 'You know I want this just as much as you do.'

'I know, and I know you're right. It's probably just an evaporation line again,' I say, but don't sound convinced.

'Let's just enjoy games night, please,' I say listlessly. 'I should be focusing on bonding with your family.' *And finding Charlotte*, I think.

CHAPTER 8

Freya throws the dice, and they skitter across the board, landing in front of me.

'Double sixes. Nice!' Stephen laughs jauntily.

I stare down at the twelve black pips. We're playing Devil's Dice, a game Stephen and his brothers made up when they were kids. In the centre of the table, an ornately hand carved wooden box with brass corners holds a stack of cards. I'm not sure where Marcel is. I haven't seen him all day, and it makes me wonder if he's off doing something to Charlotte. The thought rattles me, makes me vibrate with a frenetic energy I can't mask.

'What do double sixes mean again?' Freya asks, grinning.

'Oh come on, we played this a hundred times when we were younger,' William, one of Stephen's brothers, one with dimples and kind, dark eyes, says. He's smirking, with an eyebrow raised.

'Some of us have moved on from these childish games,' Freya counters sardonically.

Outside, hail strikes against the windows and log walls, creating a thunder that reverberates through the cabin. It's deafening, and for a while no one speaks, waiting for the sudden downpour to end. When it does, even the smallest sound seems crisp. The scrape of glass against the table as Natalia brings her wine to her lips. The rhythmic beat of Debbie's trapeze-shaped nails against the box of cards as she edges it towards Freya.

'Rolling a six is a curse. The player to your left decides something you have to do,' Stephen reminds her, but his eyes meet mine, telling me the rules of the game as we play.

'Oh right, of course. I remember now. The devil on your shoulder,' she says, looking at Ben sitting to her left. He leans in, cupping his hands over his mouth and whispers something into her ear.

I look at Stephen. 'What's going on?' I ask, watching as Ben pulls back and pushes his glasses up his long nose.

'Ben's given her something she needs to do, but she doesn't tell anyone what it is. If one of us guesses though, she loses.'

'And Ben's curses are always spicy,' Natalia says, winking a jade green eye at me.

'Oh yeah, he's a barrel of laughs.' Freya rolls her eyes. 'Anyway. Great game, guys. Last time I was cursed I never did find that pink bra ever again.' She guffaws, and there's a howl of laughter from the brothers.

I stiffen. Freya took her bra off in a *game*? With her *brothers*? That queasy feeling returns, and I take a measured sip from my glass of wine. Stephen asked me to have one. *We can't arouse suspicion*, he'd said. With each sip I take, I think of that pregnancy test, now tucked safely away in my toiletry bag so I can look at it again later. See if that line has darkened at all.

'If you are, can we just keep it to ourselves for now?' he'd asked, eyeing me. 'Please,' he'd added.

I'd been taken aback by his request. Of course I'd been planning on keeping it between us. After all this time trying to fall pregnant, I wasn't about to go and tell people until we had our first scan at least. Not even family. He should've known that. But why had he seemed so desperate for me to keep it to myself?

When I hadn't responded, he'd cleared his throat. 'It's just, my mum,' he'd muttered.

Of course it was about Ingrid. Everything seems to be.

'We wouldn't hear the end of it, Ivy. We can't let anyone suspect a thing, least of all her. Okay?'

Now, Freya's fuchsia lips pucker as she grabs the top card from the deck, her movement pulling me back into the room and out from the depths of my head.

'If you could switch lives with someone in this group, who would it be and why?' Freya reads the card aloud, placing it face up in front of her. She clears her throat. 'Ivy,' she says.

Her hazel eyes, swimming with golden flecks, cut into mine. There's nothing warm about them. I let her answer sink in.

'Why?' Ben tilts his head, stroking the stubble along his jaw.

'Why not?' Freya says, arching an eyebrow. 'She's got it all, right? Loving partner. Talent. Beauty.'

Freya's words are hollow, and I'm not sure how to respond, so I shuffle in my seat. 'Beauty? Really?' I sputter eventually, in disbelief.

Freya leans back in her seat, and I can't help but wonder why she would ever consider me beautiful. Not compared to her. Freya has something ethereal about her. She reminds me of one of the most worshipped deities in Greece, Aphrodite. The Greek goddess of beauty and desire. Every time I've seen her, she's been immaculate. She has an esoteric fashion sense of earthy colours blending seamlessly with her celestial bronze skin. Her black corkscrew curls tumble down to her tiny waist and those hazel eyes, they demand attention.

'And a loving partner, and talent,' Freya says, her tone unreadable.

'Freya, darling. You're incredibly talented,' Ingrid says softly, reaching across the table to touch Freya's arm.

'At what?' she scoffs.

'At making any man in your life run a mile.' Ben, surrounded by empty beer bottles he's sunk back, cackles.

It happens so fast. The board flips, and glasses go flying, the evening soured. I'm soaked in wine, but daren't move. Everyone remains silent as Freya gathers herself.

'You asshole,' she spits at Ben.

I can almost feel the anger vibrating from her. I'm too shocked to move, but I desperately want to reach out for Stephen's hand.

'That escalated quickly,' Natalia mutters, starting to mop up the mess.

Ingrid and Debbie stare down at their ruined clothing, bewildered. They don't move to help.

'Jesus, Freya. Grow up,' John, another of Stephen's brothers says, scooping up shards of broken glass.

'Wait. Did you do this because of the curse?' Natalia gasps, pushing her glasses up her pierced Nubian nose. 'Did you have to flip the board?'

'Shut up, Natalia,' Freya snaps haughtily, dismissing her. 'I just hope our lovely Ivy realises how lucky she is to have someone like Stephen.' Freya returns to her usual poise, but all I can keep thinking of is Freya without a pink bra.

'Still holding a torch, are we?' William grumbles, dabbing at his white shirt now splattered with a thirty-year-old Cabernet Sauvignon.

Stephen has gone rigid beside me, catatonic. I look at him for answers, but he keeps his eyes trained on the remnants of his wine. A torch? For her own brother? I don't understand.

Freya smiles wryly from across the table. 'It's not working,' she sighs.

'Giving up already!' Ben shouts, seeming to relish this. He barks out a laugh, his hand coming down onto the table. Hard.

Shooting him an exasperated look, Freya's gaze shifts, hovering over mine. I don't look away. It's chilling, the way she stares. And stares, and stares. It feels intrusive, ominous. I tremble, feeling stripped down with every second that ticks by.

'I think it might be time for some coffees,' Ingrid says, breaking the silence. She gestures for William and John to help her in the kitchen.

'Can we go and talk somewhere?' I hiss to Stephen, still frozen under the amber light from the candelabra chandelier suspended above us.

It's as though he hasn't heard me. He remains motionless, his hand limp on my thigh. I shake his arm, trying to snap him out of his daze.

'Stephen?' I say, my voice firmer now.

Freya starts laughing, a manic, unnerving sound in the otherwise silent room.

Around her, brothers, cousins, aunts and uncles seem to draw their eyes up to me all at once. A thousand spiders crawl up my spine. I don't know why, but in that moment, I feel like some sort of sacrificial lamb.

A shriek from out in the woodlands overpowers Freya's hysterics, ricocheting around us. The noise turns my blood cold.

'A vixen scream,' Stephen says, his voice low, finally raising his chin from his chest.

John re-enters the room with a tray and starts haphazardly placing mugs down in front of everyone.

'Sugar?' Andy, Debbie's husband, asks me. When I nod, he plops a cube into the depths of my mug. I watch it dissolve as it sinks into the dark, steaming liquid.

Natalia pours milk until I tell her to stop. I notice that she offers a very quick, kind smile. In her eyes, there's warmth. Understanding. It's as though she's asking if I'm okay, without speaking. I shake my head. No. I'm not alright. I want answers.

The door to the lounge is pushed open, screeching on its hinges, and John walks in with Marcel holding onto his arm.

'Ah,' Marcel says, his steely eyes roving over the tabletop. 'Devil's Dice going well, I see.' His voice is like sandpaper, and as he lowers himself into the chair at the head of the table, he regards me with a stony look.

'The game's not finished yet!' Debbie's ring-laden fingers rap against her glass as she speaks.

'It's not?' I ask, my body plunging into exhaustion at the thought of staying up any longer.

'Darling,' Ingrid says, emerging from the kitchen and placing a hand on Marcel's emaciated shoulder. 'It's only just beginning.'

* * *

Freya takes her coffee black and bitter. No fuss. I wonder if she drinks it that way intentionally, to complement the rest of her hardened demeanour.

I remain still as Marcel lays the board back down on the table and looks at his daughter. 'Now, no more tantrums,' he says, authoritatively. 'Let's play.'

There are eyes and ears all around me, restricting me from doing what I want to do. I want to speak to Stephen, to extract answers from him. But he's as impassive as ever as he passes the dice to me. I enclose them in my fist and shake, dropping them after a few seconds.

'A three!' Natalia squeals as Stephen visibly sags in his chair.

'What does that mean?' I ask.

'You have to divulge a secret you know about someone else in the room,' John says. 'And I guess as you only really know Steve, he's in the firing line!'

Everyone around the table chortles, and I think about clearing my throat and telling everyone there and then about Marcel.

About his big secret. It's the opportune moment as everyone's looking at me expectantly. But this is Marcel's family. Perhaps they already know. The sheer thought of it makes me quiver. I suddenly find myself wondering, am I safe here? Never once in my relationship with Stephen have I questioned him, but he's been acting strange for days and I think, what if something bigger is going on here?

Right now, I need to feign ignorance. Even if I am too late to save Charlotte, I may still be able to find her and somehow bring Marcel to justice. I just need to play my cards right.

Stealing a glance at Marcel, I watch his bony, shaking hand bring a glass of whiskey to his lips. Those steely blue eyes so similar to Stephen's latch on to mine and I think, *he knows*. He knows I know. I'm gripped by dread, breaking out in a cold sweat. This family, Stephen's family, is about to become mine. Through sickness and in health. Does that apply to his immediate family, too?

What if Marcel is sick? Not just with his ailments, but with something deeper? Darker. More sinister. I could never support that. But then that niggle of self-doubt returns, creeping its way up my spine. What if I'm wrong? What if, somehow, I've misunderstood things? I don't have that clarity I've been searching for, and so I make a promise to myself to try harder. To play this strange little game until I unearth the truth. Not only for Charlotte, but for Stephen too. For my relationship with him. Because he is my family, him and, maybe, just maybe, a little human growing inside me right now. Part him, part me.

'Stephen secretly loves watching *Married at First Sight* with me,' I say eventually, clenching my jaw as I hug myself.

'Boring!' Freya drawls in a grating, smug tone. 'You could at least make it something interesting. A weird little fetish or favourite sex position!'

'You'd know,' Natalia scoffs at Freya.

That's when I snap, jumping out of my seat and excusing myself from the table. As soon as I'm sequestered in the guest bathroom, I drop to the floor. Melting into the duck egg blue bathmat, I tuck my knees to my chest.

All these strange comments about Freya and Stephen mystify me. What the hell is going on? I wish Stephen would come and find me, give me answers. He's been acting odd, so unlike his usual dependable, anchored self. It's distressing, and I find myself pressed down against the cold wooden floorboards, wishing they would swallow me. I love him, I do. I want to marry him, but not here. Not anymore. Something feels off, and all I want to do is go home.

A low-pitched moan rolls through the open window, and I peer hesitantly outside. Whatever it is, it isn't human. Another woodland animal, making its presence known through grunts and growls.

I let the noise ring through my ears as I breathe in deeply through my mouth and out through my nose. *Just a few more days*, I tell myself. *Then it will all be over.* I just need to get through the next few days, grin and bear it. Suck it up. Marry the love of my life and then leave.

I try telling myself I'll never need to come back after this. I'll make excuses. But then, I shake myself. How can I be so selfish? How can I just be thinking of myself, and my wedding? Charlotte needs me. A young woman's life is more important than anything else right now, and I'm the only one who can help her.

On the off chance that there's signal, I pull out my phone, but there's still no bars appearing. I'm completely disconnected from the outside world. I rack my brain, and that's when I realise what I need to do. What my only real option is, really.

CHAPTER 9

Before I can put my plan into action, I need to make it through the night. I can't stay holed up in the bathroom forever, so I get unsteadily to my feet.

I've only had half a glass of wine, but the alcohol is coursing through my body. I feel it, or something like it, a warmth. It's prickling up my arms, weighing me down, sinking me further into myself. Despite myself, I like it. I like the way I can feel the wine swimming through my veins like a vibration. My muscles slacken and my vision blurs.

Is this my body rejecting alcohol? Another sign of pregnancy? I look in the mirror, struggling to focus, but when I do, my pupils are pinpricks, and that's when I know, someone has drugged me.

* * *

Stumbling out of the bathroom, my hand grazes along the log walls as I sail back down the hallway. My footsteps are muffled by the rug beneath me, a medley of hand-knotted wool patches dizzying me if I look down. They remind me of one of those memorial bears, a rug created from old clothing. But whose clothing? My blood curdles as I stare at the dancing textures at my feet.

Bile rises in my throat, and I grip the walls for comfort as I continue down to the lounge. A splinter catches me, embedding itself deep into my fingertip. I try to gasp, but even that, it's as though I'm breathing into a pillow, something invisible stifling me.

My head swims, like I'm in an aquarium, the water fracturing the glass. The flood gates are about to open. There's too much pressure. I'm clawing at the cords of my neck when Freya emerges from the lounge. Her slingback pumps thwack against the floorboards as she gets closer, offering a sliver of a smile. The geometric print shirt she's wearing only makes my head swirl more.

'You,' I puff.

'Ivy, you don't look well,' Freya says, but her voice is faint, as though coming from a far distance. A balmy hand meets my forehead. 'I think you need to go to bed.'

'Did you put something in my—'

'In your drink? Ivy, who do you think I am?' Freya inhales, leading me by the arm into the lounge.

The number of eyes on me as we walk in is enough to give me vertigo. The heat beating out of the fireplace pulses through me, igniting my skin. But the most perturbing of all is Marcel. I blink, trying to bring him into focus. When I do, he's sitting there at the centre of the table, one leg crossed over the other. Flames dance behind him, making him radiant. The way he pierces me with those sharp, icy eyes, it's bone chilling.

'Stephen, I think Ivy needs some water. Or bed,' Freya says.

'I'm fine,' I say, though my words are heavy on my tongue.

'Perhaps a cup of tea?' Ingrid offers, eyes wide. It makes me glance over to my coffee cup, and I wonder, did they put something in my drink?

Finally, Stephen springs up. I melt into him, having no choice but to find comfort in his familiarity. The only person I truly know here, or so I thought.

'You okay?' he whispers, steadying me.

I want to speak, to tell him no. No, I'm not okay. But instead, I glare at Freya.

'She's trying to take you away from me,' I say, trembling.

'What?' Freya asks, aghast. 'What is she talking about?'

'You'll leave me.' I crumple into Stephen, who catches me.

'Let's get her to the sofa,' Stephen says, and I vaguely notice my body being scraped up into his arms.

* * *

When I come to, I'm sprawled out on tan leather that squeaks beneath me as I move. There's a cold compress against my head, which pounds violently. My tongue is like sandpaper as I try to swallow.

'She's awake,' I hear someone say. I try to open my eyes but squeeze them shut again from the blinding light.

'I think someone had a little too much to drink.' Ingrid laughs softly.

I'm too drowsy to correct her, focusing instead on lifting myself up, but there's no strength left in me. Stephen helps hoist me up and although swaying, I manage to lock eyes with him.

'You only had the one glass, right?' he asks, his hand supporting me.

Behind him, the clock on the wall strikes one. It's been hours. How long was I out for? Most of the guests have dispersed. When had that happened?

'Ivy?' Stephen probes.

I nod, thinking back, but my recollections are soupy at best. I know though, I would have only had one glass. I'd never have had a second, not when I could possibly be pregnant. My heart vaults into my throat. My baby. I won't be able to handle it if something takes this baby from me.

'Don't take it from me,' I sob, placing my hands over my stomach. An outburst I didn't see coming.

Stephen's pupils expand as the blood drains from his face, and he grabs my hand quickly, taking it away from my stomach. To anyone else, it would seem like he's just trying to hold my hand, but I know he's trying to hide what I'm really worried about. I want to rip my hand away from him, to scream and shout and tell him to stop being pathetic. Our baby might have been harmed. Surely that should take precedence over whatever else he's worried about.

'Ivy, I'm not taking Stephen from you!' Freya laughs, her voice a serrated knife sawing through my thoughts.

Stephen's hand is still in mine, a dead weight. I wonder if I need to go to hospital, and if so, what would my excuse be? Do I even care? No. I don't. Why should I? He shouldn't either. Not when we've been trying to conceive for so long. There might be ketamine or GHB in my system. But, before anything else, I want answers. It will eat me alive, otherwise. I need to know what the hell is going on. I drop his hand, letting it fall limply into my lap.

'You were saying all these things,' I say, frowning, trying to remember. 'Talking about your bra. Wanting to know his favourite sex position.' I feel sick, but Freya sighs, a long drawn-out sound of irritation.

'Ivy. It's a game. I had to cause an argument between two people at the table. It was my curse. You were an easy target, but you didn't take the bait.'

'I knew it!' Natalia barks. 'Well done,' she adds, patting me on the shoulder.

'What?' I manage, confused.

'Devil's Dice. The curse Freya got, she had to try to make you get cross with Stephen,' Natalia explains.

'Wait, so none of it was true?' I ask, blinking in surprise.

Before anyone can answer, Debbie shuffles in with a glass of misty water in hand. 'Drink this,' she says, handing me the glass. 'Sugar water.' She smiles affably.

I'm not sure who I can trust. The glass is cool in my hand as I pick it up, bringing it gingerly to my lips. 'Thank you,' I croak, tasting sweetness on my tongue after the smallest sip.

Gradually, my body seems to shift back into itself. My temple is still throbbing, but the heaviness in my limbs has subsided.

'Is someone going to make this old man a last cup of tea before he retires to bed for the night?' Marcel grumbles.

My eyes flick over to him, so gaunt and waxen. His dowager's hump has him hunched over in his seat.

'I'll make you a cup,' Natalia says, jumping up. 'Ivy, come join me. It might do you some good to stretch those legs.' After helping me to my feet, Natalia leads me out to the kitchen. The distance from Marcel helps me breathe, releases the tension in my shoulders.

While the kettle rumbles, I try to pry some answers from Natalia. There's still so much I need to understand.

'It's nice that Stephen and Freya are so close. I certainly never had that kind of relationship with my brothers and sisters.' I laugh.

'Oh, honey, I told you that Stephen and Freya aren't actually related!'

'Course you did,' I say, remembering. A terrible jealousy swarms my insides, infesting me from nowhere. I bite at my lip, tearing off the skin and drawing blood. A metallic taste invades my mouth, and I swallow down beads of sweat.

'I don't understand, though. They're not technically related but they're . . . close? Or were close?' I ask, my cheeks growing molten hot.

'Technically, they're not related, no. Like I said, Ingrid adopted her. She tried and tried to get pregnant with a girl, but she kept having boys. It's what almost broke Ingrid and Marcel. Tore them to shreds, really. Marcel couldn't handle her obsession with wanting another child when she already had seven. Even the doctors advised her against it. Her womb just wouldn't be able to cope. I think she said it was something to do with her lining or something, it'd been stretched too thin from so many back-to-back pregnancies. She was devastated. So she adopted. Freya was already a teenager when she joined the family. Caused more trouble than she did good if you ask me.'

In my mind, I'd assumed Freya had been adopted as a young child, maybe even a baby. Knowing she was adopted as a teenager throws me.

I shake my head as Natalia harps on, struggling to comprehend what I'm being told. This is why Freya never featured in any of Stephen's childhood stories. Why hadn't he told me? Why had he kept me in the dark? His secretiveness rankles me, and it's making me wonder just how well I actually know the man I'm about to marry.

It all makes sense now, though. Of course Freya reminds me of Aphrodite, goddess of beauty and love. Aphrodite was associated with pleasure and passion. I knew I'd felt something off about Freya from the moment I met her, and now all of the dots are starting to connect.

I can't believe it. I can't fucking believe it. Of course this would happen. Swap a maid of honour for a sister-in-law (of sorts) and I could very well be living in a reoccurring nightmare.

I make my excuses and head to bed, pretending to be in a deep sleep when Stephen slinks in later that night. He doesn't kiss me softly on the forehead the way he usually does when he climbs in beside me. He doesn't even touch me. Instead, he turns off the lamp and lies there in the dark with his knees up. His silence is the most unsettling of all, but I'm too tired to have a conversation with him. I'm too angry, too scared. He must know that I'm awake too, sense my unease in the way I'm fidgeting, but neither of us break the quiet.

Questions whirl through my aching head until the early hours of the morning, when I finally drift into a fitful sleep. Is Freya planning on seducing Stephen? Will they run off together the night before the wedding? Am I going to be left alone again with an unworn wedding dress collecting dust in my wardrobe?

I can't quite face the thought of going through that again. I won't be able to handle it.

Of course the wedding is going to happen. Of course it is.

CHAPTER 10

Four Days Before the Wedding

I stir, one eye opening, adjusting to the darkness. Tapping my phone, I check the time. 04:53 a.m. I try to fall back asleep for a while, but the howl of the wind whistling through the wooden walls keeps making my eyes peel back open. Perching up in bed, I take a sip of water from the glass by the bedside. My head is pounding, and I need to pee, I realise.

As quietly as I can, I extract myself from the rickety bed and close myself in the bathroom. Gently, I pry open the box of pregnancy tests and let myself wake fully in the glaring light.

Instead of doing nothing for the next three minutes, I busy myself, brushing my teeth and splashing water onto my face. Anything to keep myself busy, to keep me from eyeballing the test, scrutinising it. But I realise when I finally look, I don't need to. This time, I'm sure it isn't an evaporation line. This is real. It's the first time in days I've allowed myself to forget all about Charlotte Walker, because in this moment, nothing else matters.

It's still faint, at first. A light, hardly detectable second line that you wouldn't see if you weren't looking properly. As time passes, it darkens, right before my eyes. I compare a photograph I'd taken of the test before to one I take now, and there's a clear difference. I still need to zoom in on the picture to be able to see it, but it's there.

The instructions tell me to discard the test after a few minutes because it might not be accurate, but the longer I wait, five minutes, ten, the darker the line gets.

I give myself a minute alone, staring down at the test with watery eyes. I stare and stare until my vision blurs. Taking one last photograph, I send it to my bridesmaids group chat and type a message I'm sure I've typed a hundred times before. It drips with desperation, but I don't care. Not now.

Tell me you see it.

I need to hear them say yes. But, of course, it doesn't go through. It goes into the ether.

* * *

I go back to bed or try to, at least. It isn't easy with the purr of Stephen's snores right next to me. My mind isn't much help, either. It's busy, careering off into the dawn as the sky turns from twilight to ochre-red.

Without the curtains drawn, I lie awake as the clouds blush, drifting behind the trees. I know it isn't possible, but each bubble and pop of my stomach makes me think, that's my baby. It's fleeting thoughts, ones I know can't be true. It's wind. Or digestion. But it's nice to pretend, if only for a few minutes.

Holding my hands to my womb, I flush. The scarlet tint to the morning doesn't last long. It changes to a mixture of caramel and rose, which follows me down the stairs and into the kitchen. As I make our morning coffee, I pause, sprinkling fewer coffee granules into my mug than I'd usually allow. Even this simple act is enough to make me beam.

I bite my tender lip, raw from the gnawing I'd done last night, wishing I wasn't so self-absorbed. Charlotte is still out there, and

I still have a plan. I just need to find the time to do it without upsetting anyone. Until I know exactly what's going on, I don't want anyone else to realise I know anything at all.

The kettle whistles, a piercing high-pitched scream, jolting me from my thoughts. I quickly twist the dial on the hob, killing the flame. As I pour the boiling water into our mugs, I still. Twigs snapping underfoot fractures the eerie silence. Raising up to my tiptoes, I lean forward and peer out of the frosted windowpane. Through the canopy of trees, the sky has turned to the palest lavender in the sunrise. It's a gentle colour, mollifying me for just a moment. But then I catch sight of Marcel. He's with Ben, stalking around beneath the beech trees, frozen leaves cracking underfoot. My brows knit. It's early to be out, unless they're going hunting again, but neither are carrying guns. Ben chucks a cigarette to the ground, embers sparking over the soil. He lets it die at his feet, spitting out a mouthful of phlegm. Charming.

I strain, trying to make out what they're saying, but their voices are too low, the same timbre as the morning crickets back home. Instead, I observe them. They're completely engrossed in whatever it is they're discussing. Marcel, wafting his hands around this way and that, seems to be doing most of the talking. Watching Ben shiver in the subzero temperature of the morning, I notice him go as rigid as his coat in the cold. Mindlessly tipping a spoonful of sugar over the coffees, I slither to the corner of the window where I can watch without being noticed.

Marcel points a finger, extending his hand out towards the direction of the tack shed. Where Marcel had been with Charlotte. Where Charlotte may very well still be. My stomach curdles, and I gag, swallowing down an acrid taste in my mouth. I don't know if I'd prefer to be right or wrong in this situation. Neither option really ends well for me.

Clapping Ben on the back, Marcel hands something to the younger man and lurches past the kitchen window. I duck behind the filmy curtain, holding my breath. Marcel seems unaware that he's being watched, hobbling back to his cabin, the one he's sharing with Ben and some of Stephen's brothers.

Ben strides off in the opposite direction with a bucket in hand, and I crane my neck to see what's in it. What could they possibly need to be doing at this hour, before anyone else is awake? I think again of Charlotte, guilt flooding through me. I haven't tried hard enough to find her, to help. I need to do more, but what if it's already too late?

Shaking the thought away, I swirl milk into the coffees. I can't think like that. I just need to try harder. Charlotte is here, on this property, I can feel it. How long can a human survive without food, I wonder. Having watched enough true crime documentaries, I should know this. At least a few days, I'm sure. So Charlotte could still be alive unless Marcel did something to her. Is Ben taking food down to her? My curiosity grows. The urge to follow Ben is strong, and I'm about to grab my coat when Stephen pads into the kitchen.

'Morning,' he croaks, wrapping his hands around one of the coffee cups on the countertop. The steam billows around the room, dancing in the rays of the morning sun. 'Chilly, isn't it?'

I quiver, a ripple working its way up my spine. Grabbing my own coffee, I nuzzle his neck, still intently watching Ben, now nothing more than a distant figure retreating to the tack shed.

'You feeling okay after last night?' he asks, his large palm resting heavily on my shoulders.

Swallowing back my anger, I close my eyes. When I open them again, Ben is gone. 'I'm fine,' I mutter.

I don't want to hold on to everything that transpired last night but I can't help it. I'm disappointed by the entire situation. Not only about Stephen not telling me everything about his family, specifically Freya, before we arrived, but also because of how he's been acting. I feel disconnected from him, like he's withdrawn somehow. Even now, standing in the kitchen watching the golden glow of the morning bathe the woodlands, I don't feel like I'm in the right frame of mind to tell him about the pregnancy test. From the outside looking in, it may seem like the perfect moment. But it isn't.

'Anything on the agenda for today?' he asks, oblivious, walking towards a calendar on our table. Since we arrived it's been filling up with notes, activities and reminders from Ingrid. He flips a page over to reveal a new day, a new schedule.

I step closer, trying to decipher Ingrid's swirling handwriting. 'Does that say: Champagne Pamper Session?'

'Looks like you're getting whisked away,' he sighs, cupping his hands over my sides and pulling me close. He bends to kiss me, but I twist away.

'Ivy?' He frowns.

'Are we going to get any time together on this trip?' I snarl, turning on my heel and stomping back up the staircase with my coffee.

As soon as I'm back in the bedroom, I regret it. We have had time together, just not as much as I'd anticipated on our wedding holiday. I'm just disheartened, about everything. About the wedding being taken over by Ingrid, about Ingrid's attitude towards me. Stephen had mentioned she could get obsessive, but so far, all I've noticed is that she has some sort of aversion, an animosity towards me. Stephen's strange behaviour, his quiet rigidness, has been getting me down. And Freya, I have this awful gut feeling that something may have happened between her and Stephen in the past. It's all too much for my already charged emotions.

I want nothing more than to take his hands and tell him about the pregnancy test. It's his news too. I hate feeling like I'm holding on to this enormous secret that's just as much his as it is mine. But my hormones are taking the reins, and I don't feel fully in control, though I'm starting to realise I might never have been in control at all.

* * *

Pulling the test from the box, I stare down at the two lines. Even darker now than they were earlier. I think about the day ahead of me. This 'Champagne Pamper Session'. More time stolen from me when I could be out searching for Charlotte Walker, who must be close to death now if she is out there, in the cold. Time is not on her side, and I won't be able to live with myself if I could have somehow helped but didn't. Yet every day there seems to be things planned, things I don't know how to get out of.

Why does the schedule only ever seem to be for me? What is Stephen going to do throughout the day? And why do we always seem separated in our activities? Should we not be together, putting together the final touches for our wedding day? Enjoying our last few days together before tying the knot? I hate to admit it, but it feels like we're being kept apart on purpose.

I wonder how I'm going to get out of not drinking at this pamper session today. I already had a glass of wine last night, and I'm terrified the alcohol will hurt the new life we've created.

I recall my maid of honour from years before, Nesta, part French part South African. She already had a son before she ran off with my fiancé and got pregnant. I vividly remember Nesta with a glass of wine each night throughout her pregnancy.

'Everything in moderation,' she'd always say. 'Don't deprive yourself. Otherwise, you'll just worry and hate pregnancy.'

I had never understood it, or her. 'Aren't you worried you'll hurt the baby?'

Nesta had placed her glass of wine down on the table and patted her stomach. 'My mother drank throughout pregnancy with me, and I turned out fine. Back then it was pretty normal for people in France, y'know. Not so much now, but one glass isn't gonna cause foetal alcohol spectrum disorder, is it?' She'd shrugged, picking up her wine again and taking a large gulp.

'Besides,' she'd continued, 'how many people go six months without even realising they're pregnant, living normally, drinking, taking meds without knowing and their kids are fine?'

I'd pursed my lips and kept quiet at that point. Our values had never really aligned, and thinking back, I'm not even really sure why we were ever such good friends. We had very little in common. Yet now, all these years later, Nesta's words ring in my ears, and just for once, I hope she was right and no harm will come to this tiny little seed inside me.

Thinking about Nesta this close to my wedding day arouses my anxiety. I place the pregnancy test back inside the box, out of sight, and tap it affectionately before walking back out into the bedroom. Stephen is there, sitting cross-legged on the bed, nursing the coffee in his lap.

'Can we restart?' he asks, his azure eyes wet.

'Have you been crying?' I ask, shocked.

'No,' he says, too quickly, throwing me an embarrassed half smile.

I feel it already, the magnetic pull towards him, the need to comfort him. But I hold back. We need to talk first, even if those blue eyes of his are my kryptonite.

'Can you tell me what's going on?' I say, eyebrows raised.

He should have told me this before we went to bed last night. I shouldn't have ignored him when he'd slipped into bed beside me. It could have been water under the bridge already. Whatever he has to tell me can't be that bad, surely.

'Come and sit here,' he sighs.

The wind outside whistles in through the cracks of the logs. My feet are heavy as I drag them across to the bed. I'm still not sure I really want the truth, but I know I need it.

'So Freya isn't really your sister,' I say. A statement, not a question. Taking the pressure off him. Letting him know I already know.

'No,' he mutters, the room turning dark as storm clouds settle outside, dark and ominous. 'She's not. Not by blood, anyway.'

The air around us seems to thicken. Even though I already knew the answer, I still feel the sting as the truth comes out of him. I blow out, my fingertips digging into the corners of my eyes.

'Stephen, I'm going to ask you something and I need you to be honest with me, please?' I stare him down until he nods. Torrents of rain hit the windows, startling us both.

'Has anything ever happened between you two?' I ask.

The oppressive stillness and the stricken look Stephen gives me answers my question, the question I needed to know the answer to, but definitely didn't want.

'Actually, don't,' I say, sharply. My face twists into disgust and I walk away from him.

CHAPTER 11

'We need to go to the hospital,' I mutter to Stephen in the bathroom mirror. There's no sunshine creeping through the blinds now, just the drab light of day. It matches the mood following our conversation half an hour ago.

He spits toothpaste into the basin and rinses his mouth, peppermint lingering in the air. 'Why's that?' he asks after a beat.

'To make sure the baby is okay! I think I was drugged, Stephen!' I say, turning sharply to face him. Hail hits the windowpanes, pelting down like falling marbles.

'The baby? Ivy, we still don't know for certain that you are actually pregnant,' he says. 'And drugged? Don't be so ridiculous! You must've had more to drink than you thought, that's all.'

I can tell from the look in his eyes, he doesn't even believe himself.

Outraged, I slam the pregnancy test I'd taken early this morning down on the countertop between us. Two solid lines are right there. It's undeniable, unquestionable. I'm pregnant. It isn't the way I'd expected to share this moment with him, but I've had no choice. Stephen stares down at the test, dumbfounded.

I want him to pick me up, to twirl me around, to laugh so hard he cries with happiness. But he doesn't do any of that.

Stephen looks dishevelled, not happy. He's not grinning ear to ear as I'd hoped. He's not the picture of a man who has just received the happiest news in his life.

'I'll get the car keys from my mum,' he murmurs, and starts walking towards the door. Just as I'm sure he's going to leave me standing there without even a backwards glance, he stops. 'This is great, Ivy,' he says.

'It doesn't seem like it,' I whisper back, but he's already left the room.

* * *

With the Mitsubishi keys in hand, Stephen leads me around the back of the cabin where a handful of cars circle the clearing in the woods.

'Thought there'd be more cars here than this,' I say, looking around us.

'Most people came in a shuttle bus, I think.' He shrugs, opening the car door for me. 'Quickly. Get in, out of this weather.'

I scrabble inside, shaking hailstones from my hair.

The car rumbles to life, pungent petrol filling our nostrils.

'What did you tell your mum, by the way? About where we're going?' I shout over the growl of the engine as we career over the rough terrain.

'Nothing much,' he says. 'Just that you wanted to go to the pharmacy after what happened last night. Said you were feeling a bit off.'

'Woah,' he says as the car veers off to the left. He fights to gain control of the steering wheel with one hand while the other shoots out protectively in an attempt to keep me safe. The car hurtles towards the trees, making him slam on the brakes. Despite his arm, I'm flung forward in the seat.

'Sorry,' he says, shaking his head. 'Stay here.' Flinging himself out of the car into the storm, he disappears round the back.

I allow my hand to trace my stomach while I have a moment alone. 'Please, please, please be okay,' I beg softly, under my breath.

'Flat fucking tyre,' Stephen shouts from outside.

A wave of terror washes over me.

'Just leave it. I'll get my brothers to help me push it back up later,' he sighs.

We start walking back to the cabin, but as we do, something catches my eye.

'Stephen,' I say, frowning.

'What?' he asks, his voice clipped.

'That car has a flat tyre too,' I say, pointing to a beat-up Toyota.

We walk around, inspecting the wheel, rubber pooled on the ground.

'So does this one,' Stephen says, walking to the next car.

All of the cars on the property have slashed tyres. Unless each car had driven over the same thing, a sharp branch, thorn or abandoned nail, someone has deliberately slashed every single car's tyre. Someone is trying to keep us all here, disconnected completely from the outside world.

'Don't say anything to Mum, please?' Stephen begs, searching between the trees, as though someone may be hiding out here.

'Why?' I ask.

'Just let me figure out what's going on. She'll only panic,' he says.

'Someone's slashed all the tyres, Stephen!' I hiss.

'We don't know that,' he sighs.

'What, so you think every single car here drove over the same rusted nail or shard of glass?' I ask.

'Or tree branch, frozen ice maybe?' he suggests feebly.

'No, Stephen. Someone came out here and took a knife to every tyre,' I say. I can tell from the deep gash I see as I bend down to inspect another tyre myself.

* * *

Stephen pushes the car back towards the others without the help of his brothers, panting, beads of sweat trickling down his forehead.

'Can I help?' I feel like I have to ask, following behind him.

'No.' He shoots me a pained smile. 'You're pregnant.'

It's the first time he's truly acknowledged it, said it out loud. My heart throbs as our eyes catch and hold.

'I'm pregnant,' I whisper back.

With the heels of his hands he presses off the boot of the car and moves towards me. I gaze at him, and despite everything, there's a flurry of excitement inside me like a winter's snowstorm. Taking me by the hand, he leads me back to our cabin. We are silent as we climb the staircase, and I tingle in anticipation.

When he shuts the bedroom door, we step into each other's arms. The sun is breaking through the clouds, rays of light streaming through the window. He kisses me, and it's the kind of kiss I've been craving from him for days. Weeks, even. It's the way he used to kiss me when we'd first met, high on life, spending weekends hiking the trails of Table Mountain and Lions Head. His mouth opens against mine, breath hot as it prickles against my cheeks, reminding me of the blistering heat of summer in South Africa. The landscape of our romance the glittering Atlantic Ocean, the sweeping Twelve Apostles Mountain range and rolling vineyards, valleys and waterfalls. Our love story comes crashing back to me in a wave of emotion as he drives me into the mattress.

My heart contracts as his tongue explores mine, hands tightening around my waist.

'Do you think this is safe?' he asks, nipping at my earlobe.

I give a frantic nod of my head, quietening him with kisses of my own. I've spent enough time researching pregnancy to know that sex is safe unless advised otherwise and I make that known by helping him unbuckle his belt.

With his fingertips prising every scrap of clothing from my body, I travel his torso until he's hard in the palm of my hand. He pulsates at my touch, moaning as I slide him inside me.

* * *

We stay cocooned in the comforts of the coffee bean four-poster bed for the rest of the morning, time running away from us.

'I should probably be getting ready for this champagne pamper session,' I sigh, planting my lips on Stephen's chest. His muscles are tense, bulging beneath me, and the last thing I feel like doing right now is leaving him. Not when it feels like we've finally reconnected.

'It's time I got going, too,' he says. 'Not sure what the guys have planned for me.'

I try not to roll my eyes as I slither out from the blankets, bending to pick up my underwear, discarded on the floorboards. I won't sour the morning by voicing my concerns: that the James family is trying to keep us apart.

Before Stephen steps into the shower he pauses outside the bathroom. He stares at me, busy fighting my way back into an underwired bra.

'You're so sexy.' He grins, satisfied.

I look down at myself and scoff. 'Really?' I can't help but notice the fluffy leg hairs I've been trying to ignore until Friday evening, the night before our wedding, and the silvery stretchmarks shimmering down my inner thighs. He's never seemed to mind my imperfections. On the contrary, he's always threatened to kiss every part of me. Warts and all, figuratively speaking.

'Really. I'm a lucky fiancé,' he says. 'And dad.'

His final two words drift towards me while he steps into the shower steam. I stand there in my underwear and smile at the outline of his body, slowly disappearing behind the condensation on the glass.

Bringing my hands to my stomach, I turn and study myself in the arched mirror. My figure, the perfect hourglass, but for how much longer? I wonder what pregnancy will do to me. I have friends who have never been the same since babies. Friends who used to wear bikinis and ooze confidence, who have become hermits in their own skin after having children. I already have stretchmarks. I'm prone to them. Taking my phone, once again checking for a signal that isn't there, I switch to camera mode. Posing, I photograph my body. Documenting it. Four, maybe five weeks pregnant. I want to take a photo like this each week, watch myself grow.

Looking at myself now, it feels impossible that there's a life inside me, little more than a poppy seed, yet already there's a heart forming, neural tubes developing. I wish my phone worked so I could look up what's really happening, get the weekly update on the embryo's growth from the Flo app. I just want to know, and to feel in control in some small way.

My fingers graze over my navel, and a surge of anxiety sweeps over me. What if the baby isn't okay? Feeling queasy, my mouth waters as I remember the previous night. I'm sure someone put something in my drink. Drugged me. There's no other way to explain what happened to me. The way my body reacted, something was in my system. I'm sure of it.

My mind instantly flicks to Ingrid, then Freya, and lastly, Marcel. I'm wary of them all, but who would have done that to me, and why? Anger rumbles inside me. If any of them have done anything to harm my baby . . . I'll . . . what? What will I do? I blink rapidly at my reflection. My mouth fills with water and I grow hot, overwhelmingly hot. For a few moments I think I might throw up. It surprises me, this sudden nausea and rage, mottled together. I don't know how to handle it, and I have to steady myself against the cool glass of the mirror.

Breathing deeply, I press my forehead to the glass. The whites of my eyes marred by fine streaks of red, the skin beneath a deep, bruised purple, making me look every ounce as exhausted as I feel.

Anger isn't going to help matters now, I tell myself. The only thing that's going to help is being vigilant. Hawk-eyed. A maternal energy, something so foreign and curious to me, floods over me. All that matters is that I keep this baby safe.

Righting myself, I peer into the bathroom where Stephen has stepped out of the shower. He stretches his sinewy body across to the heated rail and pulls off a sage green towel.

I need to appear normal, if anything to just keep him sweet. On one hand, I just want to enjoy this beautiful moment between us as we ease into the fact that we're becoming parents. On the other, I actually don't know how to deal with him. Charlotte Walker should be my priority, and it absolutely sickens me that she hasn't been. For all intents and purposes, I know I need to keep everyone at arm's length until I figure out more.

Stephen shakes out his hair in the bathroom, water droplets cascading around him.

The mounted deer head watches me as I take another photo, side on. One last photograph where the morning light is a warm caramel against my bare skin. As I look up at those tiny, glassy eyes, I shiver, thinking about what else that deer has witnessed in here. There's a wonderful ache between my legs as I shift, turning away from the deer.

'What're you up to?' Stephen asks, stepping back into the bedroom, towel around his waist.

'Starting weekly update photos.' I grin, puckering my lips as he ducks down to meet me. I can feel the callouses on his fingertips as he trails down my body. His hands have become rougher since arriving here. All that time out in nature, hunting, I think.

He snakes a hand through my curls, tugging just slightly so my head rocks back against his shoulder. Breathing in his herbaceous cedarwood and tonka bean shower gel lingering on his skin, my mouth opens with a smile.

'You can't possibly want to go again?' I murmur, but I already have my answer from the bulge in the cotton fabric.

Selfishly, I think, staying here all day would be ideal. It's all I've wanted from this trip, an unfettered day just to ourselves spent lavishly rolling around under the bedsheets, but I know we can't be much longer. There isn't enough time, and as tempting as it is, I know the moment has passed. As much as I try to lose myself in him again, Charlotte Walker's name and face have crept back into the forefront of my mind.

I'm trying to put her out of my mind, to just enjoy these last few stolen minutes with my fiancé, when I see the silhouette of a person in the trees outside the window. Someone standing there, motionless. Watching us.

I spring away from him, pointing, and as I do the figure retreats into the shadows. Out of sight.

'What is it?' Stephen asks, taken aback.

'Someone was there,' I say, my hand trembling as I continue to point out of the window.

Stephen steps closer to the window. 'Out here?' he asks, following my finger out to a ginormous tree, like something out of *Lord of the Rings*, with needle-like leaves and twisted branches.

'By the yew tree?' he says.

'That's a yew tree?' I scoff, crouching down to hug my knees. My head is spinning, and despite mustering every ounce of self-control, my eyes become wet.

'Yeah . . . why?'

I tilt my head up, locking eyes with him. 'Yew trees are a symbol of death. Of doom. Don't you know that? I knew something was wrong with this place.'

'I thought they had something to do with rebirth?' he asks. 'They practically start over from dead branches, don't they?'

'Haven't you read *A Monster Calls* or seen the film?' I ask.

'Patrick Ness?'

'Yes. About the boy with a mum with a terminal illness.'

'What does Liam Neeson as a tree monster have to do with this?' he laughs. 'I think pregnancy's gone to your head already.'

'That,' I say, 'is a tree of death, and it's becoming more and more apparent by the day that we shouldn't be here, Stephen. Something is *wrong* here.'

I hadn't wanted to talk like this. To sound fatalistic, fanciful. I know it's what some people think of me back home, that I'm odd. Eccentric. This strange girl who grew up in Southern Africa, who liked to dabble in what I'd thought was witchcraft as a teenager. Crystals, herbs, channelling energy, candles. That was my passion, before fashion. Stephen doesn't know that about me though, nor do I want him to. I grew to hate the way it made people look at me, especially men. As soon as I'd mention it on a date, my interest in magic, guys would slump in their seats, their eyes becoming unfocused. I'd never hear from them again, no matter how well the date had gone up until that point. So, it's a part of me I've always kept hidden, but it's still very much there.

Touching the carnelian beads around my wrist, I think, perhaps they did help. I'd only bought them last month, from a tiny crystal shop, pungent with frankincense and cluttered with rails of bohemian clothing I'd have once loved wearing. I'd asked the shop assistant to help me find something I could wear to help with fertility. It had been a desperate act, the only card I seemed not to have played. But getting pregnant meant everything to me. I knew it was a long shot. A one in a million chance of it actually working, but looking at the stones, smooth and polished, reddish-brown with lighter swirls swimming inside them, I think, maybe it worked. Maybe my energy has been balanced by wearing the bracelet.

The shop assistant had wanted me to do a tarot reading there and then, but Stephen had been waiting outside. I'd told him I was popping in to buy some wax melts and he'd nodded, waiting out on the pavement for me. When I came back out, I'd clutched a brown paper bag with the crystal bracelet sliding around inside it.

I remember joking with Stephen about being invited for a tarot reading, making conversation with him more than anything. But I did find myself wondering what the reading might have revealed. A big part of me, perhaps the biggest part of me, would always have a fascination with divination, astrology. The occult. It's why I felt such a strange pull towards the firepit while out on my walk with Stephen. Something had felt spiritual about the space. But if I said anything I knew the way Stephen would look at me. Like I'm crazy. It's what everyone has done to me, my whole life. It's why I distanced myself from so many people eventually. Didn't want to keep up false pretences with people that, at the end of the day, really didn't matter to me. Yet, instead, I'd managed to build a life around people in an industry so bourgeois, so pretentious, it hardly matters. People judge me anyway, just for different things.

'Ivy. Stop. It's a tree,' Stephen laughs, wrenching me from my thoughts. 'Whoever was out there was probably just one of my nieces or nephews running by.'

I nod my head, not saying I know it wasn't. Not saying I saw a figure, five foot tall, at least. Someone slender, feminine, who'd been staring towards us intently, before I had noticed and scared them away.

* * *

Knuckles drill against the bedroom door, making me break out in a cold sweat. I'd been about to leave to meet the other women for the champagne pamper session at Ingrid's cabin. All morning I haven't been able to stop thinking about the cars, and about who could possibly want to keep us all here on the property so badly. I'm starting to wonder if the slashing of the tyres is connected to Charlotte Walker. It has to be. There's been a sense of dread building inside me, a feeling that something very sinister is going on that I can't stop.

Sliding out from behind the dressing room table, I head to the door and swing it open. At my feet is a large, pale pink box.

'Stephen?' I call out but I'm answered only with silence.

Stephen has already gone, trekking down to the waterway with the rest of the guys for an afternoon of canoeing. Although who would want to do water sports in this weather is beyond me. Opening the front door this morning, freezing air and snowflakes had slipped in and I'd closed it again in a hurry. Even the quick dash across to Ingrid's cabin would require a good four layers to keep the cold off my bones.

I hadn't even known you could get down to the River Wey from here, but Stephen had run his finger along a map and shown me the trail.

My knees crack as I bend to pick up the box, weightless in my hands. Flecks of earth have been left behind, wet footprints fading back down the staircase. I shiver, wishing people would stop coming into our cabin uninvited as I kick the bedroom door closed again.

Eyeing the key in the lock, I twist it after a moment's hesitation. Without Stephen here, I feel vulnerable, exposed even in the confines of our own room. Locking the door, I feel a small sliver of control, of safety.

Dropping the box to the bed, I peel up the lid. Inside is a glittery cowboy hat with rhinestone tassels and the word 'Bride' embellished across it. *Jesus.* I lift it out of the box, revealing a tiny white satin dress beneath it. They must be throwing me some sort of hen party, I realise. A stab of disappointment pierces me at the thought of my friends not being here for it, but they couldn't get an earlier flight. They had thrown me a small soirée before I'd left, which is exactly what I had wanted. Just the four of us. No silly sashes or tacky *cowboy hats*, but an evening with a couple of bottles of wine between us and paintbrushes in our hands. We'd hired a lady who ran a local Sip and Paint, and a male model's clothing had quickly disappeared. We'd spent the evening in fits of girlish giggles, the swirl of alcohol blurring the ending of the night. It had been perfect.

Somehow, I don't think today's party is going to be remotely similar. And how am I supposed to celebrate when I'm harbouring the knowledge that someone deliberately punctured all the car tyres. Why would they do that? I shiver as the cold satin fabric of the dress delivered to me falls over my frame. It's short, barely covering my knickers. I tug it down as much as I can, trying my best to stretch the silk.

Before leaving, I slip back into the bathroom and pluck the box of Clearblue pregnancy tests from the shelf. I just need to see it again, those two lines. They are my reassurance. They anchor me.

I fold down the flaps and tip the box, so that the pregnancy test will fall into my hands. But it doesn't. One last test, still encased in its foil pouch, drops out, and I smile. I don't need this anymore.

I shake the box. My test, my beautifully positive test, falls into my hand. It hits me every time I look at it. I'm actually pregnant! How strange that is when I look at myself in the mirror and, for now at least, I look no different. I'm just me — plus some precious cargo only Stephen and I are aware of.

Nobody here knows I'm pregnant, and he's told me that we have to keep it that way.

CHAPTER 12

Ingrid's cabin is dimly lit, and I'm ushered behind thick, royal blue curtains. There's a mixture of sandalwood and frankincense in the air. Three tables are dotted around, and I'm led to the one right in the centre.

'What's going on?' I whisper as Ingrid releases the grip on my arm.

'Stephen told us this is what you'd want,' she says with a beaming smile, but there's something off about it. Her smile doesn't quite meet her eyes. 'Tipsy tarot!' She hands me a glass of champagne, the bubbles dancing up to the surface.

Taking the smallest sip to appease my future mother-in-law, bubbles pop on my tongue. Ingrid pushes me into a chair, clapping with delight, but her hands, I notice, are shaking. 'I'll admit, it's different. But we're all very excited.'

I smile nervously at a blonde woman sitting in front of a pack of weathered tarot cards.

'Write your name and date of birth here,' she says, motioning to a piece of paper, a no-nonsense tone to her voice.

My eyes dart around the room. At the other tables, Debbie and Natalia are sliding into seats across from other women. Women I don't recognise, draped in silk headscarves and heavy with gemstones. I swallow, writing my name. Ink smudges as my hand glides across the page.

'Ivy,' the blonde woman reads.

I nod, running my eyes along the deep divots in the woman's face.

'What is it you want to know?'

'I don't know,' I mutter, smile faltering. 'I'm . . . I'm about to get married?'

'I see that.'

I cast my gaze down to my ring finger, looking at the white gold tanzanite ring glinting in the glow of the flickering candles. I look back up, but the woman isn't looking at my ring. She's looking around the room, at the other tarot readers, already shuffling their decks.

'Are you wanting to know about your future with this man?' she eventually presses in a hushed voice so no one else can hear. Cocking an eyebrow, the woman waits for me to respond.

'No. I mean, Stephen's great,' I say, but my words don't come out with confidence. I'm worried suddenly, unsure of what this woman might pick up, what she'll be able to learn about my life through the cards. But a thought springs to me. This woman, seemingly unconnected to the James family, may be able to help me.

I gaze around the room again. Those getting their cards read seem completely absorbed in the moment. Those who aren't are drinking champagne, lounging around the living room engrossed in conversations of their own. No one is watching me. Not Ingrid. Not Freya. No one. I could say something to this woman, get help. It might be my only chance.

'You seem tense,' the woman observes.

'What's your name?' I ask, my fingers starting to work the piece of paper between them.

The woman leans back in her seat, looking at me curiously. 'Joanna,' she reveals. Silence follows, only filled when Joanna speaks again. 'Ivy, are you okay?'

The question stuns me, and my breath catches in my throat. I'm not sure what to say, whether to shake my head or not. So I do nothing, frozen in fear. I need a sign, some sort of green light to open up to this woman.

'Ivy?' Joanna probes, crinkled eyes searching mine.

I gulp, reaching for the pen. A simple ballpoint BIC pen, flimsy and cheap in my hand, yet so much depends on it. I'm being as subtle as I can be, so much so that Joanna doesn't even seem to notice as I press the tip of the pen to the paper. Very slowly, I start to write.

'Right, Joanna. Can you not . . . just . . . pull some cards and see if there's some sort of message?' I say, dropping the pen.

Joanna chews her thumb, sniggering. 'I need to focus on something while I shuffle the cards, love.'

I think, scrunching my brows. 'Okay. I guess . . . I guess I'd like to know about my future, with the James family.' Carefully, I rip the corner of the paper, separating the piece I've scrawled on.

Joanna pierces me with a cold glare. Her lips remain in a thin, tight line as she shuffles the cards with her long, bony fingers. 'Tell me when to stop,' she says.

I watch Joanna interweave two piles of cards. At her side lies an embroidered black bucket bag that must belong to her. It's spilled over on its side, and I catch a glimpse of a packet of slim cigarettes, a jar of Vaseline and a set of car keys that make my stomach lurch. *Focus*, I tell myself.

'Stop,' I whisper, heart pounding as I quickly push the scrap of paper into Joanna's handbag. The deck is split in two again and laid in front of me.

Joanna draws a card, turning it face up. 'The Tower,' she says. 'Oh dear.'

My back straightens, a frantic thrum in my chest. 'Wh-what d'you mean: oh dear?' I scan the card, looking at the roman numerals XVI at the top in what I think is a cloud of smoke. Lightning bolts strike the tower, and fire bursts from the windows. But the most unsettling of all, the two figures falling headfirst from the tower, plummeting to their deaths.

'Disaster,' Joanna mutters, turning another card and studying it closely. 'Everything is about to change for you. Wreckage is coming, Ivy.'

I'm not sure if this woman is legit. I'm about to get married, of course my life is about to shift. I narrow my eyes sceptically, but then what were the chances of that card being drawn? And what does she mean by wreckage? Disaster? I look down at the second card. The Ten of Swords. It's graphic, causing a tremor to run through me. A body lies face down, multiple swords stabbed through their back. *Charlotte Walker.* My brain goes there. I can't help it.

'Betrayal,' Joanna whispers.

I try not to flinch, to cower away from the image. This is my hen party. It's supposed to be fun, isn't it? It isn't supposed to conjure up visions of potential dead bodies on the premises. And what does she mean, betrayal? Is she implying that I have betrayed someone I don't even know by not figuring out how to help her sooner? Or does it mean something else? A betrayal from Stephen, perhaps? My mind flicks to Freya, but I bat it away. This isn't the time for jealousy. For insecurity. This is the time to help Charlotte Walker, if I can.

I don't want anyone to see me in discomfort while I'm having my cards read. And so, I lift my eyes back to the tarot reader, who swiftly turns another card. I stare at the word 'Death' written at the bottom of the card, at the figure riding on horseback, trampling over bodies. I shudder.

'Something's very wrong,' Joanna says, shaking her head as she fans the cards out in front of her.

Whatever she's doing, it doesn't seem like an act. Her breathing has become shallow, and her nails are tearing the thin skin at her neck, causing vicious red welts.

Joanna speaks softly, as though she knows this should be done in private rather than here in this room filled with the women of the James family.

'The life you lead, Ivy, is about to take a very different path to what you expect. You're about to be uprooted. There's about to be a big change.' Joanna jabs her finger at the Tower card. 'You shouldn't think of this as being negative,' she says. 'This tower is on fire from a strike. But, *you* could be the cause of that, Ivy. In fact, I think you're going to be.'

I swallow, frown. I don't understand. I can't make sense of any of it. I'm not someone who likes riddles, or cryptic games. I'm very much black and white, lacking the patience for any other way of being. If this woman can see the future, I need her to say exactly what she sees, not feed me messages from a tarot deck.

'Catastrophe is imminent, but for who?' Joanna asks, more to herself than to me, it seems. And once again, I shudder, wondering, is the catastrophe Charlotte Walker dying? If I don't find her in time, that's a very real possibility. I can almost feel the incessant tick of the clock in my head, reminding me, time is of the essence.

Hurriedly, Joanna turns three more cards, studying them seriously. 'You hold some power. That much is obvious,' she says. 'More power than you realise.'

I think of the note I put in Joanna's bag. I can see the ripped paper just poking out, waiting to be read. Joanna follows my gaze.

'I don't usually do this, Ivy, but I'm going to give you my number. You call me if you need another reading or to talk through this, alright?' Joanna scribbles a set of numbers down on the piece of paper on which I had written my name, sliding it across the table to me.

'Ivy! Come on, you need some champagne.' Natalia lunges at me, her glass sloshing as she drapes an arm over my shoulders.

Freya is hunkering down in the chair opposite Joanna. My time is up. Pocketing the slip of paper, I start edging away.

'You know you shouldn't drink that, right?' Joanna calls after me. As I flick my eyes up to her, she winks, and Freya frowns.

My skin crawls, a thousand critters scuttling up my spine. Joanna knows I'm pregnant.

* * *

While Freya and Stephen's sisters-in-law get their cards read, I'm whisked to another room where Ingrid and Debbie have their feet dipped in copper pedicure bowls.

'Ivy! Come,' Ingrid hollers. 'Join us.' She seems to have relaxed slightly now, no longer seeming quite as on edge, and I wonder what it was that had bothered Ingrid so much as I drag myself towards them, my feet dead weight.

'That was *different*,' Debbie says, motioning back towards the blue curtains.

There's that word again. Different. I shudder. 'Glad you enjoyed it,' I manage to say.

'Did your lady say anything interesting?' Ingrid asks, a wicked smile playing on her lips.

'Oh, yes! I found it *very* insightful,' Debbie giggles, and Ingrid keels over her foot spa with laughter.

I can't help but notice how alike they are. It unsettles me, seeing the similarities in their mannerisms and appearance. They have the same cold eyes, thin lips and cruel smirk. As they continue to cackle, tears sting behind my eyes. It's hard to feel like they're not mocking the entire thing.

I take the smallest sip of champagne before sliding the flute onto a side table, behind a prayer plant with leaves already folding upwards for the night. I'm hoping to make it look more forgotten about than abandoned.

'What did your tarot reader have to say, Ivy?' Natalia asks.

'Oh, you know. *Insightful* things,' I mutter, shooting a glance at Debbie, who stills.

Both Ingrid and Debbie settle back in their seats, kicking their feet in petal-filled water.

'Well, I loved mine. My lady, what was her name? Imogen? Said she was more focused on mediumship, whatever that is?' Natalia says.

'It means she can communicate with the dead,' I tell her delicately.

'Yes, that. Well, she was so accurate! I asked about my dad, bless his soul, and she described him perfectly, right down to the tinted glasses he used to wear! I swear, I got goosebumps.' Natalia flushes. 'Told me big things are coming my way, too.'

'Like a larger number on the scales? That *is* accurate!' Freya laughs, emerging from the curtains. A vision in a white ensemble. It makes me wonder what she's planning on wearing to the wedding.

Natalia shrivels, folding in on herself, confidence evaporating. Her face drops, and my heart plummets along with it. I feel for her. I know what it's like to be treated like this, to have no respect given to you. I want to run over to Natalia and wrap my arms around her, tell Freya how shitty that comment was, how shocking it is to treat someone like that. But I can't. Tension judders through me.

'That,' Freya says, positioning herself between Ingrid and Debbie, 'was a load of shit.'

Ingrid and Debbie set off again, childish giggles ringing through my ears.

'I don't know what you're talking about, darling. I hired the most sought-after mediumships and tarot readers in south-east England,' Ingrid splutters.

'Yes, I'm sure,' Freya sneers. 'Gave me so much clarity.'

Natalia meets my eyes. *Sorry*, she mouths. My lips twitch, and I rub my shoulder. The small satin dress feeling suddenly miniscule against my body. I'm a laughing stock, and I start wondering if this was all done on purpose to poke fun at me. It feels very much like it was. Like Stephen had mentioned tarot reading to his mum after I'd bought those fertility beads, and his mum pounced on the idea just to ridicule me. I wouldn't put it past Ingrid, anyway.

My mouth parts, and I exhale a slow steady breath, trying to compose myself. But I can't. I blaze, from the inside out, a white-hot rage making my blood boil.

'Excuse me,' I say, striding towards the curtains. I don't even know what it is I'm doing. I don't have a plan, and my entire body buzzes as I act on complete impulse.

When I burst through the drapes, the sandalwood and frankincense still linger, but the tarot readers are gone. Natalia crashes into me as she bats her way through the curtains.

'Ivy?' she says, following me further into the room. The candles are out, but the wax is still melted, hot, and silence pulses in their absence.

'They're gone,' I whisper.

The chairs have already been stacked up in a corner, the tables folded away. I rush to the window, ripping open the blinds, exposing the clearing in the woods where the cars are parked. The day is turning to dusk already, a strange pinkish hue to the sky I'm sure means the promise of more snowfall.

Scanning the cars, I try to recall which were here before this afternoon. If there are any I don't recognise alongside them. Holding my breath until my chest burns, I exhale, fogging up the glass.

'I mean, they couldn't stay all night.' Natalia nudges my shoulder. An attempt at a joke, but I'm rigid.

A glimmer of red light catches my eye through the trees. I press my palms to the glass and stare out at a car, disappearing from the woodlands.

'No,' I weep, a guttural mewl escaping me.

'Ivy! Are you alright? You're shaking?' Natalia asks, alarmed.

I feel Natalia's hands grip me by the shoulders, turning me away from the window, but I can't respond. I can't do anything. My one and only chance of getting help, has gone.

Now, my only hope is that Joanna the tarot reader sees that note I slipped into her handbag. That this strange woman with the doomsday cards returns to Shadowmoor Lodge under the only instruction I left her: Help.

CHAPTER 13

I pull at my dress, attempting to cover my exposed thighs. I'm sitting across from Debbie, who is busy sticking baby blue Swarovski crystals over the nail on my ring finger.

My nails have been filed down, painted a pinky-nude and embellished. It's far from the simple French manicure I'd have chosen for myself, but Debbie had started the design before I could say no.

'I'm a nail tech in Chiddingfold, so you leave this with me. I know what I'm doing,' she'd told me proudly as she'd pushed back my cuticles.

The stench of acetone dizzies me, but I try to ignore how nauseous I feel by getting to know Debbie more.

'So you live close by? That must be nice,' I say.

'Why would it be nice?' Debbie asks, leaning in closer.

'To be so close to your sister?'

'Oh, Ivy,' she sighs, looking at me pityingly. 'You have a lot to learn about this family.'

My spine prickles. I know I do. 'What do you mean?'

'Ingrid and I might seem to be playing nice right now, but our relationship is very up and down,' she whispers.

'Why?' I ask.

Debbie lays my fingers down inside the LED lamp nail dryer and gives me a hard glare. 'Why is your relationship with your family strained?' she counters.

'Touché,' I mutter, watching the time tick down on the lamp. I want to know more, to understand where the tension lies between Ingrid and Debbie, because from an outsider's perspective, they seem quite close. They've been drinking and laughing together all afternoon, but is it all a façade? And if so, why?

'I had a daughter,' Debbie whispers into the stilted silence surrounding us. 'Ingrid didn't.'

The room around us seems to still, everyone else fading away.

'She had sons,' I say, a statement more than a question.

Debbie nods, solemnly. 'Until she adopted Freya. Her boys were all forgotten about after that.'

I feel a pang in my chest as I think of Stephen. He's never mentioned any childhood trauma or neglect. On the contrary, he's always spoken highly about his family. But, I wonder, is that just who he is? Even on our darkest days as a couple, when we'd argued so badly we came close to splitting up, I knew he'd never bad-mouth me to anyone, never tell anyone about my less than positive traits. Like my temper. Something I've never fully been able to control when something sets me off. He's never thrown me to the wolves or made me feel ashamed. In fact, I think, straining to recall, I don't think he's ever spoken badly about anyone. Ever. Besides when he frantically told me about Ingrid getting obsessive, and could I really call that bad-mouthing? It was more of a warning.

I look Debbie in the eye.

'Even Stephen,' Debbie says, answering a question I hadn't had to ask.

My heart sinks. That poor man. My fiancé. My person. I feel a longing for him, an urge to wrap my arms around him and shield him from any hurt he could possibly face ever again. I love him so deeply, and my heart is truly torpedoed as I think again about his dad. About Marcel and what I'm sure he is somehow a part of.

Debbie slaps my hand, a quick, sharp tap. Jolting back from the depths of my worries, I realise I've brought my fingers to my lips to gnaw at my freshly painted nails.

'Don't you dare,' Debbie orders, inspecting my nails for any damage.

'Mum,' Natalia says, coming over and draping her arms around Debbie's shoulders, making the dots connect. How hadn't I known Natalia was Debbie's daughter until now? Now, it's impossible to miss. Is that why Ingrid and Freya seem so frosty, almost hostile towards Natalia?

* * *

'Ladies, dinner is ready,' Ingrid says, as Debbie applies a cuticle oil.

Leading everyone into the dining room, Ingrid seats me at the head of the table where I'm placed on show. Front and centre.

'Do you know what the guys are all doing today?' I ask, trying to hide how uncomfortable I am with several pairs of eyes feasting on me. It's like a baptism of fire. I have nowhere to go, and everyone is watching my every move.

'If they're back from the river they'll be in the barn I think,' Ingrid says, pouring a new glass of champagne and placing it in front of me. 'Adding final touches for the big day. I gave them a list of jobs that need to be done.'

It could be my imagination, but I'm sure Ingrid is watching me a little too intently as I bring the glass to my lips. I pretend to take a sip, wondering if it's a game I'll be playing all night.

'I hope cleaning that tacky Love sign is on the list,' Freya mutters, clamping her pearlescent teeth down onto her fork. 'That thing is rank.'

Everyone seems to ignore Freya's comment, focusing instead on the meal in front of them. The halibut flakes in my mouth, sweet and tender. I spear one of the roasted garlic fingerling potatoes and chew slowly to stop myself from responding.

'So, Ivy, tell me more about your bridesmaids.' Natalia grins. 'I'm looking forward to meeting them.'

'They're great,' I say, reaching out for the flute of champagne. As my fingers touch the stem of the glass I stall, remembering. I shouldn't drink.

'What're their names? What do they do?' Natalia tilts her head.

'Kayleigh, Georgie and Rosie. They're all in the fashion industry with me.'

'Interesting. So they aren't childhood friends then?' Freya hikes an eyebrow.

'Her childhood friend ran off with her last fiancé, remember?' Amber, one of Stephen's sisters-in-law, reminds Freya.

'She *what*?' Freya splutters, her eyes sparkling with excitement.

Oh God. I squeeze my eyes shut. I hadn't met Freya yet when I'd told the group about my previous engagement and how it ended. I really don't want to have to go through the entire story again, especially not at my hen party.

'The bridesmaids really ought to be wearing some sort of cerulean or glacial blue, to match the theme,' Ingrid says, in an all-too-obvious attempt to change the topic of conversation.

I swallow a mouthful of fish. 'Theme?' I ask. Part of me is grateful to Ingrid, but another part of me is on high alert. I had no idea there was a theme to my wedding.

'Hang on a minute, you were engaged before?' Freya interrupts. 'And your friend, what? Stole your fiancé?' She tries to suppress her laughter, hiding behind her hand, but she erupts. The same manic cackle as Ingrid and Debbie, parroting them. It sends a shiver through me, every one of my nerves on end.

'The theme,' Ingrid speaks loudly, over Freya. 'Is Winter Wonderland.'

The *theme* is news to me, and I'm not quite sure how to respond, but I'm grateful to not have to answer Freya's interrogations, for now at least.

'Ivy, hon,' Freya calls across the table. 'How's the champagne?'

My back snaps straight. 'It's good, thanks,' I say, reaching for the flute again. My hand shakes as I bring it to my lips. The bubbles fizz on the tip of my tongue as I pretend to take another mouthful.

Why is everyone so obsessed with my drinking? So many eyes are on me, I can't tell who really knows. Who here can tell I'm pregnant?

'This is your hen party! You should be two bottles in by now!' Freya says, an almost childlike whine to her voice. 'There you are sipping timidly and not sharing possibly the only interesting story around this table!'

I sigh. 'My ex-fiancé shagged my maid of honour. Got her pregnant,' I say, words clipped. I've only known this woman a few days, but I'm already done bootlicking her, which I feel is all I've done. Even after finding out she'd been intimate with Stephen. More than intimate, really. It's clear something more happened between them than Stephen wants to admit, and the thought repulses me.

'Wow,' Freya scoffs. 'How'd you let that happen?'

I blanch. Her insensitivity is jaw-dropping. 'I didn't *let it happen*,' I say, air quoting, and all around us the other women have grown very still.

'Well then, pray do tell,' Freya says with a smirk. If there's such a thing as Girl Code here, Freya lacks it. There is no support between us. She just wants to cast me into the fire. Turn me into the sacrificial lamb I've been feeling like I am since arriving here.

I haven't spoken about the details in such a long time, my pulse pounds just thinking of it, of the day my entire world shattered.

'She was a masseuse,' I say, slowly, methodically. 'He was a karate sensei.' It's all I can manage. I swallow, hard, gulping down air. The finer details are not welcome to me, but I know Freya won't stop until she knows the whole story.

'Right? So, your maid of honour gave him some sort of happy ending massage one day?' Freya laughs, clearly not sensing quite how hard this topic is for me.

'Something like that,' I mumble. 'I'd bought him a voucher from her spa for his birthday. I was trying to support her and spoil him at the same time.'

'And then what?' Debbie asks, blinking briskly.

'Then,' I say, a queasiness taking over my insides. 'Then he started going for massages more often. Every fortnight, maybe.'

Freya snorts. 'And you didn't realise something was happening?'

'Not at first, no. To be honest, I sensed something in the beginning. We all went out drinking once, and everyone was talking about my maid of honour, Nesta's, job. My ex was pretty drunk, but he said something I just couldn't shake.' I shiver as I recall it all. My past. The things I wish were dead and buried but somehow still manage to rear their ugly heads.

'What did he say?' Natalia asks, eyes saucer wide.

'He said no one has hands like Nesta, that no one's touch was like hers,' I say, casting my eyes down so no one can see the tears forming. I don't want anyone to know that it still hurts.

'Then what?' Freya asks, her face stony, cold.

'After that, Sean and I went to Bali. A pre-honeymoon type thing,' I say. 'It was a week before our wedding. But we just kept arguing. Fighting about the most ridiculous stuff.' I shake my head, twisting the engagement ring circling my finger. 'I started getting a bit paranoid, jealous maybe. We were on a walk down to some hidden little beach when this redhead walked by. She turned and called him by name, and he did this double take.'

'*Another* girl?' Natalia gasps.

I shake my head. 'No. I don't know. They knew each other from back home in South Africa, it was some sort of crazy coincidence. But I'd been so on edge that she set me off even more. We fought so much that he left.'

'Left Bali?' Ingrid asks, gripping the neck of the champagne bottle.

'Left the hut we were staying in, in Nusa Lembongan.'

'He left you in Indonesia, *alone*?' Ingrid asks, reaching across and touching my arm.

I nod, surprised by the cool feel of Ingrid's fingers on my skin.

'We had different flights back anyway. I had to get back sooner for work, Sean stayed to enjoy the surf.'

'Okay — so you went back to South Africa, and he stayed there in Bali,' Freya says, and the way she speaks, it's as though she's calculating something in her head.

I grow hot as the memories resurface. 'I got back to South Africa, sent him a message. I never heard back,' I say, eyes stinging.

'He ghosted you?' Freya exclaims.

I nod. 'Days went by, and there was no response. He wasn't at his house, he was just gone.'

Outside, snowflakes land softly against the windowpane. Besides the trees shivering in the breeze, it is deathly still out there. Unnervingly so.

'Wait, so you didn't even live together?' Debbie asks.

'No. We were planning to, after we got married. But we were young. I had a job and a flat of my own and he lived an hour away,' I say, hating that it feels like I'm defending myself.

'Anyway,' I continue, in the thick of the story now. 'A day before the wedding, I had to face facts. We weren't getting married.'

'He left you to deal with it. Alone?' Natalia's hand flies over her mouth in shock as I nod.

'It was hard.' My voice breaks. 'I had to cancel the whole thing by myself. Contact a hundred guests and try to explain things. Some had flown in from other countries, it was mortifying.'

Natalia swoops over and wraps herself around me. 'You poor thing,' she says.

'Obviously all the deposits were lost, but by then most things were fully paid off already. And it had been me that had paid for almost everything from my own savings, too.' I clench my fists, squeezing my thumbs inside the palms of my hands. 'Traditionally the bride's father is supposed to pay for the wedding, right? And Sean very much had that mentality, but because I wasn't close with my family the financial burden rested on me.'

Around the table, most of the women shake their heads in unison.

'Took me ages to rebuild my life.' I exhale, hoping that's the end of the conversation. Now everyone knows, I just want to move on and try to get through the rest of the party.

'So how did you know he ran off with your maid of honour?' Freya says, expressionless.

My shoulders drop. Evidently Freya senses the story isn't complete, and needs to know more. I lick my lips, cracked and dry from the bitter cold. 'I didn't, for a while. He was just gone, and after a couple of weeks of ignoring my messages even though I could see he'd read them, boxes arrived at my work,' I say.

'Boxes?' Ingrid asks.

'Boxes of my things, from Sean's house. He had them sent to my work. It was the first I'd heard from him since Bali, not that it was really hearing from him. But it was confirmation that he was done, I guess,' I say.

'What a dick,' Natalia spits, frowning. 'Champagne?' she offers, and I shake my head.

Freya sneers as she knocks back the rest of her glass and snatches the bottle from Natalia.

With my glass still full, I lift it to my lips, my hand shaking. Adrenaline is coursing through me. Suddenly, all I want is to take a long, deep gulp of alcohol. To feel the burn at the back of my throat. But instead, I grip the glass, using every ounce of willpower not to throw it into Freya's smug face.

'I didn't open the boxes for weeks,' I continue. 'It was too hard.' Even all these years later, talking about it in this kind of detail hurts like nothing I've ever felt before. It's a magnificent, sublime kind of pain that no words can truly describe.

'So when did you realise he was with your maid of honour?' Freya asks.

'Nesta didn't show up on the day of our wedding. I'd asked a few friends to meet me at a local pub and have this stupid anti-wedding party. I guess it was a way of nursing my wounds.' I shrug. 'Nesta didn't contact me at all, not even the week before the wedding when I was really hurting and needed her the most. And she was meant to be my best friend.'

'But they both just disappeared?'

I bob my head. 'Fell off the face of the earth. I mean, I knew they were both okay. They were online on WhatsApp and Facebook, posting updates and stuff. They were just ignoring me, and to be honest, it took me a long time to put two and two together.'

'Bless your heart,' Natalia sighs.

'I never actually saw either of them again. We never had any contact again,' I say, bile rising in my throat at the memory. 'I only found out about them being together when they announced their pregnancy on social media. It didn't take much to do the maths and work out exactly what had happened.'

'I can't believe you didn't work it out sooner. It sounds like it was pretty obvious,' Freya says.

I glower at her, nettled by her remark. I clamp my teeth over my lower lip, drawing blood. It's all I can do not to scream. Every cell in my body wants to dive across the table and slap Freya. Instead, I mutter two words under my breath. 'Shut up.'

'Excuse me?' Freya blinks, pitching her head towards me.

'Let's defuse this situation,' Natalia says, spilling more champagne into my glass. It overflows, golden liquid coating my hands and popping under my wrists. 'Bridal Bingo, anyone?' she says, waving a stack of cards around the table with a flourish.

* * *

Bridal Bingo is nothing short of a revelation. Most of the boxes are tame enough — we've had to mark off if we can speak more than one language, are left-handed, or are wearing black knickers. The one relatively spicy one was the sex box, and of course Freya commanded the attention of everyone in the room by being the only one to tick off having slept with more than ten people.

'Who?' Natalia begs to know, and Freya is all too happy to oblige.

'Gosh, let's see. There was Kane, Lars, Brendon, Shaun. There were two Shauns, actually,' she says, listing them off on her fingers. 'Then there was—'

'Comet and Cupid and Donner and Blitzen?' Ingrid interrupts, howling. 'I'm not sure I want to know this, Freya!'

Freya gives her a steely look. 'Kyle, Brad, Christian, Mark,' she continues as the women around the table ogle her. 'Clint, Jamie, Michael . . . and Stephen.'

It feels like she specifically saved his name for last, and she's relishing in the horror on my face. No one else seems to notice. She could be talking about any Stephen, really. But one look at her and I'm positive I know which Stephen she's referring to.

She smiles at me insidiously, picking up her wine glass and taking a sip of the crisp Sauvignon Blanc we've moved on to. 'There's more, but I lost count,' she says, almost proudly. Under her breath I hear her say, 'Stephen was the best, anyway.'

CHAPTER 14

By the time the hen party is winding down, I'm shattered. Talking about Sean and Nesta again, in such great detail, has zapped my energy. Not to mention Freya's less than subtle hint that she has indeed slept with my fiancé. Just the thought of it curdles my stomach.

I don't think I can go right back to my cabin. I'm tired of being indoors. And I'm not sure I'm quite ready to see Stephen yet, either. That man, my man, who is turning into a stranger right in front of my eyes.

As I zip up my coat over the tiny dress, I decide to take a walk down to the lake.

'Thank you for all of this,' I say to Ingrid, leaning to kiss her on the cheek.

Her skin is papery thin, cold against my own. Looking down at the glittering nail art as I pat Ingrid's back, I think about the wedding again. My Winter Wonderland wedding. How very different from anything I could possibly have wanted for myself. The South African vineyard, hot and sunny dream getting further and further away by the day.

'I'm sorry about Freya,' Ingrid says softly, glancing back into the lounge where Freya remains, hands clasped around a cup of coffee. 'Did you have a good time today otherwise?'

'Yes, thank you,' I say, lying through my teeth. I'd hated it. The company more than the activities, but Freya is part of the James family and there is nothing I can do about that.

A look passes between us.

'Not long to go now,' Ingrid says as she ushers me to the front door.

'There's really not,' I reply, a surge of adrenaline rushing through me. Soon, my bridesmaids will be here. Then things will be better. I'll have support. Feel more comfortable. And they'll help me find Charlotte Walker, if I don't find her before then.

* * *

The snow is falling faster now, pattering heavily on my coat as I crunch down to the lake. There's a soft burr coming from the barn, which is still lit up, telling me Stephen must still be in there with the rest of the guys. Good, it buys me time. A currency I'm in short supply of out here in the woodlands.

Looking over my shoulder to make sure no one is following me, all I see is white.

Even the trees have turned a strange greyish white under a blanket of snow.

The lake is covered in a thick layer of ice, dusted with snow, cracks creeping along the surface. As I edge closer, it groans, a dull lifeless sound. Knocking my knees together in the cold, I know I can't stay out here for long. I'll very possibly freeze to death, and my teeth are already chattering. But I had to come.

Stepping to the edge of the lake, I stare down at the ice florets budding from the plants, curving into delicate petals. I never realised just how beautiful winter could be until coming here. Peering down into the ice, I wonder if there's any life still down there, beneath the surface. Frogs hibernating or fish, perhaps.

It must be so completely different out here in the warmer months, when there are pops of colour and signs of life everywhere. When the crisp, cold scent of the woods is replaced with pollen floating through the warm air. When it's sweeter, and earthier than it is now. I wonder if I'll ever get to see it in all its glory. I can't quite shake the unsettling feeling that this is all very temporary, that this will never be a place I can truly call home. On the contrary, I feel like I'm in the way here. Meddling in things I should steer clear of. And yet the pull down to the lake was impossible to ignore.

I had to come, not just for my own sanity, to escape the James family if only for a few minutes, but also because it's the only place on the grounds I haven't ventured down to yet.

Continuing to circle the lake, I notice a steep dip as the trees fall away. I look back up towards the cabins, but it is still just a dazzling white, void of movement. The sky has started to shift to its evening hue. A burnt orange splashing through the clouds.

My breath hitches as I make my way towards the edge of the slope. There, concealed by trees and bushes, is another cabin. Slightly more ramshackle than the others, boards nailed over the windows, and giant holes in the wood where it's rotted away.

I look at the drop below, uncertain if I can make it down there safely from here, or if I'd be able to get back up again. Craning my neck, I check left and right, looking for a safer bit of terrain or perhaps even some steps built into the ground. It's getting too dark to see properly, and my fingers are burning from the cold. There's no way I can make it down there. Not tonight.

I turn on my heels, suddenly desperate to get away from this area, at least until morning. Sinking through the snow, I race against the setting sun, my mind whirring. Stephen had definitely told me there were only seven cabins on the grounds. Why would he lie? *Did* he lie? It doesn't look like this eighth cabin would be safe to use, so maybe he didn't think it necessary to mention. I just don't know. The only thing I am certain of is that I'm not going to ask him about it, not until I've been able to get down there and check it out for myself.

Plumes of smoke are coming from the cabin's chimney in the distance, luring me back to the warmth. Stephen must be back. I'm about to carry on in that direction when a high-pitched, ear-splitting squeal startles me. Whirling round, I rest my eyes on the stables. It's so cold the air is cutting right through my impractical clothing. The thin coat I'm wearing is useless out here, against the elements. I need to get back to the cabin, but my feet start dragging me towards the sound of the horses.

Shadow stamps his hooves excitedly as I push open the stable doors.

'Hey, buddy,' I whisper, reaching out a hand and touching the velvety soft skin by his nostrils. They flare as he sighs, deep brown eyes taking me in.

'I have a plan,' I say to him, under my breath. 'Get ready for a big ride.'

Tomorrow, I promise Shadow. Tomorrow I'll take him out of these stables and find the way back to civilisation.

* * *

A buttery aroma fills the cabin as I step inside.

'Hey,' Stephen says, coming towards me with arms outstretched. 'I want to hear all about the hen party. But first, head upstairs. Put your pyjamas on. I've lit the fire.'

In an alternate world, I'd love nothing more than to slip into my fluffy slipper socks and loungewear, curling up in front of the fire with Stephen. And I am grateful to see him trying, but my mind is ablaze, flicking between the cabin I've discovered and Freya's confession that she's slept with Stephen. Just the thought makes me push away from him. I knew it, but I didn't need it spelling out for me.

'I'll be back down in a minute,' I say, planting a small kiss at the corner of his mouth before retreating upstairs.

Scooping my hair up into a top knot, I peep a look out of the curtains, down towards the lake, staring at it curiously. I think about what the tarot reader had said to me, that disaster, betrayal and death are imminent. But that I hold some level of power. What does that mean?

Pressing up to my tiptoes, I try to see to the cabin hidden down the hill from the lake, but all I see are the bare trees standing sentry. I'm about to turn away, to tug off the ridiculous satin dress I've been made to wear all day, when movement catches my eye.

There, in the distance, a figure lurches towards the lake. I'm too far away to make out who it is, but I have a pretty good idea from their antalgic gait.

Waiting, I watch as the figure orbits the lake. They stop a while, seeming to hesitate, before they disappear down the slope towards the cabin.

* * *

Stephen has pulled me into his body in front of the fireplace. I'm trying to be present, to enjoy the heat of the flames beating against my arms. He smells so familiar, so homey to me, and yet, I feel at a loss. While pulling my sage green midi top over my head in the bedroom, a thought had struck me. Can I even marry him? I hated that moment of doubt, tried to bat it away as quickly as I could. Fought it as much as I did fight into my seamless leggings. But facing the truth, I can't help but feel like the foundation of our relationship, our friendship, is starting to crumble.

I love him, I know that. But I don't see how I can become part of the James family. It doesn't feel right, and the weight of that has me folding in on myself. There're too many skeletons in their closet. Freya and Stephen's relationship. Marcel's involvement with Charlotte Walker. The eighth cabin. Ingrid's strangeness, her obsession with family. That's what it is, isn't it? This crazy desire to keep the James family growing. That's what Stephen's been alluding to, anyway. And if that is true, then shouldn't Ingrid warm to me more? Get excited about the idea that her son is getting married and could start a family of his own.

I wish I understood this family more, but at the same time, I don't. My gut instinct is telling me to run — but then, is that pre-wedding jitters? Or something more? It must be more, because of the link to Charlotte Walker. But that has nothing to do with Stephen, surely. So what is it that is making me feel so uneasy, so eager to get away from the James family?

I wonder if others are incriminated, too, in Charlotte Walker's abduction. Like Ben. Out of everyone, I feel he'd be most likely to be embroiled somehow. I didn't like him from the moment I met him. Since my ex-fiancé and my maid of honour I'm very rarely wrong about people from first intuition. I don't trust easily anymore, but like a bloodhound, I can pick up the untrustworthy sorts.

Plucking a salted popcorn kernel from the bowl, I pop it into my mouth and chew. Stephen has my foot in his hand, and he kneads into it. All I want is to relax into him, to enjoy the massage and time alone together, but my mind won't stop.

'How was the tarot reading?' he asks, his mouth so close to my ear that his breath tickles the back of my neck.

Trembling, I lift myself up and away from him. 'Interesting,' I say, knowing I'll need to elaborate. He'll want to know, he's always been that way. Genuinely interested in every aspect of my life. I can't tell him the truth. And so, I lie.

'She told me big things are coming my way,' I say, stealing Natalia's reading. She'll never know, and neither will Stephen.

'Course there are.' Stephen grins. 'Doesn't take a fortune teller to tell you that. Especially at your hen party.' His laugh is light, and in the glow of the fire his teeth are amber.

He reaches out for me again, his hands going towards my stomach and something in me, something primal, kicks in. I don't want him to touch me. To touch my baby. *His* baby, I try to remind myself.

'Hey?' he protests, reeling back. Lifting up his hands as if to show me he won't touch me again, his eyes fill with hurt.

A heavy silence falls between us.

'Stephen, I—' I start.

'Don't,' he says, and pushes up from the floor. 'Ivy, you've been acting so strange recently. I don't know if it's the hormones or anxiety in the lead up to the wedding, but I need to know. Do you still want this?'

I'm momentarily stunned. That question. A confrontation. I didn't see that coming. It completely rips me open. My mind spirals. Days before my last wedding, I hadn't been given that option. Everything had been taken from me. Now, I'm being asked. I have a choice. Do I still want this? Is this an out? I squeeze my eyes shut, trying to understand what it is I should do.

Lie.

The word forms at the forefront of my mind. I need to lie. Clearing my throat, I force myself to look at him.

'Wait, *what*?' I spit. 'It's you that's been acting strange, Stephen. Of course I want this.' I won't tell him I've been having doubts. I won't tell him I'm scared.

'Well, good,' he says. 'I want this too.' His hand drifts to my stomach again and this time, despite the heavy thumping in my chest, I allow it.

As he pulls me back into him in front of the fire, I watch the burning logs crackle and pop.

'When do you think we'll start feeling movement?' he asks, his fingers stroking my tummy.

'I'm probably five, maybe six weeks pregnant now,' I guess. 'So not for another three months, I reckon.'

'Oh,' he says, and I feel him deflate behind me.

'We've waited this long to get here — what's twelve more weeks?' I say. 'We have to wait that long for the first scan anyway, I think.' My forehead creases with worry.

'No, we don't,' Stephen mutters, nuzzling into my neck. 'We'll go private. Book something as soon as we can. It'll be good to check everything's okay after the other night, whatever that was.'

'Thank you.' My chin wobbles as my hand goes over his and we sit there in silence until the fire dies.

'Stephen,' I say, clearing my throat as we take the bowl of popcorn back into the kitchen.

'Mm?' he grunts, wrapping his lips around a bottle of beer he's been holding and sitting at the little two-person table.

'Shadowmoor Lodge, how many cabins are there again?' I rinse the bowl out, slotting it into the dishwasher. Anything to keep busy, but even though I try not to, I look up at him.

His eyes seem to darken, the smile disappearing. 'Seven, why?' he says, straightening up in his chair.

I want to ask him if there's always been just seven, but I stop myself. I told myself I wouldn't ask him about the eighth cabin until after I've investigated. Already, I may have said too much.

'It's just such a beautiful retreat.' I force a smile, levelling my eyes at him.

'Thanks. Yeah, it is nice. Mum has turned the cabins into Airbnb lodges now, but initially, before we all moved away, the cabins were supposed to be for all of us,' he says. 'She had this crazy fantasy that all her children would stay here. A cabin each. Some kind of weird menagerie she could show off, I guess.'

Or a weird community she'd wanted to build, I think but don't say. I think about the cabins. Seven, for seven brothers. But what about Freya's? Shouldn't there be eight, in that case? Why is it such a big secret, unless something is concealed there?

The hidden cabin, so separate from the rest, haunts my thoughts all the way back up the staircase and into bed that night.

CHAPTER 15

Three Days Before the Wedding

Bacon hits oil with a vicious hiss. I busy myself making our morning coffee, plunging until the sediments of the beans are separated. Tipping sugar into the mugs, I stir, watching Stephen sort the bacon and egg toasties.

His white tank top clings tightly to his muscles as he picks the pan up and tosses the streaks of bacon in the air. The tattoo on his right arm defines his contours. A family crest I've never properly looked at, until now. Now, I lean forwards, squinting my eyes slightly. In the tattoo, branches reach out, and I count them now, for the very first time. I don't know why I haven't done it before. But there are seven branches. Seven branches for the seven brothers. Another exclusion of Freya.

If you adopt, should that child not be just as much a part of your family tree as anyone else? Knowing Freya isn't on the crest sends a rollercoaster of emotions rolling through me. I've always been empathetic — it's one of my better traits, sometimes to my detriment. But right now, as my teeth sink into the warm, doughy bread, I'm lost in my thoughts. Imagining what it must be like to be Freya, to feel so outcast by her brothers, and to not have that sense of identity that comes hand in hand with a family crest.

I wonder if Freya even knows who her real family is. I can't imagine what it must be like to be adopted. My own family isn't close, at all, but I'm grateful that I at least know who they are. Somehow, now, looking at that seven-branched family crest, I feel something for Freya, something I really didn't think I could. Sympathy. Empathy.

Is that why Freya is so bitter about everything? No. It must be more. The way Freya looks at me, it's like she absolutely despises me, maybe, that she even wants to hurt me. Swallowing back the questions plaguing me, I watch yolk bleed into the centre of the pan as Stephen cracks another egg.

* * *

Everything I need to get done before the wedding has been done, so I'm grateful that today people seem to be leaving me alone. It gives me time to think and to plan. To act.

It's still quite dark when I loop a scarf around my neck and step out into the open. The gale-force wind is buffeting around my head. Stephen left after breakfast for another hunt, dragging his gun out of the cabin with him. I set my sight on the lake and start ploughing through the wind.

It's hard to see through the hail stones that weren't forecast. They're hammering down, ruthlessly attacking me, but I keep looking. If Marcel got down to the cabin, he would've had to have used stairs, or a pathway of some description. Otherwise he'd have slipped, fallen. There must be something here, an easier way down, hiding in plain sight.

By the time I find the hillside stairs, made of concrete slabs covered in fallen leaves and twigs, daylight has broken. The hail has turned to a soft pattering of sleet, making the climb down the hill tricky with nothing to support me. But I hurry down, before someone sees me.

The cabin is even more derelict up close, trees and undergrowth pushing up through the decomposing decking. Treading carefully so not to fall through the wood rot, I make my way to a window and try to peer in. I can't see much, but it doesn't look like the cabin has been used for a long time. The room I can see is filthy. Broken china scatters the floor along with shards of glass and debris from the woodlands which must have blown in through time. The frames on the walls are slanted, but I'm too far away to see the photographs encased inside them. The room is caked in dust and cobwebs, with sheets draped over what little furniture there is inside. An old grandfather clock stands lifelessly in a corner of the room, its hands paused just past three o'clock. Shivering, I step away from the window. I don't want to be here, but I know I need to be. I need to search this cabin, even though I have no idea what I'll do if I discover Charlotte Walker inside. I haven't thought that far ahead.

From far in the distance, a gunshot echoes, rattling birds from the trees. Even though I know I'm far from the weapon, I forget to breathe for a moment. I wait until everything grows still around me again before taking a shaky step forward towards the front door.

The knob twists easily, surprising me. I'd thought it would be locked, that I'd have to find some other way in. But the door, in such a bad state of disrepair, scrapes slowly open.

Before I enter, I stall, bracing myself for what might be inside. I've seen enough true crime documentaries and enough horror films to conjure up the worst possibilities. Will Charlotte be inside, bound with the horses' reins or strangled with head collar ropes? Will she be dead, or alive?

How long does it take for a body to decompose? Surely longer in this weather. Chances are she's frozen solid, I think. Nausea rises at the thought, and I place a protective hand over my womb.

Out of all my wild imaginings, the only thing I don't expect in there is nothing. Nothing at all. Which is exactly what I find when I finally prod the door open further. No Charlotte. Not even a trace of her.

I walk inside, my weight sinking into the sodden floorboards. It's damp and musty, freezing cold from several shattered windows letting in the frigid winter air. What must be hundreds of mounted stag heads line the walls like trophies, thousands of beady black eyes staring at me blankly as I explore, their spirits seeming to linger in the air. It makes my knees wobble, a tremor passing through me as I venture further into the cabin. But there's no vile stench of a dead body, just a rundown cabin with nothing in the cupboards in the little kitchen, no water in the taps, not even a roll of toilet paper in the bathroom.

I'm about to turn to leave when I look again at the grandfather clock and frown. Something is behind it. I edge closer, a deep pounding in my ribcage. Behind the impressive hand carved clock is a door.

'Holy shit,' I mutter, certain now that I shouldn't be here. That I should leave. No one knows where I am. If I'm caught down here by Marcel, I may never be seen again. But I need to see what lies behind that door.

'Hello?' I say, barely a whisper, but only silence answers me. Silence and the watchful eyes of the stag heads.

'Is anyone there?' I say a little louder, almost starting at the sound of my own voice in the quiet.

Of course no one is here, I think. *You're being ridiculous.* But even as I think that I swear I hear something. A frantic scratching coming from the room hidden behind the clock. A rat, probably, but what if it isn't? What if it's Charlotte, unable to speak, trying to let me know she's inside?

Readying myself, I push at the clock with all my might, but it's heavy walnut wood and won't shift. I'm not strong enough and within seconds I'm puffing, overexerted. Collapsing to the floor, I rest my head against the clock and think.

After a while I head back outside, followed only by the eyes of the mounted stag heads. Circling the cabin, I locate a window I guess belongs to the hidden room. The curtains are drawn so I can't see in. I think about throwing a rock at the window and climbing inside, but if I do that, I'll zap out any warmth that room might have, and I may not be able to help Charlotte Walker right away. And I don't want anyone knowing I've been here. Sending a rock through the window will signal that someone has discovered the family secret. The eighth cabin, and the girl trapped inside it.

No, I need to be smart. If the scratching was Charlotte, that means she's alive, and that there's still time. With that in mind I hurry away from the cabin and try to scramble back up the hill, but I can't find the stairs under the new snowfall that has just begun. It's too steep to get back up without them, so I start to run, hoping to find a gradual ease in the ground I can scale.

The snowdrift is hard to work through, making me stop at a large oak tree. I grip the frozen bark and look back at the cabin.

'Oh my God,' I gasp, throwing myself behind the tree.

For a few seconds, I stay there, my chest heaving, but I need to look again. To be sure that what I saw was real. Steeling myself, I press my stomach up against the trunk of the tree and peer back at the cabin.

A number of figures are approaching. Marcel, leading the pack. Ben. Stephen's brothers, John and William. No Stephen, though, and I guess that should be of some relief.

I watch as the men look over their shoulders, stepping inside the cabin one by one. Should I go back, confront them? I think about it for a while, but then it wouldn't be good for anyone if I offered myself up to those men on a plate. If I did that, it might cost me not only my own life, but Charlotte Walker's too.

I can't move that clock by myself, but a handful of powerfully built men? They could, easily. I retch at the thought of what could be going on inside that cabin right now. I'm still deliberating on what to do when the cabin door swings back open, making me dart back behind the tree before they see me. Marcel limps out along with John and William. Ben doesn't re-emerge for some time.

While he's inside, I try to make myself believe something harmless is going on. They're setting up something for Stephen's stag party, maybe. The longer I wait though, the more I'm certain that isn't the case.

As soon as the cabin door reopens and Ben comes back out, I watch him closely. He seems to say something to the other men, shaking his head. Voices raise, loud enough to travel over to me, though I can't make out what they're fighting about. Arms gesture wildly and Ben raises his fist up above Marcel's head, making me wheeze in the bitter cold. *He's going to hit him*, I think. Before his knuckles connect, he's tackled by John and William, who pin him back against the cabin. I imagine the wood crumbling behind him.

Ben tries to wrestle with them but two against one, he stands no chance.

'This is what we do!' I hear Marcel bellow, approaching him. He carries on talking, softer now, wagging a finger in Ben's face.

I watch Ben collapse, not from a blow, but of his own accord. He crumples to the ground, head in his hands. His shoulders heave.

Whatever the hell is going on here, it isn't good. I sprint further away from the cabin, suddenly confident in what I need to do.

CHAPTER 16

Charlotte

Charlotte's ears prick up at the sound of the cabin door opening. She'd managed to kick a small stone close to it when she'd been dragged in here, a desperate attempt to be able to hear them coming back if she managed to survive, somehow.

It worked. The stone scratches at the floorboards, allowing her time to brace herself again at least. She imagines it drawing a jagged, chalk white line across the wood and wishes she'd been able to do more, but there'd been nothing else she could do. Very quickly, quicker than she could have imagined, she'd been bound at the wrists and ankles, and a dirty cloth had been stuffed into her mouth. It tasted sweet, and within minutes she'd been unconscious. She wonders if it was chloroform on the soiled rag. She's been struggling to breathe, but she can't work out if it's anxiety, panic from where she is and what's been happening to her, or if her shortness of breath is from whatever chemical the rag was soaked in. She no longer cares about the dirty cloth in her mouth. Her mouth is so dry from dehydration that the microfibre doesn't bother her anymore. In fact, she hardly notices. She's thrown up multiple times, but with the rag in her mouth she has no choice but to swallow it back down or choke on it. Some leaked through the material and has dried as it dribbled down her chin. Her lips are blistering; she doesn't need a mirror to know that. This sting is different from when her lips are in dire need of Vaseline. This is agony. Even her eyes feel inflamed but she's been crying until she couldn't anymore so her eyes may be burning from that.

Hanging her head down into her chest, she waits. Waits for the shuffle of the heavy object in front of the bedroom door and the clanging of brass twisting in the lock. But it doesn't come.

The footsteps remain out in the main room. Slow, delicate steps. Are they toying with her?

'Hello?' A woman's voice. One she hasn't heard before.

Her entire body trembles with adrenaline, her wrists juddering uncontrollably at her back.

She can just manage to see through the thin material covering her eyes. Around her, the room consists of nothing more than an old, rickety bed with musty pink covers flecked with blood. That disgusting, awful bed with the springs that pierce into her back and the flaking black paint on the metal frame. She wishes she didn't have to stare at it. She's started to find it easier to just keep her eyes closed, so she doesn't have to see it, and that makes her swollen eyes sensitive to the light of day.

She tries to swallow but there's no saliva left. Her tongue hits her palate and it's like it's rolling up against gravel.

'Is anyone there?'

Whoever is on the other side of this door doesn't know she's in here. Despite her lack of energy, her heart leaps. Someone's come to rescue her! She's about to make a sound, some sort of moan through the cloth jammed in her mouth when she stops herself. What if it's a trick? What will they do to her if she tries to escape? She's already angered them so much. And can she even make a sound, if she tries? She's so thirsty and exhausted she doesn't actually know. The screams she'd made beneath the palm pressed down over her mouth days ago had been so animalistic that she's pretty sure she's damaged her vocal cords. Yet even through the noise she'd made, no one came. Not out here deep in the woods. No one is coming for her. She'd succumbed to that fact. Until now.

In sheer panic that the woman behind the door will leave without discovering her, Charlotte starts to scratch at the chair she's been tied to.

She hears the woman pushing at whatever it is barricading her in this room. It's solid and heavy, she knows that much. Too heavy for this woman to move alone. Scratching more, until splinters of wood break off, embedding themselves under her nailbed. Ignoring the searing pain, she continues even after the woman seems to give up. She wishes she could call out and tell her it's no use anyway. They always lock the door before they leave. Unless the woman has the key, moving the object blocking the door wouldn't do any good.

The woman's footsteps retreat and Charlotte blubbers miserably. She thrashes and writhes in the chair, expending all of her remaining energy until the chair topples to the ground, sending her crashing down with it. She lands with an excruciating thud, and hears a sickening crack.

Even through the cloth, her scream escapes. The agony is debilitating, she can do no more, and so she lies there on her side, her arm radiating pain. No tears fall, she's too dehydrated, but her body racks with unruly cries.

Her only hope is that the woman heard the chair fall to the ground. Slowly, she soothes herself, staying quiet. Listening. But the woman must be gone.

It isn't long before heavier footsteps sound on the deck of the cabin. Multiple pairs of boots getting closer to her.

They're back.

The object in front of the door is moved, but even they grunt while getting it out of the way. That woman would have had no chance.

As always, only one of them enters the room. On her side, her breathing becomes shallow, anticipating his reaction to seeing her on the floor. He'll know something has happened. He'll get angry.

'I'm so sorry,' he says as he enters the room, saying what he always says before he turns to face her. When he closes the door behind him, he seems to still. 'What're you doing on the floor?' he asks.

He knows she can't respond, so he lets the silence hang in the air between them. She can do nothing but lie there, trembling on her side, bound to the chair.

'Oh, Charlotte,' he huffs, big bulky boots disintegrating the floorboards beneath him as he treads around the room. 'Have you been trying to break free?'

Her cry crescendos as he lifts the chair with her still bound to it, righting it back on its legs. The bones in her arm grind together in a nauseating, unnatural way as she flops back in her seat.

'Charlotte, my love. We've been through this. You can't do that,' he says, and his voice is gentle, the way it used to be, the way she remembers it from when they first met. A Tinder date she now wishes she'd never shown up to. All she can do is cry.

He examines her arm, and she can hear the wince he makes as he gets a closer look. It must be bad. It feels bad, broken perhaps, but it's difficult to see through the blindfold. Will he take her to a hospital? No. Of course he won't. Her body shakes as he cuts the binding from around her wrists. Her hurt arm lolls to the side, the pain wild. He clamps a hand over her mouth as she wails.

'In a few months, you can go free,' he croons into her ear. It's as though he's speaking to a child, calm and methodical.

She doesn't believe him. Hasn't believed him since she was dragged in here. She's not stupid. They will never let her go. She knows who they are, and she knows what they're doing. They'll never believe she'll keep quiet, so why would they let her go? She doesn't think she could keep quiet, not even for the sake of her own life, anyway.

She's propelled onto the bed, white-hot pain burning her arm as she squirms on the mattress.

'Hold still,' he says, peeling up her shirt.

She hates this. She wants to spit in his face and fight him off, but she can't. She's in agony, and she's tired. So tired. The pain in her arm is enough to almost make her black out.

The gel is cold enough to make her gasp aloud as he smears it over her belly. The device glides over her skin slowly, travelling across her abdomen. Like last time, there's no noise. No rhythmic thump of a heartbeat coming from her womb. He presses hard on her pubic bone, searching a while longer.

'Still nothing,' he sighs, removing the doppler after a while. 'Are you sure you're pregnant, Charlotte?'

She wants to tell him no, she's not sure. She wants to tell him she lied about the pregnancy. God, she wishes she hadn't told him she'd booked the abortion. If she'd just gone alone, terminated the pregnancy by herself and lied, told him she'd lost the baby, or maybe not even told him about the baby at all . . . maybe then she wouldn't be in this situation. But she'd only just missed her period and in sheer panic, she'd texted him. He'd come straight over to her flat with a pregnancy test and demanded they take it together.

The test had confirmed her worst fear, and she could see the life she wanted so desperately to lead slipping away from her, even as he'd smiled down at that big blue plus sign. She was too young to be pregnant, and she hadn't known him for that long. They weren't ready to be parents. She wasn't even sure if she was that serious about him, let alone if she actually wanted children. The thought had hardly crossed her mind. She was in her early twenties and had other priorities.

Her plans of travelling Europe for a year before studying law and becoming an incredible corporate lawyer would have been scuppered. So she'd booked an abortion and gone out drinking. If she was terminating the pregnancy anyway why did it matter if she drank? That's how she justified every sip of vodka she took that night, but there was still a deep sense of guilt she kept trying to wash down with more and more alcohol. She'd tried reminding herself with each sip that she didn't need to protect this little life inside her, because they weren't going to become a life.

He hadn't seen it that way, though. He'd been furious, and she's been paying the price ever since.

'Why isn't there a heartbeat?' he hisses. He's growing red in the face, a vein threatening to burst at the side of his temple.

She tries to shrug but it sends a shooting pain all the way up to her neck so that every nerve in her body stands on end. A garbled response escapes from behind the rag in her mouth.

He sighs, irritated, and rips out the cloth. It's the first time she's been able to breathe through her mouth in days and ravenously she drinks in the air.

'Why isn't there a heartbeat?' he repeats.

'I-I don't know,' she manages to croak. Her tongue sticks to the roof of her mouth as she tries to speak. 'Please. Water.'

He produces the bottle of water he keeps in his coat pocket and brings it to her lips. She keeps her hands at her sides as she's been trained to do, sipping thirstily at the water.

'Answer the question,' he demands.

'I don't think you can hear a heartbeat in the first few weeks of pregnancy,' she says. A guess. She knows nothing about pregnancy.

She wants to tell him that maybe the baby has died because of how she's being treated. She isn't getting enough food or water for herself, let alone for the baby that should be growing inside her. But she knows that this baby is the only thing keeping her alive. He wants the child he believes is growing in her womb, and so she begs him for more water.

'I need it,' she says. 'For the baby.'

Water spills over her chin, soaking her clothing. She doesn't care. She gulps and gulps, lapping up as much of the spring water as she's able to.

'Enough,' he says, taking the bottle away although it's still half full.

It's enough to make her sob again. He's giving her just enough to keep her and the baby alive.

CHAPTER 17

Ivy

I haven't asked Ingrid if I can go for a ride this time. The horses seem pretty neglected as far as I can tell. They may have food and water, but no one ever seems to be paying them any attention.

They don't seem to leave the stables, which I find odd considering they're supposed to be racehorses. Shouldn't they be exercised regularly? I don't even think they are groomed properly. Their hooves don't seem picked, their manes and tails seem matted, and from the last time I saw Shadow, I remember dried dirt clinging to him. He hadn't been well kept. There was no healthy shine to his coat, no clear vision in his beautiful eyes. They were caked in dirt, and so I bring a sponge with me from the cabin to wipe away the debris from his eyes. I wonder if it's just like this through winter, or if Ingrid has given up on these horses entirely.

Shadow whickers as I approach him, his ears perked. After giving him a clean, I lay the saddle pad over his back and heave the saddle on top. He nickers as I stroke his shoulder blades, calming him before attaching the girth.

My eyes scan the area. I can't see anything suspect — there's no one in here, no sign of a struggle. It should make me feel better, but I'm jumpy. My every nerve standing on end.

Just as I'm putting the bit into Shadow's mouth, something behind me crashes, banging and clattering to the floorboards. Whirling around, all I see is the rotted wood of the tack shed, fungus growing in every direction. Has someone followed me here? One of the men from the cabin?

Trembling, I tie Shadow to a beam, but the timber is spongy and decayed. I grimace but manage to loop the rope around the wood. Checking Shadow's secured, I move towards the back end of the shed, in the direction the noise came from.

'Who's there?' I call out, my voice muffled in the dampness of the shed.

There's no response, though I don't expect there to be. I'd made sure no one had followed me back to my cabin where I'd quickly changed and grabbed the sponge to clean Shadow. I'd checked over my shoulder while sprinting to the stables. If someone had been following me, they were incredibly discreet. I hadn't noticed anything.

But there's a noise now, and my unease isn't tempered by my fading confidence. I can almost feel a breath on the back of my neck as I edge closer to the back of the shed. It's there that my gaze lands on something jarring. The bucket, lying on its side, abandoned. One look and I know it's the one Ben had taken from Marcel. I peer inside it, at the remnants of carrots and apples. Segmented into crescents, the grains of the apple aged to a dark brown. Horse food. My eye twitches as realisation dawns.

Mirthlessly, I let out a laugh. A dry, cough-like splutter. I'd thought Ben was taking food to a missing girl, a missing girl I'm starting to wonder if I ever saw at all. Is there really someone in that eighth cabin? Or do I still have what my teachers used to call an *overactive imagination*? I can no longer tell. I'm confused, my mind spinning.

Had the person I'd seen in the car with Marcel been someone else? Someone here? It wasn't Freya. Nor was it Natalia or Debbie.

That, I'm sure of. But there are other family members here. Had I confused one of Stephen's cousins or sisters-in-law for Charlotte Walker, the missing woman? Ben had just been coming to feed the horses, after all. That's why the bucket's here. It all makes sense. And now, before I go too far, I'm trying to talk sense into myself.

A rat scuttles out from behind the bucket, halting at the sight of me. Whiskers twitching, the rat stares at me with shiny black eyes. I shake my head. Nothing sinister has been going on at all. Yet, the image of that girl in the passenger seat of the car is seared into my retina. She had looked so much like the girl I'd seen in that newspaper article. Was it some sort of Baader-Meinhof phenomenon? Had I simply stared at that article too long? At that photo of Charlotte Walker? I can almost pass it off as that, in fact I want to. But, what about the clothes? I *had* her clothing. That couldn't just be coincidence.

I squeeze my eyes shut, trying to block out the relentless part of my brain still screaming at me to help this missing woman. Buckling to my knees, I let myself do the one thing I've always promised myself I'd never do again. I dig my fingernails deep into my forehead, piercing flesh I always cover with my hair. My fingertips inch closer to my hairline and before I can stop myself, I scrunch a fistful of hair into my hand. When I pull, I don't feel the pain it brings with it, I feel a release. A cathartic, otherworldly release alleviating all of my frustration, if only momentarily. The instant throb from my scalp brings me back into myself, placating the palpitations in my chest.

I touch the fine strands of hair wrapped tightly around my fingers, too many to count. Crushing them into my palm, I watch my knuckles turn white, hating that I'm doubting myself. I can't allow that to happen. I won't. I might have mistaken the bucket of horse treats for something more sinister, but I'm not mistaking the rest of it. Charlotte Walker is here, dead or alive, in that cabin by the lake, and I will not stop until I find her. I need to stick to the plan.

Picking myself back up from the ground, I discard the clump of hair that rolls away like tumbleweed.

Once I've adjusted the stirrups, I mount, pressing my heels into Shadow's sides.

'Let's go,' I whisper as Shadow trots from the shed.

I knew I'd be quicker on horseback. As soon as we're out in the open, we're cantering. As I'm suspended in the air, slamming back down into the saddle, I plead. *Let my baby be okay.* I know this is dangerous, stupid even, but I also know it's the only way out of this retreat to get help for Charlotte. Especially with all of the tyres slashed on the cars, this is my only way out of here. I'd go slower, but I'm petrified of being caught, and so I careen on.

As we charge through the woodlands I think of the eighth cabin. Of the clock concealing whatever lies behind that door. I think of Ingrid's words. '*She's definitely different,*' she'd said. And, '*She's not his usual type. At all.*' I think of Freya's admission. '*Clint, Jamie, Michael. . . and Stephen.*' The way she had said his name, with a hiss and a sultry bite of her lower lip. Just the thoughts anger me enough to drive my heels further into Shadow's sides, making him pick up the pace.

Watching the retreat fall away, I hold tight as Shadow gallops through the woodlands. My ludicrously glitzy nails dig into the palms of my hands as I clasp the reins. Ice particles hit my exposed cheeks as I speed away from Shadowmoor Lodge. Every stride the horse makes edges us closer to Dorking, the only town I know around here from the taxi ride. Childishly, I'd thought the name unfortunate when I'd read it on a road sign on the way here. Now, the town of Dorking may very likely be my only chance of saving this woman.

Shadow's hooves are blasting into the frozen earth, getting further and further into the depths of the woods when a gunshot reverberates around me, shaking the branches of the trees. A second explosion ricochets around me, then a third. Shadow falls forward, a sharp, heart-shattering cry coming from deep inside him. He crashes to the ground, taking me down with him. For a breathtaking moment, I think I've been shot. It hurts all the way down to my diaphragm. I try to swallow air, but I can't, and it makes me clutch helplessly at my chest. Slowly though, the spasm from having the wind knocked out of me eases and I sip in a lungful of air so cold it's enough to turn my organs raw.

Rolling over, I check on Shadow. He's still down, panting heavily.

'No, no, no,' I scream, ignoring the pain radiating up the side of my body from the fall. Scrambling over to him, I place a hand over his heaving chest. Huge, scared eyes penetrate mine as his rapid breath heats my face. 'Shadow,' I whisper, brokenly. *Sorry*, I think. *Sorry, sorry, sorry.* If I'd just left him in the stables, he'd be okay. Oh God, what have I done?

My eyes rove over his body, searching for a wound, a point of entry where the bullet may be, but I can't find one. Just as I'm starting to think he might be alright, footsteps make me pivot. The colour drains from my face as Marcel emerges from the thicket, a bolt action rifle aimed in my direction.

I stare right down the barrel of the gun, wondering if this is how I die. I've always wondered how the inevitable would find me, chase me down. I've always hoped to grow old. To fall asleep and never wake up, the way everyone must surely want to go. That or doing something that they love, but for me, death by sewing machine doesn't sound quite as poetic. I've always been terrified of getting sick, of watching myself deteriorate or, worse still, lose myself to some kind of mind-altering ailment. I never expected *this*. I've escaped death by gunshot once, though it had come at a price, and perhaps naively I'd decided the chances of facing the barrel of a gun again would be slim. Even in South Africa, but certainly not in England.

'Are you going to shoot me?' I rasp, still fighting for breath.

Marcel parts his lips, about to speak, but another voice interrupts.

'Ivy?' Stephen calls, crashing into the clearing with Ben on his tail. 'What the hell are you doing out here?'

Marcel lowers his weapon, exhaling in irritation. I break eye contact, looking back down at the horse.

'Shadow,' I tremble, not daring to remove my hands from his side. I can feel his ribs jutting out, sharp under my touch.

Stephen runs over, crouching down. 'Are you okay?' he asks, assessing me.

I nod, though I don't know if I am.

'What happened? Was he shot?' Stephen places a hand on my shoulder, loving, warm, pacifying. His touch puts a chink in my armour, and I loosen under the contact, just slightly. He's my fiancé, and I'm sure he'll keep me safe, no matter what. He knows I'm pregnant, and he's wanted this baby for so long that I know he will do anything to protect me and our unborn child.

'Was he shot?' he says again, more urgent now.

I nod again, shivering. Stephen curses under his breath, retracting his fingers from me and redirecting his focus to Shadow.

'Ivy, I can't see a bullet wound,' he says. 'I think he's just in shock.'

'Because one of *you* shot at us,' I spit, glaring up at Marcel. I know it was him. The barrel of his gun may well have been smoking for all of my certainty.

John and William enter the clearing now, followed by their other brothers. Uncles and cousins are in convoy, all halting at the sight of Shadow on the ground. Stephen is gently moving each long leg to check for sprains.

Marcel sticks his nose up, sniffing the burnt gunpowder permeating the air.

'This,' he says, measuredly, 'is hunting land. You shouldn't have been here.'

I cross my arms, seething. Not even an apology. He seems indifferent. There's no remorse or concern, and I'm convinced if Stephen hadn't come barging through the trees when he had that he'd have shot me. I stare at the gun in his hand, at his finger still idling on the trigger.

'He's right Ivy,' Stephen says, his hand still resting on Shadow. 'You knew we were hunting today. Why would you come out here, especially on horseback? I told you last time how dangerous it is.'

'I know. I just—'

'Just what, Ivy? Didn't think, again?' Stephen's voice is rising.

Winter could melt from the heat of my flaming embarrassment. He's scolding me in front of everyone, like a child chastised for wandering away from their parent. I try to remind myself he's reacting this way out of love, that he just doesn't want anything bad to happen to me, but it's still mortifying. I hate that he's speaking to me like this in front of everyone else.

Men with guns close in on me, and I feel a surge of panic as I take in their blood-splattered clothing. A sudden thought crosses my mind. Are they really hunting deer, or is something more sinister going on? It's a ridiculous thing to think and I try to dismiss it, but it's there now, another thing to torment me.

'Are you . . .' Stephen starts, his voice falling away as his eyes leave mine and land on my stomach.

'I'm fine,' I say quickly, before anyone else can pick up on what he's asking me. But I can't be sure. I've had a fall. I've been drugged, and been galloping on horseback through the woodlands.

I've been shot at. Is the baby okay? I've been such a fool, and I'll never be able to forgive myself if I've lost the one thing I've always hoped for and dreamed of. My hand impulsively goes towards my womb, and I place it there before I can stop myself.

Marcel's watchful eyes narrow. He's noticed.

Stephen stands, letting out a long stream of vapour as he sighs.

'We need to get back to the hunt,' he says, hoisting his rifle bag back over his shoulder.

'Wait. Wh-what about Shadow?' I stammer as he starts to walk away from the clearing. 'Is he hurt?'

He stills. 'Shadow's fine, just in shock,' he says, taking one last look at me before stalking off into the trees.

* * *

My chance of getting out of here on horseback has been sabotaged.

When Shadow finally recovers from his state of shock, I lead him back to the stables and untack him slowly. My forehead rests against his own and I breathe in his dusty, woodchip scent. I almost got us both killed. The sickening realisation that Marcel had deliberately aimed and shot at me makes me shake. My hand won't steady as I run it through Shadow's mane.

Had he really not realised it was me? Could he really have thought I was a deer? I must have been a good thousand feet away from him when he'd put a cartridge into the chamber of his gun, pressed his cheek into the stock and squeezed the trigger. He'd had me in his line of sight, and he'd fired the round right at me. Intentionally. I'd have been magnified; I saw the scope he was using. I may not like guns, but I know enough about them now. It's something I'd forced myself to confront after what had happened to me in South Africa. Facing my fears, I'd called it.

Weekends had been spent at shooting ranges, if only to feel in control over the one thing that had made me lose control of my bladder and made me do the most hideous things with a vile man whose face I'll never know. The mask he'd worn the day he'd hijacked me had hidden any defining features I needed to find him. He was just a faceless figure with a gun. And the father of the child I lost early on in pregnancy.

The memory comes back to haunt me now and my hand rakes into my scalp, gripping at strands of hair. My face is still pressed into Shadow's, and I scrunch my nose, about to pull out a fistful of locks, but something makes me stop.

Shadow's doleful eyes don't leave mine. My heart sinks as I realise the path I'm going down. I won't allow myself to slip into that horrible, dark place in my mind again. Shadow nudges affectionately into me, and it's almost as if he's encouraging me to keep strong. Keep going. Don't give up. If I give up, Charlotte Walker has no chance and neither do I.

I think again about what happened today. I'd been racing through the woods, through the ancient beech trees, when I'd heard the gunshot. The bullet had penetrated the trunk of a tree just behind me, causing Shadow to rear up and spin. I'm sure the second bullet hit the ground right next to us. I saw the ground explode, the dirt flying into my eyes. I remember the blast of the frozen earth right by Shadow's hooves. It had been enough to send him crashing down.

Under the guise of hunting deer, Marcel had feigned innocence. But no. Marcel had known it was me. He'd shot right at me, maintained his focus and shot again. He'd been trying to execute me.

CHAPTER 18

I need to come up with another plan. The tarot reader hasn't come back with a fleet of police cars; in fact, she may not have even seen the note slipped into her bag. It could've fallen out or been flattened at the bottom of the bag by whatever else was in there. Her phone, cigarettes, the deck of cards. The note isn't something I can rely on to help me now.

Even if Joanna has found it, would she link it back to me? In my mind, I like to think that Joanna would see the note and instantly have a sixth sense that something is wrong at Shadowmoor Lodge. But I know the world doesn't work like that. Rarely do things play in my favour, things don't just fall into place. The world is about overcoming hardships, proving you can withstand the trials life throws.

With two days to go until my bridesmaids arrive, I'm very much alone out here in the ancient woodlands of Surrey Hills. Alone to deal with the James family who, I'm realising, have some very nasty skeletons in their closet.

'I'm so sorry,' I murmur to Shadow before leaving, the other horses watching on curiously.

* * *

The door opens with a dull crack as I get back to the cabin. The floorboards bend beneath my feet. I'm pacing, breathing fast, squeezing my fingernails deep into the palms of my hands to stop them from travelling up to my hair and ripping out giant chunks.

The brittle wood foundation makes creaks and pops, groaning in protest under each step I take. How the hell am I going to get out of here? I could leave on foot, but the acreage of woodlands stretches for miles. It would take hours to get to Dorking or any other town close by, and if I got lost out there in the middle of such an unforgiving winter I'd surely freeze to death before someone finds me. *If* they find me. And what about Stephen? I'm not sure if I can risk upsetting him even further. His patience is wearing thin with me.

When I look at the time, I'm surprised that it has only just gone midday. My eyes burn, like I've opened them under the ocean for too long. They're heavy, begging to be closed. *This is pregnancy*, I remind myself. This is what I've always wanted. But I know it's more than that. I'm tired because of the fatigue following the adrenaline rush. I was almost killed. Of course I'm tired.

As much as I want to do more, I find myself collapsing down onto the mattress and curling into a tight ball. I'm asleep before my eyes have even had a chance to flutter closed.

I'm jolted awake by the bedroom door slamming. Blinking quickly, disorientation takes hold. It's dark outside. I must have slept for hours.

Stephen comes in, heavy footed. 'Hey,' he grunts, heading right to the bathroom and turning the shower on. Dried blood, the colour of rust, falls off him in clumps. 'Been field dressing,' he explains as I stare down at the scattered ashes of blood dusting the floorboards.

A frown forms on my face. I have no idea what that means.

'Gutting deer,' he says, shedding his shirt and kicking off his trousers. They land in a pile in front of me, but I'm too repulsed to pick them up the way I usually would. Not that he'd expect me to, but I've always liked to think we work best as a team.

When he steps into the shower, the water pooling at his feet turns a dark reddish-brown. I step away as he lathers shampoo into his hair, the woodsy smell already drifting through to the bedroom in wisps of shower steam.

'Think you'll be ready for dinner in five minutes?' he calls to me.

'Dinner?' I ask, though I already know what he's implying. We're going over to Ingrid's for another family meal. And his question is rhetorical. He doesn't mean it. I know he expects me to go. He's telling me: be ready in five minutes.

I inspect myself in the mirror. No. I'm not ready. My makeup has rubbed off from sleeping the day away, my hair is knotted, and my clothing is creased. 'Yep,' I shout back through gritted teeth.

* * *

The concealer is cakey on my nose, no matter how I try to blend it in. In this weather my skin is dehydrated, zapped of moisture. Part of me thinks I should just go into the bathroom and use a face wipe to rub the makeup off. I'd look better bare faced than like this, and that's saying something. But there's a part of me, a deeply insecure part, that decides to tip the bottle of foundation onto my hand and start dabbing the liquid over my face. I won't be able to stand being in Freya's presence if I haven't at least tried to make an effort.

Stephen stalls as he opens the bathroom door, looking me up and down.

'You look nice,' he says. His tone is still gruff, and he doesn't quite meet my eyes. My eyes that I've painted dark in a moody Kate Moss fashion. War paint. I've curled my lashes and swept the mascara out at the corners. I've also managed to change, to slip into a little black dress I now realise I won't be able to wear for much longer. Already it feels a little tight on me.

I don't respond to him; I merely look at his reflection in the mirror as I glide a burgundy lipstick over my 'o' shaped mouth.

'I don't know why you're angry at me,' he huffs. 'If anything, I should be mad at you!'

Replacing the cap on the lipstick, I place the tube back on the side table and turn to face him. I smooth down my dress and take a deep breath in. 'Stephen,' I say.

He doesn't move, but his eyes trail down my body, devouring my every curve. 'Ivy,' he replies, his Adam's apple bobbing as he swallows.

It would be easy for me to lose my tongue, to tell him how angry I am with him. What's hard, is refraining, and that's exactly what I do.

'We should go,' I say, dropping a faux fur coat over my shoulders.

We haven't spoken since the shooting, but I don't want to. Anything I say will only fall on deaf ears. *I need to go to the doctor. We need to check the baby is okay.* It's no use. The cars can't get us anywhere, and I'm too terrified to mount a horse again after being shot at.

'Ivy, you should know something,' Stephen says, his voice stopping me as I'm walking towards our bedroom door.

'What?' I say, turning to face him.

I'm sure he's going to tell me that he knows I've seen the eighth cabin, confess to whatever it is that's going on down there. But then, I'm also sure that Stephen doesn't know anything about that. I know him. He's my fiancé. I *trust* him, don't I? I'm suddenly not so sure.

'There's a storm coming.' He winces, and seems to force himself to meet my gaze.

'A storm?' I ask, not understanding the severity of his words although it's written all over his face.

'There's been a severe weather warning announced.' As he says this, he stands with his hands wedged deep into his pockets.

'As in, a *blizzard*?' I ask, my voice rising an octave.

'Most likely, yes.' He dips his head, once again avoiding eye contact.

I stride towards the bedroom window and peer outside. Meaty, low-lying clouds hover over the woods, dark grey, almost black.

'No,' I whisper, gripping at a strand of hair that has fallen over my eyes. I tug, not hard enough to pull out the hair on my already scarred scalp, but enough to hurt.

The doctors warned me if I carry on, I'll get bald patches. It had got so bad after the hijacking that I'd even started tearing at my eyebrows and at the fine, delicate hairs above my top lip. That was before I met Stephen. Since meeting him I've come off the anxiety medication that helped control my urges. I haven't needed it since. I've felt safe, and happy. Until now.

'Ivy, it means the other guests might not be able to get here for the wedding.'

'My bridesmaids?' I choke, not wanting to believe him.

'Everyone,' he says.

'The wedding's still two days away. The storm will pass. There's time for them to get here!' I cry.

'I think you might need to ready yourself for doing this without them.' He sighs.

'No!' I shake, and pull. I hear the follicles tear, as if in slow motion, as I bring my fist to my face. There in my hand is a handful of hair, not just a few strands but a thick clump. I've drawn blood, my scalp warms with red beads and the feeling is euphoric, if only for a few moments.

'What're you doing?' Stephen asks, alarmed. His nose has scrunched up in disgust. He doesn't know about this, about how bad my mental health was when we'd first met.

I had been going to tell him. I'd thought it only right. But we'd met and it had been so lovely, and I hadn't done anything like that for a while at the time. So I'd glossed over it. I'd told him about the hijacking, of course. But my mental health never came up. When he'd asked if I was okay, I'd said yes, because I was. And as our relationship progressed, I'd only improved. Even when our struggles to conceive started, I didn't fall back into old habits. I hadn't needed to, because I had him.

Now, I don't know if I do have him. Not in the way that I used to.

'I-I don't know,' I mutter, dropping the hair to the floorboards and hoping he'll forget what he's just witnessed.

He doesn't. He grimaces, looking down at the ball of hair on the floor.

'Ivy,' he says slowly. 'A warning like this wouldn't have been issued if there wasn't a real concern.'

It takes me a moment to process this information. This storm, this blizzard . . . it means my bridesmaids aren't going to make it. It means the tarot reader won't be able to arrange help even if she does see my note. It means no one is coming. No one is going to help me.

CHAPTER 19

It's only when we're inside Ingrid's cabin that I wonder how Stephen managed to hear about a weather warning on the news. How he'd managed to be privy to that kind of information when there's no signal and no Wi-Fi on the grounds.

There *must* be a signal somewhere out in the woods, way up high on a hill maybe. In the direction the men have been for their hunts. Or maybe there's a radio somewhere that can tune in to a certain frequency. I don't know, but I'm determined. While the night plays out in front of me, I plot my next move.

The first thing I'm going to try tomorrow, two days before the wedding, is search for signal around the hunting grounds. Storm or no storm. I need to try.

Stephen circled everything for me on a map when we'd arrived, shown me where they go to hunt. There are several hilltops in the area, so I'm going to try each and every one of them.

The weather warning either came through on his phone while he was out there hunting, or they'd had a radio out there which had picked something up. Either way, I need to find out if there's a way to connect to the outside world and get help. Though at this stage, I'm not even sure what I'll be calling for help for. Myself? My baby? Charlotte Walker? All of the above? If I actually get through to someone, I'm not sure what I'll say to make sure it doesn't all come out in a garbled mess.

* * *

Halfway through dinner, spinach and feta stuffed chicken breast wrapped in bacon, there's a knock at the door.

'Ivy,' Ingrid says, her mouth forming a tight line as she looks at me from the doorway. 'Someone is here to see you.'

I drop my cutlery, my heart skyrocketing. My bridesmaids. One of them, at least. One of them made it. Thank God. I rise from the table, apologising as I leave behind quizzical looks in my wake. When I get to the front door, however, it isn't Kayleigh, Georgie or Rosie. It's Joanna, the tarot reader.

'What's this all about?' Ingrid asks, hot on my tail. My eyes grow wide.

Joanna clocks my expression, my alarm at Ingrid being right behind me and it causes her to straighten a little. Stand her ground. 'I was wondering if I could have a word with Ivy,' she says.

I part my lips to respond but Ingrid beats me to it.

'Is this about her tarot reading?' she asks, a nervous laugh rippling from her.

'Joanna, please. Come in,' I say, and start to open the front door wider to let her inside.

Ingrid's hand clamps down on the frame, stopping me. 'We're right in the middle of dinner!' she says.

'This won't take long,' Joanna says, dancing from foot to foot in the cold. Behind her, her black Volkswagen Beetle rumbles, the engine still on, headlights shining brightly onto the deck.

'Make it quick,' Ingrid says with a sigh, strutting back down the hallway and into the dining room.

I'm not sure whether to be relieved that Ingrid's gone or not, but before I can think about it too much, Joanna speaks.

'Was this you?' Joanna produces the slip of paper I'd tucked into her bag.

I nod, too afraid to speak.

'Help?' she reads, piercing me with a mystified look.

I don't know how long I have alone with Joanna, and so I know I need to be quick. Seize the moment.

'Something's going on here,' I say quickly, hushed and frantic.

'I don't understand?'

'The James family. Something is wrong here.' I falter, struggling to articulate what I really want to say.

'I sensed that, when I arrived.' Joanna nods, and lifts her head up to inspect the cabin. 'I could feel it in the woodwork. Something dark.'

Her words make my skin pebble.

'From the moment I arrived, I wanted to leave,' she says, shivering as she glares at me in the shadows. 'And now I'm back. Because of this.' She holds the piece of paper up in front of us, between her thumb and forefinger.

'So, tell me, Ivy. How can I help you?'

'Joanna,' I whisper. 'I think something really bad is going on here. Something to do with that missing local girl, Charlotte Walker.'

Recognition ignites Joanna's deeply grooved features, but as it does, footsteps make both of us whip our heads in the direction of the woods.

The earth splits beneath boots, the cracks ringing loudly throughout the otherwise silent night. Not even the tawny owls I've become so accustomed to are out tonight.

'Please,' I hiss, grabbing Joanna's hands. They're unbelievably cold in my warm palms. 'You need to help me.'

Marcel appears from the darkness, ascending the stairs to the decking.

'Ivy,' he wheezes, gripping the banister.

I want to tell Joanna everything, there and then. Explain how Marcel shot at me. That he had wanted to kill me. But I can't. Not in front of him.

'Marcel.' I nod, stiffly.

When I hadn't seen him at dinner, I'd thought he must have tired himself out hunting and had assumed he wouldn't be coming tonight. Seeing him now, fury stews from my insides.

You shot at me, I think, seething.

'Is this one of our esteemed wedding guests?' he asks, his words laced with sarcasm. 'Just missed the storm, didn't you?'

'This is Joanna. She did our tarot readings at the hen party,' I explain.

'Ah,' Marcel says and his facial expression twists from hospitable to utter distaste. 'And what is it you're doing here now?' he asks, addressing Joanna directly.

'I have a message for Ivy,' Joanna says, simply.

'A message.' Marcel plays the word on his tongue, thoughtful.

'From the other side.' Joanna sinks her hand into her handbag and produces a sharp amethyst pendant dangling from a silver chain. She holds it out in front of Marcel's face, and I can't help but notice how it starts to sway angrily despite the lack of a breeze.

'For heaven's sake,' Marcel scoffs, rolling his eyes. 'I'll be inside.' He slams the front door behind him, leaving us both standing stock-still out on the decking.

'Thank you,' I breathe, finally breaking my gaze from the crystal to Joanna, who shrugs in response.

'Easiest way to get rid of someone,' she says. 'In this field you get to learn pretty quick who believes and who doesn't.'

'I believe.' My voice shakes. I'm still speaking quietly, afraid of people listening in. Our voices could easily travel through the quiet of the night, into the dining room window that I know is cracked open. I have to be careful.

'I know.' Joanna nods. 'Ivy. I want to help you. What's going on?'

'You're going to think I'm completely mad,' I sigh, looking back over my shoulder to make sure we're alone.

'Does that matter?'

'I guess not,' I say, biting my lip.

'I think Marcel, that man you just met, I think he's responsible for the disappearance of Charlotte Walker.'

There. I've said it. It's out there now. Someone else knows. Saying it out loud, it's like the heaviest load has been taken from my shoulders.

'That's a serious accusation, Ivy,' Joanna warns. 'What makes you say that?'

I notice Joanna fumbling with her handbag, her wrist trembling as she checks the time. This woman is scared. Out of her depth. She's probably wondering why the hell she decided to come back here, to get involved. I would have the grace to feel bad if she wasn't my only hope.

'I saw her, in his car. With him.'

Joanna's mouth falls open. 'When?' she manages to ask after a while.

'This week. Just a few days ago,' I say. 'I'm sure it was her,' I add, noticing Joanna's sceptical frown.

'And y-you think Charlotte is here?' Joanna asks, her voice wavering. It's the first time I witness her composure slip.

Joanna looks over her shoulder, back towards her car, grumbling in the frigid night air. She wants to leave, I can tell. She's wishing she'd never driven back here, into the depths of Shadowmoor Lodge. But it's too late now.

I nod in answer to her question. Scared but confident. I'm sure, Charlotte is here.

Joanna rubs the pendulum in her hand. 'This is a tool I use for divination,' she explains. She closes her eyes and lifts the amethyst up to the moonlight.

The rhythmic thump of my chest is dizzying. I want to ask her what she's doing, to tell her there's not much time, but I'm too afraid to open my mouth. Looking back at the cabin, I'm certain a curtain falls back over the window looking out to the decking where we are. Someone is watching us.

'Joanna,' I force myself to say, but Joanna's eyes don't even flicker in acknowledgement. Whatever she's doing, she's focusing all of her energy into it.

A minute ticks by before Joanna blinks. 'I need to sit down,' she says.

I lead her to a chaise sofa, and we sit opposite each other.

'I'm going to start asking simple yes or no questions, Ivy,' Joanna says. 'If the pendulum swings clockwise, that indicates a yes. Anticlockwise is a no. Understand?'

I nod, unsure where this is going. Joanna extends her hand, holding the pendulum out in front of us.

'Is anybody there?' Joanna asks softly.

We both watch the pendulum, and for a while, it does nothing. The night is still, not even a whisper of a breeze. Then, the pendulum starts to swing. I don't believe it at first. I look at Joanna's hand, sure she's manipulating it. But her hand is motionless.

'Is this Charlotte Walker?' Joanna asks, and the pendulum starts to sway in the opposite direction.

'Is Charlotte Walker here?' she asks, her tone strengthening now.

The pendulum starts swinging erratically. I study it closely. It's spinning clockwise.

'I don't understand.' I shake my head, lifting my eyes. I wait for Joanna to meet my gaze.

'The pendulum connects with spirit. Spirit is telling me Charlotte Walker is here.'

My stomach drops. I've been right all along. 'But the spirit isn't Charlotte Walker?'

Joanna shakes her head, no. 'This place is swarming with spirits, Ivy. Angry, resentful spirits.'

My skin crawls at Joanna's words. 'Does that mean Charlotte Walker's alive?' My pulse pounds.

Before Joanna can answer me, the front door cracks open. The sharp click of Freya's heels sound against the deck. 'Ivy?' she calls out into the night.

'Take this,' Joanna mutters, enclosing the pendulum in my hand. It's surprisingly hot in my palm. 'I'm going to get help. I'll be back.' With that, she rises.

'You,' Freya says in recognition as Joanna hurries past her.

I watch as she gets into her black Beetle and throws the car into reverse. I want to wrench open the car door on the passenger's side and go with her, I want to beg her not to leave me here alone — but Freya is here, so I hold my tongue.

'What was she doing back here?' Freya asks, and it almost sounds accusatory.

I think quickly. 'She said she had a message from my grandmother who passed away a long time ago.' As I say it, I pocket the pendulum.

'Urgh!' Freya raises an eyebrow. 'What a con.'

I ignore her, pulling open the front door and leaving Freya behind as I head back inside.

* * *

'Who was that?' Stephen asks as I position myself in the chair next to him.

I explain the same story as I did to Freya and I'm met with the same disbelieving look.

'Weird,' he says. 'You okay? That's pretty creepy.'

Stuffing my hand in my pocket, I roll the amethyst around my fingers and nod. Yes, I'm okay, because someone is going to get help. I'm not alone in this anymore.

* * *

After Ingrid has sliced up a sliver of cheesecake for everyone, Stephen excuses himself from the table. He's never had a sweet tooth, but as I cut into the biscuit base, I wonder where he's gone. I heard the front door open and close. The cold night air drifts all the way in and wraps around me. I don't take a bite of the cake. Instead, I push it around the plate with my spoon, waiting for Stephen to come back. The pendulum, as dainty as it is, feels weighty in my pocket.

Watching the minutes tick by, I start to wonder if Stephen is coming back. So when the door to the cabin flies open and Stephen clomps in holding onto the neck of a beer bottle, I'm stunned. I'm about to go up to him and ask him where he's been when I feel a hand on my arm.

'Ivy,' Ben says, drawing my attention away from the group.

I turn in his direction, clutching the stem of a wine glass that has sat in front of me all night, untouched.

'Help me clear these.' He nods towards the plates in front of us.

Together, we stack everyone's plates. I notice Stephen crouched over the fireplace, throwing logs onto the flames. Marcel is sitting in his tartan armchair, stroking a thumb along his jaw. They're discussing something, and Stephen seems agitated. He's tossing more logs into the fireplace than there needs to be, making smoke billow out.

'Ivy?' Ben breaks my concentration, and I look up at him, realising I've still got a stack of plates in my arms. 'Let's go to the kitchen,' he says.

I have no choice but to follow him. When we get to the kitchen I stand with my feet shoulder width apart, squaring up to him. I'm not going to let him intimidate me, no matter what he does.

'Ben.' My tongue does a sharp flick as I sound out his name. He reaches out for me, and I try to flinch away, but he holds me tight.

'You need to stop,' he says, his hand hot against my skin.

'Stop?' I echo.

'Stop prowling around. Stop looking,' he says, his eyes beseeching. 'Please. For your own good. Before something really bad happens here.'

I'm not sure what to say, or what to do. I stand there, dazed for a few moments, before I simply turn away from him and walk out of Ingrid's cabin. I don't stop to retrieve my coat or to say goodnight to anyone. I just leave, unable to spend another minute there in the cabin or to be in the presence of anyone in the James family.

CHAPTER 20

Two Days Before the Wedding

In the morning, I extricate myself from under the covers and sherpa fleece blanket while Stephen snores softly. I leave him to sleep off his hangover, padding into the bathroom to splash water onto my face.

My body is yearning for a run. I feel it, that cry for aching muscles in my legs. To have my feet pounding against the hard earth again. I need to hammer out the festering truths I've discovered before they spread into every part of me.

I know the rule with exercise is that if you were doing it before pregnancy, it's considered safe. Bethany Hamilton only stopped surfing in her final trimester, so I am confident a run isn't going to do any harm to the baby.

Changing, I lace up my running shoes, throwing a quick glimpse at Stephen's lifeless form. All night I dreamed of Freya, with Stephen. Every time my body would shut down, I'd find myself entangled in a hellish nightmare, watching the two of them become intimate, right here in the cabin, out in the woods by that disturbing firepit and down at that eighth cabin, in the room hidden behind the grandfather clock. I couldn't escape it. Their cries of pleasure still rang inside my head long after I woke.

Anger and betrayal bubble inside me. How could he have kept this from me? And how am I meant to act around Freya now? I can't look at her without imagining her with Stephen. It's an image I could've done without. But wouldn't I have rather known than be kept in the dark? I don't know which would be worse. I sigh, quietly slipping from the bedroom and heading downstairs.

Outside, crystalised cobwebs string across the cabin like banners and the trees are silhouetted against a ruby-red sky. A blood moon. I swallow back the sense of foreboding it brings with it. The storm hasn't arrived yet, and for that I'm grateful. It'll make the journey into the woodlands easier, at least.

My eyes are wet, whether from the shock of the change in temperature as I stepped outside or from my raging emotions, I can't tell. I start to run, steadily at first, keeping an even pace. Instead of having my AirPods jammed in my ears, I'm moving along to nothing more than the eeriness of the woods. Trees creak and groan in the wind, and frozen leaves rustle as they skitter across the path in front of me. Before long, I'm sprinting, trying to get away from my own imagination. From the imagery in my head of Stephen and Freya, together. I squeeze my eyes shut, trying to force the thoughts out, but they keep coming. I can't even explain why it's rattling me, only that it is. This week was supposed to be about me and Stephen, no one else. It was our time to celebrate our relationship with loved ones, and perhaps naively, I thought that once we arrived, nothing would get in the way of that. But of course something did. Something always crops up to destroy everything I work hard for. The impulse to howl out into the morning twilight like a wild dog foaming at the mouth is hard to control.

I try to inhale the icy cold air, but my throat constricts. My emotions are running riot, and I can't grasp onto anything to stabilise myself. My foot catches on a tree root that has risen to the surface of the soil, in search of oxygen. I trip, stumbling forwards, and come down hard. My elbow connects with a jagged rock, searing pain vibrating through me. Stuttering for breath, I swallow down a sob.

As I lie there on the cold, hard earth, I realise I'm drenched in sweat. Heat is trapped inside my thermals, and the urge to claw my way out of the clothes overwhelms me as I lift myself from my knees. The wet has seeped through my leggings, leaving me soaked through and shivering.

Looking around at my surroundings, I try to orientate myself, but everything looks the same out here in the woods. The cabins and stables have already sunk far behind me, and as the snow starts to plummet down, I realise that I am lost. The fall had spun me round, and I can no longer be sure from which direction I came.

'Fuck,' I mutter, fumbling for the phone in my pocket. I hold it up as high as my outstretched arm will allow, paying no attention to the incredible pain shooting from my elbow. A bar jumps up onto the screen, just one, but it's there. My stomach flips, and in my excitement, I shout out loud. But it's short-lived. As soon as I look again, the bar is gone. Was it a trick of the light? Was it ever there at all?

Growling in frustration, I unlock my phone to check if any messages came through, but there's nothing. Sighing, I stuff my hand back into my pocket, rummaging between the amethyst, lint and the set of the cabin's keys. Pulling out the folded map Stephen had given me when we'd first arrived, I trace the route I ran with the tip of my finger and try to work out where I am now, but there's nothing around for miles. Just tree after tree in every direction I turn, and in the thickening snow even the path is starting to disappear beneath a blanket of snowflakes.

The snow starts to blow wildly, slapping at my face as I wander through the woodlands, no longer sure if I'm even on a trodden path. I shouldn't have come out here, I know that now. I should have listened to everyone last night, realised the severity of the blizzard that was stopping our wedding guests from getting here. Ingrid had told everyone this storm was going to be the new *Big Freeze*. I didn't know what that meant and had looked at Stephen for answers.

'One of the worst winters in the United Kingdom, it happened in the sixties I think,' he'd said quietly.

'Or is it the new Beast of the East?' Freya waggled her eyebrows at us, amused.

I had assumed that was another notable storm of some sort and had tried to ignore the grin that had crept up on Freya's face. I could tell she was enjoying this setback in our wedding. *Couldn't have planned this better myself*, I imagined Freya saying.

As much as I'd hated being around that table last night, I'd do anything to get back there now. Back to the warmth and security of the cabins. I'm horribly aware of how alone I am out here, and suddenly I wonder when Stephen will wake up and notice that I'm gone. Will he come searching for me? If he does, will he even find me?

My hand stays glued uselessly to my womb as I struggle on. *What have I done?* In a frighteningly short amount of time, I can no longer see a few metres in front of me. The blizzard has changed into a complete whiteout. Blundering on, I have to guide myself with my hands out in front of me. The cold makes my bones ache, not just my elbow from the fall, but all of me. Even my thermals are futile out here.

The ground crumbles beneath my running shoes, sending me crashing back down. My spine scrapes against the earth, jagged rocks digging into my back as I slide down a slope. When I hit even ground, I lie there hurt and shaking, my hands quivering as my nails dredge up dirt and snow. For a while, I can't bring myself to move, terrified by the very daunting realisation that I am far away from my fiancé, from the cabins, from anyone at all. I am truly alone out in the middle of a blizzard, injured, my back cut to ribbons. Pregnant. What the fuck have I done?

Just as I'm thinking this, I spot something. Something big. It's almost totally submerged in snow, but small patches of black are still peeking out. I drag myself towards it, my hand reaching out and touching the cold hard rubber of a tyre. Looking up, I realise it's a car. A black Volkswagen Beetle. It's plummeted into a ditch, the bonnet crunched up against a beech tree.

My heart races, and despite all of the agony I'm in, I pick myself up and stagger to the car. I quickly brush a layer of snow from the driver's side window and peer inside, expecting to find Joanna slumped over the wheel, but instead, the driver's seat is empty.

* * *

With the storm quickly intensifying, I claw at the handle of the car door. I have no choice but to climb inside and protect myself in the sliver of warmth and safety the car can provide.

When I'm inside, I notice the key is still in the ignition, but the engine has long since died. I try to restart it, but it sputters in protest. There's no way I'm going to get this car started. My eyes look longingly at the vents, trying to imagine the warm gush of air that would normally filter through.

My body is still quivering, though I'm no longer sure if it's from my abrasions or a cold like nothing I've ever experienced creeping right into my very core. Twisting round, I check the backseat, wondering if Joanna has curled up there but there's no body huddled on the upholstery. Where the hell is Joanna? Had she swerved to avoid a deer and skidded off road? Would she have attempted to walk back to the cabins on foot that late at night?

There are other things on the backseat, and I ferret about, discarding books on crystals, oracle cards and an ice scraper. There's a cloth I recognise that had been strewn over the table at my tarot reading which I grab and wrap around myself, though it's of little use. The material is thin, almost see-through, but it provides a shred of extra warmth that I can't refuse.

As I continue to root through Joanna's belongings, I'm surprised to find her handbag amongst the items. Would she have really walked off into the density of the woodlands without it? I feel like it's an invasion of privacy, but I unclip the clasp and dig inside. The first useful thing I pull out is a bright yellow lighter. The second is some sort of handmade smudge stick, an herbaceous bundle bound together with string that smells heavily of lavender.

Gripping both the lighter and the smudge stick, I look out of the car window, my heart sinking. In the whiteout, I don't think anyone will be able to see the smoke if I light the stick. I don't even think it would produce enough smoke to gain anyone's attention this far away anyway.

Casting the stick aside, I lean into the backseat again and grab one of the ivory pillar candles I'd seen. It's difficult with my hands growing numb but I manage to flick the spark wheel on the lighter after a few attempts and create a flame. Briskly, I put the flame to the candlewick and watch the small fire dance. I never thought I'd be so grateful for such a small amount of heat.

Placing the candle onto the dashboard, I carry on looking for anything I think might be useful. I haven't tried the boot yet, but the thought of stepping back out into the blistering cold of the blizzard is far from appealing.

After a while I accept the car holds nothing else to my advantage other than shelter from the storm. I try to remember what I know about blizzards, but in the freezing temperature my brain is struggling to function. Blizzards, I think I recall, last roughly for three hours. Maybe less. I can stay in the car for a few hours, wait for it to pass. There's a handful of candles in the back and while it isn't much, the gentle heat seems to comfort me.

I rapidly grow tired, my body expending all of its energy shivering and shaking. As the minutes tick by I start to have very real concerns of developing hypothermia. As much as I fight it, I soon succumb to sleep, my eyes flickering to a close.

CHAPTER 21

When I wake, I blink in confusion. It takes me a full minute to remember where I am, and how I got here. It's still light outside, blindingly so from the snow, but I have no idea how long I've been asleep for.

The storm seems to have passed as outside is eerily quiet and still. Ice has started forming on the windows inside the car. Wax from the candle has melted all down Joanna's dashboard, and the flame has been extinguished. I grope around for the lighter and relight the wick, my movements rigid.

The door handle feels frozen as I grip it. Ice splinters as I try pushing open the door, but it won't budge. With a sickening twist in my gut, I lurch to the passenger side and tug on that door handle, but I'm met with the same resistance. I've been snowed in. The car may be covered in piles of snow. Even if someone can see down into this ditch, the chances of them seeing the car under all of the snow is minimal.

I am trapped. With no food, no water and worse still, no heat. I start to cry, and the tears are so hot against my frozen cheeks that it burns my skin. As I sob, I twist the engagement ring around on my finger and think of Stephen. He must be out searching for me by now. I wish I'd told him I was going for a run. At least then he'd have some inkling as to my whereabouts.

But then, out here at Shadowmoor Lodge, there's nowhere else to search than the woodlands. It's just unfortunate that the woodlands span for miles in every direction, and Stephen will have no idea where to start.

* * *

I'm on the third candle by the time daylight starts to disappear. There's been no sunshine, no hope of any of the snow melting away throughout the day as I sat there at a loss for what to do.

Surely Stephen would have called a search party. The family would have spread out, covering all ground. Someone has to be coming for me soon. I have tried to get out, bashing myself up against the door, but the blizzard has barricaded me inside and my strength is no match against the depth of the snow.

With my clothing still wet from slipping down the slope, I decide to peel off the layers and hang the clothes over the car seats. I'm sure they won't dry, but once they're removed from my body, I huddle into the dryness of the cloth I found in the back, and a small sliver of the chill is lifted.

I need to get out. If I get out, I may stumble across a search party. If I don't try, if I stay here in this car, I will surely die. Once again, I look around. The tempered glass of the car windows is too strong to shatter easily. I need to find something with a pointy edge to weaken it. Digging back in Joanna's bag, I hope to find something like a pocketknife, but the only thing with a pointy edge I produce is a pen. Although I know it won't work, I start trying to chip at the corners of the glass with it, but soon exhaust myself.

I know my legs are much more powerful than my arms, especially now I've hurt my elbow. Leaning into the driver's side door, I use all of my willpower to pummel my feet into the passenger side window. I kick and kick, but the glass doesn't budge. With no other ideas, I start to scream. My voice rings out into the woodlands until I'm hoarse.

* * *

It's pitch black when I next stir. I've been drifting in and out of sleep for what feels like days but it must only be an hour or two, really. Opening my mouth, I make one last-ditch effort to call for help. That's when I hear it, the snapping of twigs and crunching of earth underfoot. I won't allow myself to believe it's a wild animal. The steps are human, I'm sure of it. Ignoring the pain radiating up my arm, I start to slam my palms incessantly on the car window.

'Please!' I cry out, unsure if anyone will be able to hear me under the snow, but I have to try. 'Please help me! I'm here!'

The steps grow hurried, closer. Someone is definitely here. I'm saved.

'Oh thank God,' I sob, slapping at the glass again and again to be sure they've heard me.

The snow is being swiped away. I keep calling, keep smacking, it's all I can do, I can't stop. The first face I see isn't one I'm expecting. I was hoping for Stephen, to feel rescued and safe, found. To feel his face against mine, to be wrapped in his arms and get warmed up. I wanted to hear his voice, just to listen to him reassure me that I'm going to be okay. But the face staring in at me from outside the car is one of the last I'd expected or wanted to see. Freya's face.

Standing agape, Freya takes a step back as if in shock. With her jarring, cold eyes fixed on me, Freya seems to take a moment to assess the situation. When she takes another step back my insides roll. Very briefly, I'm sure Freya is going to leave me there. Walk away and pretend she'd never seen me. But then Freya's head swivels in the direction she'd come from, and she starts to call out for help.

I hear more footsteps, and voices speaking frantically, but they're too muffled to make out. My vision is starting to blur, the adrenaline too much, but I can just make out Ingrid and Debbie approaching the car window. And before I allow myself to close my burning eyes, I hear the sharp, high-pitched trill of a whistle blowing.

CHAPTER 22

One Day Before the Wedding

When I stir, I'm petrified to open my eyes, too scared to go back to being inside that freezing cold Beetle out in the woods. I'd been oblivious in my sleep, away somewhere else. Somewhere warm and secure.

I want desperately to fall back asleep, to let my dreams whisk me away to a safer place, but then I hear the tick, tick, tick of a clock and my eyes fly open. For one very brief, awful moment, I think I'm in the eighth cabin. That they've brought me here while I was out cold. But as my eyes adjust to the surroundings, I see the blazing fire and slowly I come into myself.

I'm lying on the sofa in our cabin, Stephen draped over me, breathing heavily in his sleep. It's swelteringly hot under the piles of blankets on top of me. Wiggling my feet, I'm horror-stricken when I can't move them. Do I have *frostbite*? Am I going to lose my toes? How serious are my injuries? I try to sit up, but Stephen's weight is too much for me to shift. I'm still too weak.

Looking up at the clock ticking away unawares, I notice that it has just gone one o'clock in the morning. A day before our wedding. The day all of our guests are supposed to arrive. How different things are now to when we first arrived here. No longer am I excited about getting married. All I want to do is go home, to leave Shadowmoor Lodge and never come back.

'Hey.' Stephen rubs his eyes.

I try to speak but my throat feels raw.

'Here,' he says, passing me a glass of water from a side table. 'Drink this.'

Taking the glass, I take small sips, inspecting the gauze dressing over my hands. Someone has treated my wounds. Slowly, I push myself up to a seated position and instantly my vision blurs.

'Easy,' Stephen warns, steadying me as I sway.

Closing my eyes, I listen to him sigh. A deep release. We sit in silence for a few minutes, alone in our cabin. The flames gently pirouette in the fireplace, the wood hissing and popping. I look at anything but Stephen because I know his silence means something. I can tell by the way he's interlaced his fingers and is staring at his feet.

'Ivy,' he eventually says when he clears his throat. 'What the hell were you thinking?'

I don't know how to answer him. Every time I open my mouth the words disappear.

'You're lucky we found you when we did, y'know.' He shakes his head at me. 'Much longer and you'd be in a body bag.'

'I was looking for a signal,' I admit after another mouthful of water. 'I wanted to try and contact my bridesmaids, see if they'd managed to get here for the wedding before the storm.'

It's a lie, but Stephen's eyes crinkle, softening as he pulls me into his arms. 'Oh, my love,' he whispers.

It's only then that it hits me. I'd been in the black Beetle, crumpled against a tree.

'Joanna?' I croak. She has to be okay. The only reason Joanna came back here was to help me.

'We can't find her,' Stephen sighs, cupping my hands in his. 'We've searched, Ivy. She must've found her way out of

Shadowmoor Lodge. She'll be fine.' He refuses to meet my eyes as he speaks, and his words are flat, lacking promise.

'But she left her bag in the car. All her things,' I say, shaking my head. I don't believe Joanna left Shadowmoor Lodge; I'm not even sure she left her car willingly after she crashed.

'What do you want me to do, Ivy?' Stephen barks, dropping my hands into my lap. 'Go out there in the middle of the night? In the pitch black? It's a death sentence.'

'You would for me, if I was out there, wouldn't you?' I challenge, locking eyes with him. My fiancé, the guy I have always thought would do anything for me. Yet now, I'm not so sure that's true.

'Ivy, we don't even know if she's out there!' he implores.

'She crashed her car, Stephen. She's out there, probably hurt!'

He turns away from me, chucking another log onto the fire. 'We both need some rest. We can look in the morning, at daylight.' With that, Stephen pulls a blanket over himself and leans back in the armchair opposite me, closing his eyes, bringing an abrupt end to our conversation.

* * *

When next I wake, the fire has long since danced its last *pas de deux*. The logs have turned to ashes and there's a chill in the air. Stephen isn't in the armchair, and sunlight is bleeding into the lounge. As I sit up, the lacerations on my back scream in protest. My skin feels tight, the scabs splitting back open after an evening of starting to heal. Wincing, I lean forward and chug the fresh glass of water Stephen must have left by the sofa for me.

Voices out in the hallway make me still. Barrelling laughter I don't recognise travels through to the lounge. Quietly, I pick myself up on shaky legs and make my way to the door. I stay hidden, but glance around the corner.

'Some storm that was,' a man is saying, the buttons on his shirt straining over his midriff. 'You're lucky your wedding can still go ahead.'

I gulp. Can it? Can our wedding really go ahead? I thought my past had been a shambles, my first wedding being cancelled one week before the big day, but this? One day before the wedding? My heart physically aches.

'I know, Charles. We're very lucky,' Stephen replies. 'If the storm had happened today, I'm not sure what we'd have done. We're very grateful to you for coming out and getting the car.'

'Good to go, boss,' I hear another, younger male voice say in a cracked drawl. His cap is on sideways and there's grime smeared on his overalls.

'Right. You all keep safe, and enjoy your wedding,' Charles says, his voice dripping in a southern English lilt. He claps Stephen on the back and heads out the front of the house.

Stephen follows, and I creep along the hallway to a window. Charles and the young boy he's with climb into a pickup truck, and on a platform on the back sits Joanna's Beetle.

I rush to the front door, colliding with Stephen.

'You're up,' he says.

'Wh-what are they doing taking Joanna's car away?' I stammer.

'You've slept half the day away, babe,' he says. 'We found Joanna. She's fine. She asked us to tow her car back to Dorking for her.' His eyes shift as he speaks, and his hands seem restless, stuffing them in and out of his pockets.

'Joanna's fine?' I ask, squinting up at him. I'm not sure why, but I can't quite bring myself to believe him.

'Yes,' he says. 'Shaken, but she's fine. Already back in Dorking.'

'How'd she get there without her car?' I ask. 'All the other car tyres are slashed.'

Stephen sighs. 'Ben ran up to one of the hills, found a signal. We called an ambulance, Ivy. I didn't want to tell you and worry you because she's absolutely fine, just spent a night out in the cold so she needed checking over. Okay?'

I don't believe him, and I've lost count of how many times I've been untrusting of him in these last few days. 'You promise me, Stephen? You promise me, she's okay?' My lip trembles as I speak.

I have absolutely no way of finding out if Joanna is alive, if she got out of the woodland safely after crashing her car. She was the only person who knew of my suspicions and who was going to get help. Without her, I feel completely isolated.

'I promise. She's fine,' Stephen says, but his voice is high-pitched, false.

As I stare at him, letting his lie cement between us, I feel the divide. An awful, twisting shift in our relationship. We no longer tell each other everything. The trust is gone. Perhaps, I think, reminded of Freya all of a sudden, it was never there at all.

CHAPTER 23

Ingrid arrives at our cabin not long after I've warmed myself up in the shower. Before she got there, I'd stood under the flow of the water for a while, the steam rolling off my freshly scrubbed skin. I'd allowed myself to cry, huge heaving sobs as my hands held the tiles tacked to the wall. I'd cried even through my relief when I'd worked up the courage to check my toes. I'm not going to lose them. They'd just been tucked under so many blankets that I couldn't feel them when I'd been lying on the sofa. There is a strange tinge of grey to them though.

'It's okay, they'll get back to normal soon. Just keep warm,' Stephen had said, rolling a pair of woolly socks over my feet and squeezing gently. 'We probably don't have long before the masses arrive to check in. Do you want me to light the fire again? Get you anything?'

I'd shaken my head, trying to throw him an appreciative smile. 'I'm fine,' I'd said, but I hadn't sounded as reassuring as I'd have liked.

* * *

Ingrid, of course, notices my eyes, like swollen pig slits, from the second she arrives, and surprisingly, she seems almost nurturing towards me.

'That was quite a scare.' She nods, her hand patting my back as she embraces me.

I can do nothing but breathe in the overpowering musk of her perfume, too afraid to say a word in case I start to cry again.

Debbie and Freya swagger in behind her, brazenly opening cupboards, making themselves cups of tea.

'Sorry.' Freya smiles when she notices me watching her. 'I'm all out.' She plucks a Tetley teabag from our box and drops it into the same mug I've used every day of our stay here so far. It makes me run my tongue across the back of my teeth and sigh. I won't be using that mug again.

'Where's your ring?' Debbie asks, pointing out my naked ring finger.

'Oh, I must've left it in the bathroom after I showered,' I mumble, dropping my gaze down to the pale skin where my ring usually sits.

'Her hands and feet are a bit tender after being out in the storm,' Stephen explains, reaching out and placing his hand over my wrist.

I'm grateful to him, for feeling like he's got my back, and once again it makes me waver uncertainly. Can I trust him? Before I can even entertain the question, Ingrid interrupts my thoughts.

'Are you sure you're up for this wedding?' she asks, her question so bold that we all snap our heads up in her direction.

'Of course she is,' Stephen says tersely, watching his mother crack open windows and dry mugs on the draining board.

I play with my ring finger, with the skin soft, hating that Ingrid feels she can do whatever she wants here, in what should be our cabin. I know it's Ingrid's lodge. I know I'm a guest and I shouldn't complain, but I can't stand how overbearing the women in this family are. I also don't like that Stephen has spoken for me. He hasn't even asked how I'm feeling, but then would he really expect me to be feeling any other way twenty-four hours before our wedding? Less than that, really. In what world could I call everything off now?

'Well good. Your mother's put in enough effort for this event,' Debbie says sanctimoniously, placing her cup of tea down on the coffee table.

'Now,' Ingrid says, cutting through the awkward silence. 'As is custom the night before a wedding, the bride and groom must be separated.'

My heart drops. *Oh no.*

'Don't look so crestfallen, Ivy,' Freya sniggers. 'It's only a few hours apart. I'm sure you can handle it.'

'D'you really think this is a good idea? After everything she's been through?' Stephen asks, his arms sliding around my waist.

'My God, you two are as bad as each other,' Freya retorts, rolling her eyes as she struts away, leaving her tea untouched.

'Ignore her.' Ingrid flashes me a small smile. 'Look, you two have some dinner. Enjoy the last few hours together, then head off to your separate cabins for the night. Next time you see each other will be at the altar!' She winks, but I'm sure she looks as anxious as she does excited. There's a nervous tick in her eye.

'Stephen, you'll be bunking with your brothers. I'm sure they've planned a few things for you throughout the night. And you . . . ' She turns to me. 'We'll try and keep you out of trouble.'

Before we can answer, Ingrid and Debbie scurry out after Freya.

'I guess that's that, then,' I say, puffing out a long breath.

'Promise me you won't do anything else stupid tonight.' Stephen frowns, pulling me into his chest by the nape of my neck. 'You won't go off into the woods? You'll stay inside, warm, safe?' His eyes don't leave mine until I nod. And this time, I mean what I say. The day is already fading and there's not a chance I want to be in that amount of danger ever again.

'Good. I really don't want to leave you out here. I don't like it.'

I want to tell him I don't like it either. I want to beg him not to leave me, but I also know that I'll finally be able to breathe with him gone. I'll be able to think. Because right now, I'm not sure if he's smothering me intentionally or not. Is he even smothering me? All I know for sure is that I feel like I'm under a microscope. Like he's watching my every move. But is that out of love? Is it to protect me? I'm questioning everything and it's both exhausting and overwhelming. My eyes sting as I close them briefly.

'Hey, if you're up for it why don't we cook something together, enjoy our last evening before the ceremony,' he suggests.

'Before we become husband and wife,' I say, trying the titles out on my tongue.

'Would the future Mrs Ivy James care to join me in the kitchen?' he asks, extending his hand.

He looks at me expectantly and I place my hand in his, getting to my feet. Together we head towards the kitchen, but as we do I can't seem to shake the sense that I'm being guided there. Shepherded, like a lamb being led to the slaughter. It isn't the first time I've felt like some sort of sacrifice at Shadowmoor Lodge, and I'm guessing it won't be the last.

'Here's your ring by the way,' he says, guiding my engagement ring right back down the length of my finger. I try to smile gratefully.

Grabbing a bulb of garlic out of the fridge, Stephen pulls off two cloves, crushing them under the flat side of the knife in his hands. I didn't even see him retrieve the knife from the magnetic rack. It just seemed to appear, in his hand.

'Can you tear off some sprigs of rosemary?' he asks, nodding at the fridge again.

I yank the fridge door open and hunt for the rosemary.

'Oh, can you take the chops out too?' he asks.

I take out the rosemary and lamb chops and slowly start picking at the herb.

'You're very quiet, darling,' he says, positioning the knife down between us. The steel glints, sharp and shiny.

Though I'm not sure it was a question, I answer him anyway. 'It's just been an exhausting few days.'

Towel-drying the chops, he takes a pinch of salt and sprinkles it over the meat.

I reach for the blade, ready to roughly chop the rosemary but he stops me.

'I'll do that,' he says, pushing my hand away from the handle of the knife. As if he doesn't want me touching it. I stand, shell-shocked, subtly shaking my head. *Snap out of it. He's being completely normal*, I think.

When he picks the knife back up, I swallow hard. I'm trying to ignore it, but something feels very off. Is it just pre-wedding jitters, or something more?

'You've definitely had an eventful few days at Shadowmoor Lodge, haven't you?' His lips curl up as he speaks. Rolling the herbs, he starts making crosswise cuts in a precise, rocking motion with the knife.

'Sorry,' I mumble, though I'm not sure why I'm apologising, and he glances up, questioning it too.

'Don't be sorry,' he says, his eyes gleaming. 'Be careful.'

'What?' I whisper, trembling.

'Be careful,' he says again. 'Next time you might not be so lucky.' He turns away from me, pulsing polenta in a blender.

He transfers the polenta to a pot of boiling water and whisks it together, all the while I stand there motionless, his words replaying in my head. *Next time you might not be so lucky.* What does he mean?

As he works, I'm hyper aware of the knife, still in his free hand. He hasn't put it down. I feel ridiculous for thinking it, but ever since I came back from the blizzard he's shifted again. Become cagey. The weight of the secrets hanging between us are decimating our relationship right before my eyes. Our entire stay at Shadowmoor Lodge has affected us in ways I can't begin to understand, and I find myself wishing we'd never come, not for the first time.

The chops are as big as his hands as he picks them up, rubbing the herbs over them.

'Can you put some butter in the skillet, please?' he asks.

I drift towards the butter dish and carve two tablespoons from the block. They blend together, melting steadily in the pan.

'Our last meal before we're married,' Stephen says, breaking the silence between us.

I nod. I want to ask him if there's any way of postponing the wedding. Of waiting until my bridesmaids and the other guests can get here. It's the only excuse I have. To tell him that I need them here. I need my friends, to be around people that aren't related to the James family. That part, at least, is true. What I can never tell him is that I can't do it without my people because I'm not sure if I can trust his family.

My mind flicks to Joanna and I hope, I pray to whatever God is out there that Stephen was being truthful. Joanna has to be okay. Because if she's really back in Dorking, that means she will still get help, surely. No one here knows that I told Joanna my concerns about Charlotte Walker or the James family, and Joanna wouldn't have said anything to the family when they found her. I'd made it clear how scared I am alone out here.

Stephen lays the chops in the butter, and they sizzle and spit in front of us. I draw my eyes down to the meat, turning golden in the pan.

'Can you set the table?' he asks, one of his hands slithering up my back.

I shiver, backing away from him. 'Sure,' I squeak, ripping two placemats out of the drawer next to me.

* * *

'Y'know we don't have to do this if you don't want to, Ivy,' Stephen says, but his words seem laced with an icy warning.

'This?' I ask, slicing through a juicy chunk of fat, severing it from the lamb and putting it to the side. Stephen usually admonishes me for it. Plucks the fat from my plate, tells me it's the best bit. But today he doesn't. Today he stares at it, the juices sluicing into my asparagus.

'The wedding,' he says, eyeing me testily. 'I know how much having your friends here for the wedding means to you.'

Despite his solicitous words, I can't help but feel like it's a test, one that if I fail could derail any hopes of me escaping Shadowmoor Lodge. And so I look up at him, smiling broadly, and say, 'Of course I still want to get married, Stephen. It's unfortunate they can't be here, and I'll admit I am disappointed, but it can't be helped.'

This seems to be the response he was looking for. He leans back in his chair, bringing a glass of Merlot to his lips and takes a long sip. What he doesn't realise is that I'm waiting, biding my time for our wedding day. Because while my friends might not be able to catch their flight to get here, the blizzard has passed now. Roads will be opening back up. Our caterers, DJ, celebrant and other local guests will be arriving in the morning. There will be an abundance of cars, of people I can turn to for help. It's my last chance. So I sit across from Stephen, twisting my engagement ring around on my finger and chew a mouthful of lamb steadily between my teeth, the perpetual ticking of the clock once again the only sound in the room.

A rap of knuckles on our front door makes us look up.

'I'll get it,' Stephen says, springing from the table. 'Probably Mum again, come to whisk me away.' He gives a dramatic eye roll on his way out the door, one I return half-heartedly.

With him gone, I sit with my plate of food in front of me, the rosemary and garlic lamb chops, roasted vine tomatoes and creamy polenta turning cold. My stomach growls, but I can't bring myself to eat any more of it.

I hear the front door of our cabin creak open and brace myself for an onslaught from the James family. I'm not looking forward to another evening trapped with those women, but I've long since realised I don't have a choice. That I'm just a pawn, positioned wherever Ingrid feels is best. Usually as far away from Stephen as she can manage.

The familiar chime of Kayleigh's laughter sends my pulse skyrocketing.

'I can't believe we made it,' I hear my bridesmaid say. She's here. Kayleigh is here at Shadowmoor Lodge.

Leaping from the chair, I fly through to the hallway, ignoring my body's cries of pain. Pummelling right into my best friend's arms, I breathe in her gentle floral scent, burying myself in her auburn waves. I can hardly believe it when I see Rosie and Georgie hovering behind her.

'You're here,' I choke. 'How did you—'

'We arrived before the storm hit, just before they redirected all the Heathrow flights,' Kayleigh says, glossy lips breaking into a grin. 'We were lucky, really.'

'Very,' Stephen replies, his hand in his beard.

'We had to wait the storm out before we could get here though. We were so worried we'd miss the wedding,' Georgie says, her tawny hair shining under the moonlight.

'Are you okay, Ivy? It looks like you've been crying?' Rosie, always the empath, asks. She eyes me suspiciously, her face, makeup free as always, a picture of concern.

'Oh, I'm fine.' I force myself to smile, but the quiver in my voice betrays me. I don't want to say anything about what's been going on until I have them alone. Away from Stephen, who is standing at the front door, blocking the entrance.

'She's not fine,' he says, and we all turn to face him. 'Ivy went for a wander and got lost in the woods during the storm.'

My friends' mouths drop open simultaneously.

'Ivy! Are you hurt?' Georgie picks up my bandaged hand gently, sapphire blue eyes searching the rest of my body for more wounds.

'I'm fine, really! Just happy you three are here now,' I say. 'C'mon, let's get you all in out of the cold.' I turn to re-enter the cabin and look up at Stephen, towering over me.

For a moment, I don't think he's going to move. He seems to stand there, motionless, before he flicks his eyes off into the distance. He scans the surroundings briefly before coming back into himself. His mouth fractures from a tight line into the smallest smile, and he stretches out to grab Kayleigh's suitcase.

'Here, let me take that,' he says before leading us all inside.

CHAPTER 24

The wheels of my bridesmaids' suitcases roll down the cabin hallway as Stephen gives the short tour.

'I'm sorry, we didn't think you were coming so we haven't set anything up for you,' he admits as we stop in front of the door to the spare bedroom. He pushes it open to reveal a room much smaller than our own, equipped with nothing more than a pinewood bunkbed and forest green futon by the window.

'We did try to call and text, but nothing was going through,' Rosie says, holding her old, battered iPhone up.

'There's no signal out here,' Stephen and I say in unison, looking at each other awkwardly.

'I'll need to run over to Mum's, grab some linen. I'll let you all catch up.' He pecks me on the cheek before turning to go. 'Won't be long,' he adds, before he leaves.

'Well, this place is a bit . . .' Kayleigh pauses. 'Creepy,' she whispers, low enough to make sure Stephen won't hear her remark.

I wait until I hear Stephen wrench open the front door and slam it behind him. Treading to the window to be sure, I watch as he strides through the snow towards Ingrid's cabin.

'You have no idea how happy I am to see you guys,' I finally say, and my body starts to tremble.

'I know! We tried everything to get here sooner but—' Rosie stops. 'Ivy, you're shaking?' she says.

'What's going on?' Georgie demands, looking around the room as if she too can sense the danger.

'Right. You aren't going to believe me, but just listen, please,' I start, dragging a hand through my hair, still damp from the shower. 'There's this girl, Charlotte Walker.'

'That missing girl? She's all over the news here, her face was everywhere in WHSmith when we went in there to buy some snacks,' Kayleigh says with a frown.

'Yeah, her,' I say quickly. 'Well. She's here. At Shadowmoor Lodge.'

'Wait, what? She's hiding here? Why?' Rosie gasps.

'No, she's not hiding here. She's here . . .' I pause, unsure how to phrase it. 'She's here against her will.' I look up at my friends and watch their faces transform to looks of confusion and concern.

'I don't understand?' Georgie says.

'I'm sure Stephen's dad abducted her. She's being held captive in this creepy secret eighth cabin no one knows I know about,' I divulge.

'Ivy, that's crazy,' Kayleigh whispers, but her eyes twinkle with fear.

'I saw her,' I say firmly. 'In Stephen's dad's car when I was out on a horse ride. Ever since, weird things have been happening here. I've been shot at—'

'Shot at?' Georgie cries, bewildered.

'Ssh! Please!' I put my trembling finger to my lips to silence them. 'Please help me.'

'What're we supposed to do? There's no signal out here,' Rosie murmurs, close to tears.

'Did you rent a car?' I ask, checking out the window for Stephen. He's already trudging back, a pile of blankets and sheets in his arms.

Rosie shakes her head. 'We got a taxi here,' she says.

'Fuck,' I hiss, letting my head hang low.

'What about Stephen? Does he know what's going on? Can't he help?' Georgie asks, chewing on her lip.

I sigh. 'I haven't told him. There's been other stuff going on. Too much to explain right now, but it's made me wonder if I can trust him. So I haven't said anything to him about it,' I confess.

'We need to get the fuck out of here,' Georgie mutters, and as she does, we all turn at the sound of Stephen's boots thundering up the staircase.

'For the bridal party. Only the best Egyptian cotton.' He grins, showing us the sheets with a flourish before depositing them down on the futon. He stills as he notices our expressions.

'What's up, ladies? Christ, it looks like you've seen a ghost,' he says, nervous laughter bubbling out of him. 'Wait, have you?' His brows crease.

'No.' I let out a giggle, too loud, too sharp. 'No, I just shared our news with them, that's all,' I say, placing a hand over my stomach.

All three of my bridesmaids' eyes widen further.

'We're going to have a baby,' I say, a quivering smile tugging at my lips.

'W-we can't believe it!' Rosie stammers.

'The most amazing news!' Kayleigh nods. 'Congratulations!' She steps forward and hugs Stephen.

'I thought we were keeping that between us, babe?' Stephen's eyes narrow. 'Until we know the baby is okay.'

'I'm sorry, I got excited.' I throw an apologetic shrug his way. 'They're my best friends, Stephen.'

He nods curtly. 'Well, I'll let you guys catch up, I guess. I'll be over at John's cabin if you need me. My mother and the rest of the posse should be here soon for some festivities, I'm sure.'

At the doorway, he stops. 'I can't wait to call you my wife,' he says, looking me up and down before leaving.

* * *

As soon as he's gone, Georgie rips her phone from her pocket and starts swiping frantically.

'There's no signal,' I remind her.

'So what do we do?' Rosie asks, tugging at strands of her hair.

Watching her do it makes my hand drift up to my own hair, now falling in waves down my shoulders. I let my hand trail up the back of my neck and start to dig my nails into the soft skin just below my skull.

'Stop,' Kayleigh says stiffly, pushing my hand away. 'Don't do that.'

I want to be grateful to her, but in that moment all I need is to feel that comforting swell of my skin as I tug my hair out by the root.

'Are you really pregnant?' Rosie whispers.

I bob my head. 'I am,' I say, watching nervously for my friends' reaction.

'Oh, Ivy. That's fantastic.' Tears spring to Rosie's eyes. 'I know just how much you've wanted this.'

'Can we talk about that later?' Georgie snaps. 'We're trapped here with a potential murderer!' She starts to pace with her phone in hand.

'Georgie's right. Congratulations, darling, but we need to figure out what to do,' Kayleigh says, pressing her lips together. 'You need to tell us everything.'

I try to tell them everything. To not leave out a single detail. By the time I'm done, they look awestruck. We've congregated in a circle in the centre of the spare room, and as we stand staring at each other a strong gust of wind thrashes tree branches into the bedroom window. The glass threatens to splinter, trees straining at their roots.

'Right,' Georgie says slowly, stepping forward. 'Here's what we do. We wait. We pretend absolutely everything is fine. Got it? Then later, when everyone's asleep, we head down to this eighth cabin and move that clock. Check what's behind there.'

'And what if it is Charlotte Walker? What if she is behind that door?' Rosie asks, holding her breath while she waits for an answer.

In the silence that follows, the wind howls, sending a chill down my spine.

'Then—' Kayleigh starts but pauses at the sound of the front door creaking open on its hinges. 'Then we take this family down.'

CHAPTER 25

The piercing staccato of heels cuts through the silence, the clattering of several pairs of shoes echoing down the hallway.

'Ivy?' Ingrid calls from the bottom of the staircase. 'We're all here.'

I look at each of my friends in turn as I hear the chatter and laughter of the other women. Glasses clink and plates rattle as things are brought into the kitchen downstairs. 'We can do this,' I whisper. 'Let's just go down and pretend to have a good time.'

'Ivy!' Ingrid calls again, shriller this time.

'Coming,' I shout back, trying to force enthusiasm into my voice.

* * *

Everyone is bustling about downstairs, setting up a selection of hors d'oeuvres. Drinks are being poured, a party commencing.

'Come, Ivy. Don't be rude. Introduce us to your friends.' Natalia bumps shoulders with me, casting a huge grin to my friends.

'Sorry. Natalia, this is Kayleigh, Rosie and Georgie,' I say by way of introduction.

'Gosh, you're all so tanned!' Natalia chirps. 'You can tell you're not from here. Look at my pasty skin.'

Rosie smiles brightly, instantly drawn in to Natalia's warmth. I meander away as they chat, following Kayleigh and Georgie, who are moving slowly in the direction of the alcohol.

'Don't suppose you can have one.' Georgie dips her head towards my stomach, making me lurch.

'No one else knows,' I hiss. 'Please don't make it obvious.' The one thing I haven't told them is how Stephen warned me about keeping the pregnancy between ourselves. Amidst everything else, I'd clean forgotten.

Shame washes over me as I realise just how often I forget I am pregnant. I haven't got used to the idea yet, and until I see that little flicker of a heartbeat at an ultrasound scan, I'm not sure if I can fully accept it.

'All the more for me,' Kayleigh says, sucking back a glass of champagne.

* * *

'This is a mash up between trivia and beer pong,' Natalia explains. 'But with prosecco.' She places a ping pong ball into my hand. 'As the guest of honour, you can go first. Throw a ball into one of the other side's prosecco glasses and they have to answer a question about you!'

I steady myself, eyeing up one of the twelve flutes on the other side of the table. When I throw the ball and it lands with a splash into the glass in the centre, I blink in surprise. My team holler and cheer.

'I'll take this one.' Freya steps forward and plucks up the prosecco. She downs it in one fell swoop, then looks squarely at me as she produces the ping pong ball from her pouting mouth. 'What's the question?' she asks with a smile.

Natalia flaps around with a clipboard. 'Okay, Freya. How did Ivy and Stephen meet? Was it A) through internet dating, B) through work colleagues or C) at a garden centre?'

Freya chuckles. 'Let's see. I highly doubt Stephen works in fashion so it's not option B. I'll go with option C, at a garden centre,' she says. 'Because it's boring.'

I bristle. Of course Freya had to make a remark like that.

'Internet dating, actually,' I reply bluntly. 'Stephen had just moved to South Africa and was looking to meet someone. It was all a bit of a whirlwind romance really, we just connected straight away.' I watch as Freya's smug expression sours.

'He just fit right in as well, didn't he, girls?' Georgie says, rounding in on Freya too. She's always been the feisty one amongst my friends, helping with any battles that were ever picked.

Ingrid beams, oblivious to the tension brewing. 'He has always been the easiest to get along with from my brood.'

'Unlike some, it seems,' Kayleigh mutters under her breath.

'What dating site was it, Ivy?' Natalia asks.

'Hinge,' I say, smiling at the memory of the day we'd been matched. Until Stephen, internet dating back home had seemed pretty dismal.

I had still been reeling from my ex-fiancé's betrayal and wasn't sure if I could ever put my trust in a man again. I hadn't told Stephen about my past, not at first, scared he'd think of it as emotional baggage. Which it was and still is to some extent. I don't care what anyone says — something that life shattering isn't something you ever truly recover from. I've just learned to move on, to build up trust again. Stephen has been as patient as a person could be with me.

There's a nauseating drop in my stomach again at the thought of our relationship. Now that we finally have everything we want: a baby on the way, a wedding tomorrow. Yet there are secrets, lies, distrust, all of them having taken root here at Shadowmoor Lodge. I wonder, briefly, if we do leave here together as husband and wife, can our relationship ever be the same again? Just as I'm pondering that, Freya interrupts my thoughts.

'My turn,' she says, a slur to her words. Like mother like daughter it seems, even if they aren't technically related.

'Sure you don't want me to throw?' Debbie asks, her eyebrow raised.

'I'm not completely inept,' Freya snaps, tottering forward in a ridiculous pair of heels. Instead of aiming at the flutes, her stare lands on me and she throws the ping pong ball. Hard.

There's a collective intake of breath as the ball hits me in the centre of my forehead.

'What the fuck?' Georgie demands while I stand there shell-shocked.

'Sorry, slipped.' Freya smiles sweetly.

'My fist is gonna slip into her face in a second,' Georgie murmurs.

'Alright, ladies. Come on,' Ingrid says nervously, picking up the ball which has rolled to her feet. She brushes it off and chucks it across the table. Prosecco spatters the tablecloth.

'I feel like asking you three questions about Ivy is unfair. You have an advantage over us,' Debbie says.

'Depends on what the question is.' Georgie shrugs.

'Alright then, I'll ask one. How many times do you think Stephen's cheated on Ivy? Is it A) once, B) twice, or C) three times?' Freya grins wickedly.

'Freya!' Ingrid admonishes her. 'Don't be so ridiculous. Stephen hasn't cheated on her!'

I glare at Freya. Stephen hasn't cheated on me, I know that. But now the seed has been planted, and it makes me want to throw up.

'Stephen doesn't have the cognitive capacity to form a true attachment to someone. Of course he's cheated,' Freya says.

I dash to the bathroom and start to dry heave into the toilet bowl. Freya's cattiness has knocked me off-kilter, and I wonder if she gets some sort of cheap thrill from poking at me like this.

When I summon up enough courage to re-enter the room, Ingrid scoops an arm around me and offers me a glass of water. Freya narrows her eyes, watching us closely as Ingrid strokes my back. I want to tell Ingrid she's making it worse. I can feel Freya's resentment growing as she glowers at me from across the room, her jealousy raging from her pores.

CHAPTER 26

I'm glad that the evening winds down fairly quickly. No one seems to want to stick around long after Freya's outburst. The sausage rolls are left untouched, growing stale on the kitchen counter.

'I am sorry about her,' Ingrid whispers as she leaves, shamefaced.

'It's not the first time she's apologised for Freya's behaviour since we've been here.' I sigh, closing the door to the cabin behind Ingrid and turning to face my bridesmaids.

'Right, gear up, everyone. Scarves, gloves, coats, boots,' Georgie orders, sliding on her mitts. 'We're going for a walk.'

'Shouldn't we wait a while, till everyone's asleep like you said before?' Rosie asks hesitantly.

'I don't know about you, but I wanna get out of here as quickly as I can,' Kayleigh replies, rubbing her arms.

'Going down to that cabin doesn't mean we'll get to leave any sooner though,' I tell them seriously. 'If anything, it might make it worse.'

'Worse how?' Rosie asks, knitting her brows together.

'We could be caught going down there. Or they could figure out we've been there, see our footprints in the snow or something? I don't know . . .' I exhale, pulling on a pair of leg warmers.

'At least by going there we'll get some answers, right? From there we can come up with a firm plan,' Georgie says. She's ready to go, waiting at the front door for the rest of us. 'Hurry up,' she says without trying to hide the indignation in her tone.

Reluctantly, we finish wrapping up and quietly sneak away from our cabin and off into the woodlands.

* * *

The trek back to the eighth cabin in the dark is near impossible with no carved-out pathway. My legs burn as I wade through the snow covering the ground.

'Down there?' Rosie gulps when we're at the lake, the icy surface glistening under the light of the moon, now beginning to wane.

I bow my head apologetically. 'There are steps somewhere,' I say, trying to orientate myself. I start stepping blindly down the hill, my feet searching for the steps I know are there, buried under the snow.

'Ivy, don't slip down there. You've got enough scrapes and bruises already,' Rosie reminds me worriedly.

'I'm fine. I just need to find where we're going,' I say, squinting in the darkness, but as I do, I feel my boots slide. I crash to the ground, submerged in a blanket of snow. My spine, already tender, cracks against a rock and I cry out in agony.

'Ivy!' Kayleigh gasps, skidding down the hill after me.

'Careful!' Rosie hisses, looking down at us in panic.

'C'mon,' Georgie says, grabbing Rosie's hand, and together they climb down the side of the hill.

'Are you okay?' Kayleigh sobs, reaching me and helping me up.

'I'm fine,' I lie, trying to brush myself off. My body aches, every muscle, every bone.

'The baby?' Rosie asks as she reaches us.

'I can't think about that right now,' I say, my tone hardening. I can't, because if I do, I'll break apart. This poor baby trying to form life inside me has already had to deal with so much, and I really have no way of knowing if she's okay. She. For some reason, I keep thinking of the baby as a girl. A mother's instinct, perhaps.

I place a hand over my stomach.

'We need to carry on. Let's go,' I say, limping away from my friends.

They follow closely behind me, and soon, the shadow of the eighth cabin looms over us.

'This place gives me the absolute creeps.' Rosie shudders, staring up at the dilapidated cabin.

I twist the handle. It's unlocked, just like it was before, and I allow the door to swing wide open.

'Jesus Christ,' Georgie whispers, staring inside.

'Are you sure we should go inside? Shouldn't we just wait until morning? Get help then?' Rosie asks, her eyes shimmering.

'We're here now. Come on,' Kayleigh says, stepping a foot over the threshold. The floorboards moan under her weight.

'I really don't want to do this,' Rosie says, but she follows behind her.

As soon as we're all inside, we stare at the grandfather clock blocking the door.

'What if she's dead?' I ask, my fingers scratching at my scalp.

'What if she's not?' Kayleigh counters.

'Help me push this thing,' Georgie says, rolling up her sleeves in front of the clock.

Even with four of us, it won't shift.

'It's useless,' Kayleigh growls in frustration. 'My hands are actually starting to blister already.' She holds up her palms, wincing.

Rosie wanders off into the depths of the cabin, into the rooms I've already explored.

'What about this?' she says, coming back after a few minutes, a hank of rope in her arms. 'We could tie it around the clock and pull?'

My panic peaks. 'If it falls and gets damaged, they'll know we've been here,' I say, biting at my lip.

'Wait,' Kayleigh says, snapping her fingers. 'I've got an idea.' She darts to the entrance of the cabin and peels up the sodden doormat from the floor.

'If we tie the rope around the clock, Ivy and Rosie can pull. Georgie and I can try to hold it so it's tipped slightly on its side, then one of us can kick the mat underneath it. That might make the clock slide across the floorboards a bit easier,' she says with a shrug.

'Worth a shot,' I say, watching Rosie wrap the rope around the trunk of the clock.

I'm astonished when the plan works. It isn't easy, but together we manage to move the clock just enough to reach the doorknob. As I suspected, however, it's locked.

'I knew this would happen,' I seethe. 'What the hell do we do now?'

I'm painfully aware of how silent it is, of how my voice rings throughout the cabin. Even the creaking of the trees has seemed to come to a stop. Worst of all, I can hear none of the scratching I'd heard the other day to make me confident that someone is inside that room. It is deadly quiet. Either I was wrong, or the person inside must have perished. It's entirely plausible in this weather, being cold enough to make my skin blister and blue. I'm shocked I haven't been left with chilblains from the night outside in the blizzard.

'We turn this place upside down for a key,' Georgie mutters and stomps off into the kitchen.

She's tearing open cabinets and drawers, but there isn't much to rifle through.

'Can we pick the lock?' Rosie asks.

'With what, a twig?' Kayleigh scoffs, surprising me by how harsh she sounds.

'She's just stressed,' I mutter to Rosie as Kayleigh stalks into the lounge.

We trail behind her and I bend to inspect a dusty box. When I blow away the cobwebs and dirt I see it's a Monopoly set.

'Well this is fucking creepy,' Georgie says from over my shoulder. She snatches the box and flips it over. 'This is a personalised Monopoly set,' she tells us.

We gather round and lift the lid. Miniature model versions of the cabins at Shadowmoor Lodge are dotted around the board, all but the eighth one. The tokens are all handmade tiny figures, each resembling a member of the James family. My skin crawls as I hold a miniature version of Stephen in my hands. It's uncanny. They're made of something weighty, like silver. There's a lot more than the standard six in the original game.

'Why's it creepy?' Rosie tilts her head.

'Look,' Georgie says, jabbing her finger at the board. 'There're the cabins, right? The cabins of Shadowmoor Lodge, but they're the only actual properties. Everything else is a person.' She wipes the board, her hand coming away grimy.

'Bernadette, Chantelle, Kae,' she reads, wiping at the board some more. 'Francesca, Tilly. They're all women.'

'So what, the game is to buy a cabin and then a bunch of women?' Kayleigh shudders.

'Something like that.' Georgie swallows.

An awful sense of dread washes over me as I glance over the rest of the board.

'There's an Ivy here, look.' Rosie points at one of the blocks.

'What the hell is this?' Georgie grimaces, looking through the rest of the box, but there's no set of rules we can find.

'I honestly don't want to know,' I say.

'It's some sort of twisted game Ivy . . . and you're a part of it,' Georgie says, replacing the lid and sliding the box back under the coffee table.

'Was there a Charlotte on the board?' I breathe heavily.

'I think so,' Rosie squeaks. 'I think I saw a Charlotte.'

'Whatever's going on here, I don't like it. It's getting more fucked up by the second,' Georgie whispers.

'Guys,' Rosie cuts in. We turn to look at her. She's holding up a set of keys.

'Where'd you find that?' Kayleigh asks, grabbing the keys from her.

'Over there by the mantelpiece,' she says.

I fight off a tremor. We need to be more vigilant. I hadn't even noticed Rosie wandering off.

There are three keys dangling from the rusted chain. Three chances of getting into that room. We head back over and slide the first key in the lock. It jams and takes Rosie a few seconds to pull it back out again.

'Let me,' Georgie says, taking the keys from her. She looks at them closely, then at the shape of the keyhole. 'This one,' she says, inserting the key.

The door clicks open, and we all hold our breaths. The smell that comes wafting out as we manage to crack open the door is enough to make us all recoil. It's not a smell of decay exactly, but of faeces, urine and stale sweat mottled together. It takes a while for our eyes to adjust to the darkness. All of the windows are boarded over, keeping out any hint of moonlight.

There's a dull, amber glow coming from the corner of the cabin, helping my eyes to adapt to the surroundings.

The first thing I notice is the heat in the room; it's substantially warmer than the entrance we've just walked through. The second thing I notice is a gentle whir, and I follow the noise with my eyes. It's coming from the direction of the amber glow which I think must be some sort of electric heater. I take a tentative step towards it, realising the glow is coming from some LED flames. The heater is plugged into the wall, and it surprises me that this cabin in the state it's in has electricity. The amount of heat being pumped out of such a compact machine is impressive.

My eyes swivel at the sound of Kayleigh's voice. She's pointing a quivering finger to the back corner of the room where the silhouette of a woman is just visible.

'Oh my God,' Kayleigh gasps.

'Oh my God,' I echo.

The woman is sitting in a chair, *bound* to a chair, I realise as I take in the woman's hands tied behind her back.

'Ch-Charlotte?' I swallow, my breath caught in the back of my throat. My heart is racing so much I can feel my pulse pounding in my temple.

'Ivy,' Georgie hisses in the dark. 'You were right.' She's visibly shaking, the confidence she's exuded since she arrived diminished in an instant.

In the chair, the woman's head lolls and for a gut-wrenching moment I wonder if we're too late. Is she dead?

As if we all realise the severity of the situation at the same moment, we scramble over to the woman tied to the chair and crouch down in front of her.

'She's cold as ice,' Rosie whispers, touching the woman's hands.

There's a blindfold over her eyes, and a rag stuffed inside her mouth. I'm about to rip the material out when Kayleigh stops me.

'Wait. What if she screams? Someone might hear her.'

She's right. It's late and the woods are quiet. The woman's scream could carry right across the lake.

Instead, I hover a finger under the woman's nose.

'She's breathing,' I say with a sigh of relief. It's faint, but it's there. A delicate warm breath against my skin.

I look around, noticing buckets in the room. The stench gets worse the closer I go. Peering inside, I realise this woman has been untied and made to use these buckets to go to the bathroom for days. But as I glance back over to her, I guess whoever comes down here to help her relieve herself doesn't come often enough. Her clothes are damp with her own urine, soiled and stained too.

Very carefully, I peel up the blindfold. The moment I do, I recognise the woman's face. It is Charlotte Walker. She has been at Shadowmoor Lodge all along, just as I'd suspected. But why? Why is Marcel keeping her down here, alive? A sudden movement makes me leap back in fright.

'Who the hell are you?' Charlotte cries out from beneath the rag wedged into her mouth. It's muffled but I can just make out her words. She's startled, looking between us like a frenzied wild animal as she's woken from her sleep. She thrashes around in the chair, trying as best she can to cower away from us.

'Wait. Please!' I beg. 'We're here to help.'

CHAPTER 27

Charlotte

'Wait. Please! We're here to help.' Charlotte can hear desperation in the woman's voice. Pleading with her to keep quiet.

They say they're here to help her, and Charlotte wants to believe them. She does. But what if it's another mind game? Looking at them, she notices they're all around her age. Late twenties, early thirties at a push. And they look genuinely terrified, shocked to have found her here.

It feels like it's been a long time since she last heard a female voice, but she lost track of the days pretty quickly in here. She might have been here three days, or a week. She's really not sure. The lack of lighting has made it difficult to tell. The windows have been sealed shut, to keep people from peering in, she guesses. And that makes her wonder just what brought these women here.

'Charlotte? Charlotte Walker?' The same girl speaks again. Her voice is soft, soothing, and it makes her want to lean into the musical quality of it. She has an accent. Australian, maybe. She can't tell, can't bring herself to concentrate enough to pinpoint it. Her focus is on figuring out who these women are, how they got here and how on earth they found her.

Charlotte nods slowly, tears streaming down her cheeks. Adrenaline is coursing through her, making her tremble, and she's embarrassed too. Sitting there in her own excrement. She knows she stinks, she also knows she shouldn't care. But she does, she does, she does. It's mortifying, and she feels the blood rushing to her cheeks.

'I can't believe we've found her,' another of the girls is saying, shaking her head in disbelief.

'I knew it! I knew it!' the girl that asked her if she was Charlotte Walker says. She has her hand clasped over her mouth. If these girls are acting, they're good.

'We're going to get you out of here,' a woman with a short, pixie cut says. She's fiddling with the bonds around Charlotte's wrists.

She tries to ignore the pain as she tugs at the restraints. 'Cable ties,' she hears her say. 'They're cutting right into her skin.'

They seem to come together, suddenly. Stand away from her while they talk among themselves. She wants to scream at them, to cry and beg them to help her, but she stays silent. Listening.

'We can't untie her. We can't bring her back to the cabin with us, not tonight. It's too risky.'

'Why? She needs us, Georgie.'

'What if they come back here tonight and find her gone? What happens then?'

'But . . . she'll die down here!'

'Don't be ridiculous, Rosie. She's survived this long.'

'Georgie's right. She has a heater in here. She'll make it through the night.'

Charlotte's heart plummets. They can't leave her here. She can't handle one more second stuck in this awful place. She starts to flail in the chair, making as much noise as she can. Before they got here, she didn't think she had any energy left in her, but here it is. This is survival mode, kicking in.

'Stop her! Quickly. Stop her.' The girl she thinks is called Rosie rushes over to her, stilling her by her shoulders.

'Charlotte, calm down. We aren't going to leave you here.' She pauses. 'For long. We're going to get you out of here. We — we just need to be smart about it.' The tremor in her voice tells Charlotte she's speaking the truth.

With her chest heaving, she tries to regain composure.

'Charlotte, we're going to take that rag out of your mouth, okay? Please, don't scream. I promise you we're here to help,' Rosie says, looking over at her friends for validation.

There's a mixture of head shakes and nods, making Rosie pause. She's definitely not the one in charge here, but she seems nice, and the warmth of her hand against her skin is comforting. When she retracts her hand, Charlotte wishes she could pull it back, like a child not yet done with a touch from someone they love. The moment the contact is broken, she feels alone again.

'Can we just speak to her? She deserves to tell us her side of the story,' Rosie says, pleadingly.

One of the others strides up to her. The one with the pixie cut. 'Scream and this is going right back in your mouth,' she warns.

Charlotte nods again, a silent promise that she'll remain quiet. She won't jeopardise this.

She gags as the rag is pulled out of her mouth, the way she always does. Her mouth is dryer than she's ever felt it and as she tries to move her tongue to speak, it sticks to her palette.

'Water,' she utters hoarsely, tilting her head in the direction of a trough at the other end of the room.

'Of course,' Rosie says, scuttling over to the water.

There's a plastic cup bobbing on the surface and Rosie scoops some water inside it, bringing it over to her lips. As she downs the contents of the cup, she closes her eyes. It must have been over twenty-four hours since she's had water.

'You want my side of the story?' she asks, and they all bob their heads. 'Before I say anything, I need to know who you are, and what you're doing here?' She doesn't trust them. Not yet. And she isn't going to tell them anything until she's sure they aren't here to cause her more pain.

CHAPTER 28

Ivy

Charlotte wants to know who we are, and I can't say that I blame her. The poor thing is absolutely terrified, half-starved and freezing cold despite the heater in the room.

'I'm Ivy. This is Kayleigh, Georgie and Rosie.'

Charlotte remains silent, eyeing us suspiciously.

'I'm — I'm getting married here. Tomorrow,' I admit. I'm not sure if I should say that, if the admission will make things better or worse but Charlotte's eyes widen in horror, giving me my answer.

'You're marrying one of *them*?' she spits. 'Which one?'

'Stephen. Stephen James,' I sputter.

Charlotte blinks at me in the darkness, taking the name in. 'I don't know who that is,' she says.

'One of the brothers. But he lives overseas, with me.'

'And you guys?' Charlotte pivots her attention to the others.

'The bridesmaids,' Kayleigh explains.

'Charlotte, we have no idea what's going on here. But we know something is very wrong, and we want to help,' I say, bending in front of her. I try as best I can not to gag at the smell coming from her as I place a hand on her leg. 'But to help you we need to know everything.'

Charlotte considers us, strapped to the chair with cable ties digging into her wrists. 'This family . . .' she starts. 'The James family? They're sick.'

Her words make a scream claw at my throat. Fear blooms from my insides as I wait for Charlotte to continue. She requests another sip of water first, which Rosie brings to her lips.

'From what I gather, the James family have some sort of obsession with . . . with procreation,' Charlotte says. 'I'm pregnant.'

'That's why they're keeping you here?' Kayleigh asks, starting to fidget. She's twisting her head in every direction, clutching at her arms.

'I think so. He keeps putting this doppler on my stomach whenever he comes down here. He gets angrier every time he doesn't find a heartbeat.' Tears pool into the globs of mucus on her face.

'He?' I ask, expecting her to say Marcel. It's the only name on my mind. His face, burned into my memory from when I was up on horseback.

'Ben. Ben James,' Charlotte says. 'I'm his ex-girlfriend.'

Ben? For a moment, I don't understand. But then the first conversation I had with him comes hurtling to the forefront of my mind.

'*Wouldn't hold your breath, we broke up.*' I heard him say that as I'd walked up to him and Stephen on our first night here. When I'd asked what had happened, he'd seemed so standoffish, and it had made me instantly dislike him.

All he'd said was, '*Well, Ivy, she was a lying bitch. That's what happened.*'

I want to ask Charlotte what he'd meant. I want to ask her a million things, to try and make sense of all of this. I open and close my mouth like a fish, trying and failing to form any words.

'What about Marcel?' Georgie asks. 'Ivy told us she saw you with him, that you were in his car?'

'Wait, that was *you*?' Charlotte cries. 'God. I've been hoping the person I saw on that horse would recognise me. It's been my only hope.' Her chin quivers.

I squeeze my fingers tight, so the blood pools at the tips.

'It's all of them, all of the James men,' Charlotte says, her nose running. 'They're all involved.'

We all turn rigid. A sudden whistle of wind, creeping in through the rotting wood, makes us all whip round. I clutch my womb, wanting to tell Charlotte there's no way all of the James men can be involved. Especially not Stephen. But even the other brothers. I've been getting to know them. But there's no denying it. They're embroiled in some sort of pregnant woman fetish.

'I'm pregnant too,' I whisper into the gloomy room, which is starting to spin.

'Then you're as dead as I am,' Charlotte says, exhaling slowly. 'They won't let you leave, y'know?'

'Yes, they will. We're here,' Georgie says, adamantly.

Charlotte shakes her head. 'They'll kill you all.' She's sobbing, drool and snot dripping down her chin.

'No, they won't,' Rosie says, and I turn in surprise at the strength in her voice.

'Are the women involved?' I ask, my words weighted down with fear.

'I haven't seen any women,' Charlotte says, her greasy black curls swinging as she shakes her head.

'Does that mean we can trust them?' Rosie asks.

'We trust no one,' Georgie says firmly. 'Ivy, tomorrow you put that wedding dress on. You play it completely cool. We can't risk the family cottoning on that we know. We wait, okay? And when we work out who we can trust . . . we go to them for help.' Her voice is shaky, her eyes moving erratically.

Kayleigh nods. 'Worst-case scenario, we steal one of the cars that pull up and we get to Dorking as soon as we can to get help.'

I glance back at Charlotte, and I hate what I have to do but there's no other way. I pick up the filthy rag, holding it between my fingers. 'I'm going to have to put this back in your mouth,' I say with a wince. 'We need to leave, make it look like we haven't been here.'

Charlotte's eyes grow huge, and she starts trying to scream but I jam the cloth between her teeth before her wail has any force to it. I hate that I feel like I'm the bad person here, that I'm doing this to Charlotte, but I need Charlotte to remain here, tied to the chair. We need to lock the bedroom door and slide the clock back into place, leaving the cabin as though we never entered it.

'I swear to you, we'll come back for you,' I say, my voice cracking as Charlotte's head falls.

* * *

'It makes me sick, thinking of her down there in that cabin by herself,' Georgie says, her lip curled in disgust.

'There's nothing we can do till morning,' I mutter. My mind is still reeling. I can't believe I was right all along. Charlotte Walker is here, and the James family is involved. I'm slowly resigning myself to the fact that I won't be getting married in the morning, that putting on that Pnina Tornai wedding gown will all be for show.

It was my dream dress. Being a fashion designer, I could have created something similar myself, but I just couldn't get that dress out of my head. The dress from the designer I used to watch with glowing admiration when I was just a girl, my obsession with fashion just beginning. Stephen had surprised me with a flight all the way to New York so that I could try it on, and when I did,

I couldn't leave the store without it. I'd never wanted to have to slip my head out of that gorgeous halter neckline again. I wanted to live in it, shimmering under the water crystals that covered the dress head to toe. And now, I'll be putting that dress on but not for the reasons I've always dreamed of. At some point tomorrow, I'll have to shatter my future with Stephen. Tell him I can't marry him and destroy his entire family.

I convulse, wishing I could know for certain if Stephen is involved in whatever is going on. I hope not, because if he is, that means I've been creating a life with a complete psychopath. But he was a part of that board game, a solid silver token made to look just like him. Why would that be there if he isn't involved? And who are the other women's names across the board? My head aches with questions.

'You okay, honey?' Rosie says, sidling up beside me.

We're sitting in front of the lit fireplace, all of us just staring blankly into the flames.

I shake my head. No. I'm not okay. I'm the furthest thing from okay. And I can't stop worrying about Charlotte, down there in that cabin bound to a chair. She's cold, sitting alone in the dark. A sitting duck, waiting for Ben to visit her again.

'I think I just need to go to bed,' I say with a sigh, the pendulum from Joanna warm in the palm of my hand. I've been holding it for hours like some sort of comforter.

'We should all go to bed,' Kayleigh says, taking the black cast iron poker and spreading out the embers of the fire. She takes the pot of ashes that has been perched by the fireside and sprinkles the contents over the cinders.

'I don't want to sleep alone,' I say as we reach my bedroom door.

'And you shouldn't have to,' Kayleigh says, pulling me into her arms. 'Come on. Grab your duvet. Come bunk with us.'

Collecting the sheets and a pillow, I head to the guest bedroom and start setting up a makeshift bed on the floorboards.

'Don't be silly,' Georgie says, placing her hand on my shoulder. 'We can share.' She pats her single mattress and beckons me over.

It's a squeeze, but I don't care. I nuzzle into my friend's warmth, who is lying there in the dark stroking my hair, soothing me to sleep.

CHAPTER 29

The Wedding Day

I lean against the kitchen counter, a mug of coffee in hand. My bridesmaids and I are clad in our pyjamas, hair scraped back. We're all wearing masks of dread, our faces drained of colour.

'You know I love you, Ivy, but I'm starting to wish that storm had stopped us from getting here,' Kayleigh says, standing motionless in front of the window.

Rain is lashing down so hard it's carving lines through the earth.

'Thanks,' I mutter, resting my head on Kayleigh's shoulder. 'Did any of you get any sleep last night?'

My bridesmaids' heads tick side to side like a metronome. We look out at the storm clouds, black and heavy overhead.

'It's supposed to be good luck to rain on your wedding day,' Rosie says, trying to inject hope into her words.

The rain counters the blood moon from a couple of days ago, bringing contradicting beliefs of bad luck and good.

'It's not my wedding day though, is it?' I murmur, finishing my coffee and rinsing out the mug.

'Oh God, darling. I'm so sorry,' Rosie gasps. 'I didn't even think . . . how're you feeling?'

I feel my poise slip as my chin trembles. 'Broken,' I admit. 'I'm about to lose everything.'

'You don't know that,' Georgie says, her words tender. There's a softness in her eyes that isn't usually there, and that almost makes it worse for me, because I do know that I'm about to lose everything. I know that there's no coming back from this. I'm about to discover the truth the James family have been hiding, one way or another, and my relationship with Stephen will be destroyed. I'm about to lose my fiancé.

'At least this time I know it's coming,' I sniff. I've never liked to dwell on things or make myself feel like a victim, but it's hard not to now. Watching my first wedding and fiancé dissipate was devastating enough, but to have to go through it again? It's a sick, cruel joke.

'We don't know Stephen is part of this yet,' Kayleigh reminds me.

'He's part of that game, right? We all saw that. That means something. It means that whatever is going on here, he's involved.' I blink back tears, staring at my bridesmaids. 'Let's go. People will start arriving soon. We need to get ready.'

* * *

In my figure-hugging gown, I twist and turn in the mirror. If I look close enough, I feel like I can see the start of a bump. But it can't be. It must be water retention. Still, the dress is breathtaking and my eyes sting at how beautiful I look in it.

Kayleigh, Georgie and Rosie knock at the door, all sucking in their breaths at the sight of me as they enter.

Their chiffon bridesmaids' dresses are stunning, the flounce sleeves hanging off their shoulders. They walk towards me, surround me.

'Babe, you look truly gorgeous.' Rosie smiles. A sad, sorry smile. A smile I've seen before, last time.

'So do you guys,' I manage, burying my face into our group hug.

'Ivy?' Ingrid's voice calls from downstairs. 'Ivy, happy wedding day! Now come down please. Lots to do!'

My shoulders drop. 'And so it begins,' I say, my eyes closing as I exhale. We trail down the staircase, and Ingrid gives us all a once-over, her nostrils flaring.

'Well, don't you look . . . fancy,' Ingrid says, raking her gaze over me with a wince. Ingrid is dressed in a Grecian floor-length dress with an empire waist and a cape overlay making her look regal. I'd have expected no less.

'You'll need a dressing gown on if you're keeping that on. Don't want Stephen catching sight of the dress before you walk down the aisle!'

'Are you taking her somewhere?' Georgie asks, measuring Ingrid with an icy glare.

'Yes,' Ingrid says, lifting her nose up at her. 'As mother-in-law of the bride, we've some final things to take care of together before the ceremony.'

Last night, huddled around the fireplace, one of the things we'd discussed was making sure we weren't separated at Shadowmoor Lodge.

'We need to be strategic, like in a game of Monopoly,' Georgie had said.

We assess each other silently now, our plan already crumbling.

'Chop, chop.' Ingrid snaps her fingers, motioning towards the front door.

'She can't go out in *that*,' Rosie protests. 'It's pouring with rain. She'll get drenched.'

Ingrid waves her off. 'We have umbrellas.'

I see no way out of this. I try and fail to come up with an excuse to stay behind.

'Why can't we come?' Georgie asks, standing her ground.

'It's a family matter,' Ingrid says, her lips pressing into a tight line. 'Why don't you three entertain yourselves with a bottle of sparkling cuvée. It's from a vineyard right here in Surrey, you'll love it.' She wrenches the neck of a bottle from a wine rack and passes it to Kayleigh.

'Greyfriars cuvée. A blend of Chardonnay, Pinot Noir and Pinot Meunier,' she reads, eyebrows raised.

'It's award winning. Enjoy it,' Ingrid says, the cape of her dress flicking behind her as she turns to go.

'I don't really feel like drinking. I'd rather stay with Ivy,' Georgie says firmly.

Ingrid's eyes roll to the back of her head. 'As I mentioned,' she says, her voice clipped, 'this is a family matter.'

'It's fine,' I cut in. 'I'll be back soon.'

'Ivy, no.' Kayleigh eyes me nervously.

'Save me a glass of cuvée.' I smile queasily and head upstairs to slip into a fluffy fleece bathrobe.

Before going back downstairs, I pull out the pendulum from the bedside drawer. I still it, watching closely as the gentle sway comes to a stop.

'Am I safe to go with Ingrid?' I whisper. For a moment, the pendulum does nothing, as though considering its response, but slowly it starts to spin clockwise. I wait, letting it get faster and faster. I try to recall what Joanna had said. I strain to remember until I hear Joanna's voice, echoing in every chamber of my brain.

'*If the pendulum swings clockwise, that indicates a yes. Anticlockwise is a no. Understand?*'

If I'm to believe Joanna's words, then the pendulum is answering yes. I'm safe to go with Ingrid. I breathe out, looking at the deluge of rain hammering at the windowpanes. In the distance, I can see the other cabins. Stephen is out there, in one of them. He'll be trimming his beard, pulling on his navy suit. Perhaps even reading through his vows one last time. He has no idea what's coming, and really, neither do I.

CHAPTER 30

'Where are we going?' I ask, following Ingrid out the front door.

'To the barn,' Ingrid says, picking the hem of her dress up as she steps down into the squelching mud.

I do the same, feeling ridiculous in such an extravagant dress paired with a battered pair of black Hunter Wellington boots. As we pass by the lake, I fight to not turn my head in the direction of the eighth cabin, but I can't help myself. I crane my neck and come to a standstill. Someone is down there. But when I blink and look again, there's nothing but the trees swinging wildly in the wind down there. All I can do is silently pray that Charlotte is still okay, that she made it through the night and that nothing sinister is going to happen to her before I can get help.

'Ivy, do keep up. We'll catch our death out here,' Ingrid calls.

You have no idea, I think, looking forward and marching on. The fairy lights strung across the outside of the barn are twinkling brightly beneath the brooding sky. It looks stunning, and I get a jolt of hideous realisation. My wedding here isn't going to happen. I wish it would stop hitting me. I wish I didn't care so much, but I do.

When we get inside, escaping the rain, we stand at the long table holding an impressive looking wedding cake on a rustic, three-tiered wood slice stand. Ingrid slides a manila envelope across to me. 'Your wedding menu,' she says by way of explanation, delivering a scathing smile.

I hate the way Ingrid looks at me, even now when I know I won't ever become her daughter-in-law. The need to be liked and accepted is so strong inside me it almost hurts.

I brace myself, not sure what to expect. I've been so busy focusing on everything else that I haven't even thought to ask about the food for the wedding day. I vaguely remember a phone call here or there with Ingrid running ideas by us. But in all honesty, I'd clean forgotten people eat at weddings, as ridiculous as that sounds. It's been the last thing on my mind in the grand scheme of things.

I hesitate but slowly slip the paper out into my hands. It's shiny and smooth to the touch.

'Recycled silk.' Ingrid beams, nodding at the menu.

Timidly, I lower my gaze to the calligraphy font and peruse the courses. There are things on there that I've never even heard of before. The sage dauphinoise, caviar torte and petit pois á La Française are one thing, but bee pollen? On a menu? What is *that*? It's far too extravagant for me, but I smile as I look up at Ingrid.

'It's perfect.' I whisper the lie, tucking the fancy paper away again. Out of sight, out of mind.

I don't say what I feel. That with every detail of this wedding, it's as though I'm losing a piece of myself. It's gorgeous, and I couldn't have done better myself for someone else's wedding, but it's not what I ever wanted for myself. I wanted nothing more than a barbecue, something rustic. Something less luxurious, because luxurious isn't me, despite the gown I'm wearing. People often get the wrong idea about me. They think because I like fashion, I'm superficial, pretentious even. That couldn't be further from the truth, but this menu doesn't portray that. This menu is overindulgent, and it isn't how I want people to see me, but that doesn't matter anymore anyway. Today, no one will remember it as my wedding day. It'll be a day they'll never forget for sure, but for all the wrong reasons.

I wonder, as the rain pelts down on the rooftop, just how far into this wedding we're going to get before it all comes to a head. My bridesmaids, my skeleton crew, are already dressed and ready to go.

Ingrid's eyes linger on me and she opens her mouth, seeming like she wants to say something, but she stops herself.

'Is everything okay?' I ask her, my anxiety building.

Ingrid clears her throat and starts distributing the menus on the tables around the room. 'I thought we should have a little chat, before the ceremony goes ahead,' she says slowly.

'About what?' I ask, the hair on the back of my neck standing on end.

'Ivy, this family—'

She's cut off mid-sentence as the doors to the barn fly open and at the sight of her son, Ingrid swallows her words.

'Mum,' Stephen says loudly, over a roll of thunder. He turns his attention to me, his expression seeming to melt at the sight of me. 'Ivy, you look . . .' He stops, considering me. 'Breathtaking.'

He's in his suit and I can't deny that he looks detrimentally handsome. I can feel my knees wobble as he walks towards me. I want to run up to him and wrap my arms tightly around his neck but at the same time I want to scream and run away from him. It's a disconcerting feeling.

'Thanks,' I mutter pathetically, looking down at the bathrobe I'm wearing over my wedding dress.

He presses a kiss to my forehead, an arm slithering around my waist. 'What're you both doing in here?'

'I was just showing Ivy the menu. Caterers will be here soon,' Ingrid stammers nervously.

I look between them. There's tension there, something brewing. Words are left unspoken as a look I can't quite decipher passes between them.

'Surely that could've waited, Mum. We have to get ready for the ceremony,' he snaps. He lets out a puff of air, his chest deflating as he faces me. 'You should go back to the cabin, my love.' His eyes are hard, willing me to defy him.

For the first time, the way he towers over me, his height intimidates me. I'm scared of him. I'm scared of this entire family. Stuck between the two of them, I find myself wishing I hadn't come here alone, without my bridesmaids.

'Wait!' Ingrid cries. 'Stephen, please.' The anguish in her voice is enough to chill me down to the marrow.

'Don't do this,' Ingrid begs.

My breath hitches. 'Don't do what?' I ask.

'Nothing! Leave,' Stephen says. 'Now.' His hands are on my arms, fingers digging down to my bone.

'Stephen, stop. You're hurting me,' I gasp.

Georgie bursts through the barn doors at that moment, Kayleigh and Rosie right behind her.

* * *

'Get off her,' Georgie screams, hurtling towards us.

Stephen jerks away, raising his hands. 'Woah — what's going on here?' He looks genuinely shocked, his eyes wide, a strange half smile playing on his lips.

'I think you should be the one to answer that,' Kayleigh says, reaching me and holding onto my other arm.

'My mother was about to give away a bit of a surprise I've planned for Ivy, and I'd very much prefer that she didn't,' he says, his words short, cold. 'And now, I've already said too much. So if you don't mind, can you escort the bride back to her cabin so I can have a moment alone with my mother?'

'What surprise?' Rosie asks, her eyes flicking between everyone.

Stephen sighs, exasperated. 'We've been planning to get the horses in here. I know how much Ivy loves them. I was going to ride in on a horse and I needed my mother's help with it,' he says, looking down at the ground. 'Because I don't know how to ride.'

His answer makes a deep part of my heart swell. If he's lying, he's good. Even his ears have tinged pink. I look over at Ingrid who remains expressionless.

'What were you going to say, before Stephen got here?' I ask her.

Ingrid's eyes dart up. 'Nothing. Nothing important,' she says, shrugging it off.

* * *

The whole way back to the cabin, I can't shake the feeling that Ingrid was trying to tell me something important. Warn me about something. It gnaws at my insides. The way she clammed up the moment Stephen came in, and Stephen's tight grip on my arm. I can't make sense of any of it, and besides my bridesmaids, I'm becoming acutely aware of just how much I can't trust anyone.

As I climb the steps leading up to the cabin, I notice a pair of boots toppled haphazardly by the front door.

'Someone's here,' I whisper to Kayleigh, cocking my head towards the shoes.

Creeping closer to the door, I wish we hadn't drawn the curtains before I'd come down in the wedding dress. There's no way to peer inside.

'Be careful,' Georgie says as I put my hand on the doorknob.

It turns in my hand, unlocked. I'm sure we locked it before we left. The beating of my heart is erratic as I poke my head inside.

'Ivy! Hi. I've been sent over to come keep you company.' Natalia beams, her eyes glittering with a deep purple eyeshadow. 'I know I'm not part of the bridal party, but I hope you don't mind.' She tips a flute glass to her lips. 'You lot are much nicer to be around than Freya,' she adds with a flush.

Taking another sip, she notices the girls staring at her silently.

'Hope you don't mind. Helped myself to a glass!' Her smile is so open and warm, so unlike the other members of the family that I can't help but soften towards her.

'You're welcome here,' I say gently, nodding my approval towards my friends. Natalia isn't like the rest of them. She's inherently good. But still, I can't risk her finding out what we know, and now that she's here it's going to make communicating with my bridesmaids ten times harder.

'Join me for a pre-wedding drink?' Natalia asks hopefully.

'Sure!' I show my teeth in an attempt to smile. 'Rosie, mind helping me pour us all a glass in the kitchen?'

Rosie scuttles behind me into the kitchen, leaving Georgie and Kayleigh with Natalia.

'Rosie, we need to keep Natalia distracted, okay? She can't know what's going on here, just in case she's a part of it,' I hiss as I pour four glasses of cuvée.

Rosie nods fearfully.

'Now that people are going to start arriving, I'm going to try and sneak out. I'll have to find help . . . alone.' I sigh.

'But we said no separating,' Rosie says, chewing at her lip.

'We haven't got a choice, Rosie. It's easier for one to sneak out than two — let's be honest. And I know who not to trust here. You don't. Yet. I like Natalia, but she might've been sent here to . . .' I pause. 'To *babysit* us.'

Rosie grabs one of the flutes and downs the glass. 'Sorry,' she mutters, refilling the glass with the rest of the cuvée in the bottle. 'I don't know how much more I can take.'

'I'm sorry for dragging you all into this,' I say brokenly.

'Into what?' Natalia's voice comes creeping into the kitchen. She hangs on the doorframe, her glass empty in her hand. A flicker of something passes over her features. It's subtle, but it's there. Suspicion. Distrust. And something else. It's the same sort of look I've seen in Freya's eyes before. Something that looks a lot like loathing.

'Just practising my wedding vows!' I say quickly, lifting a glass to my lips. I take the smallest sip. 'Sorry for dragging you into all of this, into my world of fashion and crappy reality TV.' I force out a laugh.

'It's good!' Rosie says, nodding her head a little too enthusiastically.

'Funny,' Natalia says carefully, approaching the counter and lifting up the empty bottle of cuvée. 'Thirsty, I see!' she says, grabbing another bottle from the wine rack and unwrapping the foil.

'Maybe we should save the rest of the drinking for after the ceremony,' I suggest meekly.

'Nonsense! It's your wedding day, drink up!' Natalia grins, tilting her head towards my full glass.

'I don't want to stagger down the aisle,' I joke, making myself wink and hoping Natalia can't see the quiver in my hands, the pulse in my neck. The nerves ooze from the pores in my skin.

'Excuse me,' Rosie says softly, slipping past us. I hope she's going to the others, to tell them of the plan.

Natalia turns to follow in her footsteps, but I call out, stopping her in her tracks. I need to buy Rosie time.

'Can you help with my dress? I have it on, under this,' I say, pointing at the bathrobe.

Natalia's eyes light up. 'Really?'

I pull at the string tied around my waist and reveal the dress.

'Ivy!' Natalia says hungrily, like a moth to the flame. 'It's incredible.'

For just a moment, I allow myself to feel like my wedding is going to go ahead. To think that this is the reaction I'll get from a barn full of guests as I walk in, bouquet in hand. I want to hold on to this moment, for the little girl in me that has always wanted this. I breathe the moment in, holding it close, then I turn my back to Natalia, showing her the plunging back and the crystals cascading down my spine.

'Can you help me with the zip?' I ask. 'I need the bathroom.'

Natalia scoots closer, delicately working the zip down to the small of my back. 'There,' she says, stepping back.

I thank her and head to the bathroom, closing myself in. Pressing up against the door, I wait, listening for the sound of Natalia's footsteps. At first, I don't think they're coming, I think Natalia is standing there, waiting for me. But eventually, I hear her retreat back to my bridesmaids.

Hurriedly, I zip the dress back up as far as I can reach. Bunching the train of the dress in my hand, I slip quietly out of the bathroom and pad down the hallway. I hold my breath as I pass the lounge. Natalia has her back to the door, making it easy for me to sneak past, but before I do, I capture Kayleigh's attention. I can't speak, but my eyes burn into my friends. Kayleigh tips her head just slightly, just enough for me to notice. A goodbye, of sorts. A good luck, I'm sure.

CHAPTER 31

Breaking free from the cabin, I sprint as fast as my heavy, water-logged boots allow me to go. I know my time is limited, that Natalia will notice my absence within minutes. I need to be quick.

Cars are bottlenecked through the woodlands already, guests and staff starting to make their appearance. I didn't have time to grab the bathrobe or a jacket, and my skin is already turning numb, the cold working as an anaesthetic.

I'm not really sure where it is I'm running to, until I realise, I'm going in the direction of the horses. Reaching the tack shed, I pause to catch my breath. The air feels like sharp icicles stabbing at my airways and the rain is already starting to weigh my dress down. I push open the tack shed, desperate for a moment's respite from the storm.

Out of the wind, I perch on a bucket upturned on the floor, no longer caring if it stains my dress. That doesn't matter anymore. I let my head fall into my hands and start first by massaging my temple, but soon my fingers creep up towards my scalp.

Letting out a growl of frustration, I rip my hands away. I stun myself when no hair comes away in my clenched fists. I've fought the urge, controlled it, and that feels more powerful than the pain itself. Standing on shaking legs, I start to head towards the door, knowing I need to continue, but I stop. There's a big black bag in the corner of the shed, some sort of canvas duffle bag. I'm sure it wasn't here last time I was here.

Cautiously, I step towards it, my knees wobbling. It looks stuffed full and as I bend to inspect it, I notice how hard whatever is inside it is. It isn't full of something soft, like clothes or blankets, but something solid.

Trying to keep logical, I tell myself it must be old tack gear. A saddle, maybe. But as I unzip the bag and gaze down, I taste bile in my throat. I buckle forward, then, horrified, scramble away from the bag, clawing my way to the wall. Pressing my back up against the damp wall, I stare at the bloodied arm that has thudded like a dead weight out of the bag.

* * *

I know I have no choice but to find out who the body in the bag belongs to. My first thought is Charlotte, but the skin tone is all wrong. This arm is pale, the skin almost porcelain compared to the deep espresso shade Charlotte has.

Swallowing down my disgust, I drag myself back over to the bag. The crystals on my dress scratch and scrape along the floor as I move. As I continue to unzip the bag, I'm careful not to touch the arm.

The next thing I see is clumps of blonde hair, matted with the strands clinging together with something dark and hardened that flakes beneath my fingertips.

I gag as I brush the hair out of the face of a woman, not recognising her at first. The impossible angle of her features makes it hard to place her. But then, with terrible clarity that paralyses me, reality hits. It's Joanna. It's as though she has been frozen, her mouth hanging open in a haunting silent scream. The lips are white, and her limbs are beginning to stiffen. Rigor mortis is just starting to set in. I'm surprised by how quickly I seem to become desensitised to the dead body, but because of her doll-like colouring, rigidity of her form, and with no foul odour, I can almost make myself believe it isn't real. But it is. Joanna never left Shadowmoor Lodge. Stephen was lying. I let a howl escape me — one I can't control.

I touch the tarot reader's shirt, where a bullet hole has punctured the material and her ribcage. Her blood already congealed. There's no rise and fall of her chest, no sign of life.

This is all my fault. Joanna would never have come back here if I hadn't asked for her help, but I did, and Joanna tried. She crashed her car into a tree in the middle of a blizzard and got hunted down deep in the woods. Now she's dead. Murdered.

'I'm so sorry,' I say, squeezing my eyes shut. I can't look anymore, but I shut Joanna's soulless eyes before zipping the bag back up.

Racing back through the clearing in the woodlands, I'm aware that if someone looks out of their cabin window, they'll see me. I'm impossible to miss in my shimmering white dress, though it is already ruined. Mud has seeped up into the hem, quickly spreading. As I sprint, the train snags and tears on rocks and trees, crystals scattering along the forest floor, but I don't stop. I careen on, needing to make it back to my bridesmaids before something happens to them too.

The door to the cabin is ajar as I reach it. Crashing through, I call out for them.

'Kayleigh! Georgie, Rosie?' I can't keep the shrill, high-pitched tone from my voice.

There's no response. The cabin is hushed. My bridesmaids are gone.

Heels click against the floorboards, and I twirl around, eyes wide with fear. I have just enough time to grab the bathrobe, cinching it around me with the belt to hide my appearance before Freya saunters into the room.

She's in a sage green dress that flutters behind her. Her waist looks unnaturally skinny in the corset bodice. With her hair scraped up into a slick, high ponytail, I notice just how sharp Freya's jaw is, and the severe edges of her cheekbones. When she turns, her long hair falls over one of her bare shoulders and I get a clear view of the back of her neck. There, inked right at the nape of her neck, is the James family crest. But instead of the seven branches I've seen on Stephen's crest before, there's an eighth branch, jagged and rough. As though she'd drawn it on herself. It reminds me of the lightning bolt from the card at the tarot reading.

'Look at you.' Freya hikes an eyebrow up. If she notices the muddied train of the gown pooling out from under the bathrobe, she doesn't say anything.

'Your makeup is a bit smudged,' she says, pointing to my face.

I ignore her comment.

'Where're my bridesmaids?' I ask coldly.

'They've gone to get ready for the ceremony,' Freya answers, giving me a quizzical look like I'm completely dense. 'The guests are arriving. You aren't getting cold feet, are you?' She smirks in amusement. 'It's not too late y'know.'

'You'd love that, wouldn't you?' I can't help but bite back.

Freya lifts her chin, glaring down the length of her nose at me. The beating rain eases, gradually turning to the most delicate patter, hitting the surface of the frozen lake.

'He won't stick around. He will leave you, Ivy,' Freya says, and even though I shouldn't care anymore, the words still cut me. She continues to speak before I can respond.

'He takes no responsibility for his actions. He got me pregnant, Ivy! And what did he do? Reacted like the world was coming to an end. He was *horrified*, like having my baby would be the most awful thing in the universe,' she cries. 'Lucky for him,

I lost the baby. Just a few weeks into the pregnancy. It was like Stephen seized his chance and abandoned ship.' Her nose crinkles. 'I should've let Ingrid know back then that her precious son isn't quite as innocent and perfect as she likes to think he is.'

The ground seems unstable underfoot. I need to sit down, yet I do nothing but stand there, swaying as I listen to her speak.

'Our baby had meant more to me than anyone here knows,' she says, pointing her finger as she pirouettes around the room. 'That baby meant truly becoming a part of the family. I'd be a James, linked finally by blood. But the baby just couldn't fucking stay. Everyone leaves me in the end!' Tears fall down her face, streaking her makeup.

I can't process this. Not now. Maybe not ever.

'I think you should leave now,' I respond, no longer caring about keeping the peace. There's no love lost between us anyway. Freya's lip curls. 'You're digging yourself your own grave,' she says.

I let her words settle, wondering just how true they are as I watch Freya stride away. The James family crest on the back of her neck slowly disappears with her.

CHAPTER 32

With Freya's words still taunting me, I'm forced to move forwards. I need to continue like I'm about to say: 'I do.' I need to keep putting on a front.

Switching the wellington boots for wedding shoes, I buckle them up and walk to the window. As soon as I'm sure Freya's gone, I leave the cabin, making my way to the barn, slipping and sliding over frozen patches in the ground.

I hold the train of the gown so it doesn't drag through the mud any more than it already has. My heels, white pearl banquet sandals, are difficult to walk in, and I can already feel blisters starting to form. But I march on. I know when I reach the barn, I'll suss out someone who will help me. It isn't just the James family anymore. The lodge has opened the floodgates, and swarms of people have already appeared. There's a rumble of chatter coming from within the barn and it sends a thrill through me just to know other people are here now.

The caterers are already here, setting up the gazebo. Sumptuous scents are starting to swirl through the air, unseen but sinking deep into the bark of the trees. I eye them all suspiciously, wondering if I can trust any of them. They're carting food from a blue van with a catering company logo printed across it. I'm about to start striding towards them when one of Stephen's brothers, Martin, approaches them.

I whirl around, darting behind a tree before he notices me. He starts directing them in through the barn doors as they carry huge stainless-steel containers in with them.

Without much of an excuse as to why I'm here early, I need to try and remain hidden, but I also need to get into that barn and scope out the guests. Part of me hopes that my bridesmaids are already trying to figure out who they could turn to for help, if they're in there. But they don't know any of these guests. They'll have no idea who is who. I need to get to them, and fast.

At the entrance to the barn there's a wooden crate with a blackboard perched alongside it. Written in chalk: *Put your phones in here.*

I don't quite see why phones would be an issue during the ceremony, considering there's no signal out here. To stop people taking photographs, perhaps. There's a number of devices piled on top of each other in the crate already. I'm about to walk past, ignoring it, when a bald man in a tuxedo stops me in my tracks.

'Phone?' he says gruffly.

'I'm the bride,' I laugh, motioning to the dress.

'I see that,' he says, eyes so dark I can't see the pupils in them as they scan me. 'I've been under strict instructions that *no one* brings phones into the barn.' He holds the palm of his hand out in front of me.

I want to argue with him, but I don't have the time. Turning sharply, fists clenched, I walk up to the crate. Sliding my iPhone out of the clutch bag I'm carrying, I drop it into the box. It's no use to me anyway. The phone beneath mine, an old, scratched Samsung, lights up. I peer at the screen, checking I haven't somehow turned the camera on or unlocked it. My stomach clenches as I stare at the phone, a slow, prickling sense of dread creeping up my spine. A woman smiles up at me in the background of the Samsung. The corkscrew curls and big, shining eyes are unmistakable. They belong to a face that has haunted me ever since arriving at Shadowmoor Lodge. One of the wedding guests has a photograph of Charlotte Walker saved as the background on their phone.

It must be Ben's phone. Charlotte had said they had dated, and that she was pregnant with his child. She thinks that's why she's here. Held captive to keep the baby growing inside her. She'd warned me that if the James family finds out I'm pregnant, they'll keep me here too. But at the moment, I am one step ahead of them. I know about Charlotte and about their sick, twisted game with pregnant women. I'm connecting the dots by myself already, and while I don't know exactly who those other women are on that personalised Monopoly board, I'm sure they were all pregnant too.

There are so many children running around the grounds of Shadowmoor Lodge. I had just assumed they were Stephen's brothers' kids when we'd first arrived. Now, I'm starting to wonder if something more sinister is going on.

Staring down at Charlotte's pretty face, I fight the urge to pick up Ben's phone. I wouldn't be able to get into it anyway. It's locked with facial ID password protection.

The bald man observes me closely, and I throw him a small smile as I turn away from the crate.

'Can I go in now?' I ask. I'm desperate to get inside, to see my bridesmaids if only to make sure they're alright.

'Bit early, ain't ya?' he asks, folding his arms. Whoever this man is, I won't be trusting him.

'I need my bridesmaids,' I say, trying not to tremble as our eyes drill into each other.

Eventually, he nods and parts the barn doors, but as he does Ingrid shrieks from behind us.

'Ivy! What're you doing? It's not time for the ceremony yet, the guests will see you.' She hurries over to me and covers me with her own jacket.

I exhale, my breath trailing out in front of us. 'Ingrid,' I say. 'I need my bridesmaids.'

'Well, I'll get them for you then. But you can't be here, not yet!' Shooing me away, I'm left out in the cold, watching the caterers continue to offload food from their van. *Something blue*, I can't help but think bitterly as I press my fingernails to my scabbing scalp. I won't pull, but just digging my nails into the skin there feels like a release. My hair is hardened from hairspray and my fingers come away sticky. It takes me a moment to realise I've drawn blood that rolls down my fingertips and into the palms of my hands.

* * *

'Your bridesmaids, forgive me, I've forgotten their names,' Ingrid says, flustered as her dress flaps in the wind. 'They've said they'll meet you back at the cabin. Head back there, before you catch a chill. I'm surprised you aren't sick already after being stuck out in the blizzard the other night.'

I swallow, and for the first time I notice the swelling in my glands. I'm hot, despite being in nothing but a dress.

'You do look a little pale, you know. Are you sure you're alright?' Ingrid asks, stepping closer. She reaches out and touches my arm. 'Your skin's all clammy.'

'I'm fine,' I lie, and then add, 'thank you.'

I'm not fine. I thought the trembling was from nerves and that my body aches have been from the fall, but now I realise I have a fever, and it's getting worse by the second.

'Go back to the cabin, love. I'll send them your way,' Ingrid says, swivelling her head. She looks back towards the barn and then over my shoulder. Finally her eyes lock back on mine.

Marcel barges out of the barn and starts to tread towards us through the snow. I can see his eyes roving over my body, taking in the mud splattered over the gown. His pace quickens.

'Run,' Ingrid cries.

CHAPTER 33

I'm not sure why I listen, if it's the sheer panic etched into Ingrid's eyes or something else, but I run. Run away from the guests and anyone who could possibly help me inside of the barn. While I let my legs carry me, hitting the wet earth as I go, I wonder just how dangerous Marcel is.

I want to look back, to see what's happening between them. But I find that I can't. My focus is on the hordes of other guests arriving and parking up closer to the cabins. I head in that direction, but as I get closer, I realise I'm not sure who the majority of them are. All I know is that all of them are somehow connected to the James family, or they wouldn't be here. Being from overseas, I'm at a disadvantage and that means trusting any of the guests is risky. My best hope is for a member of staff, if there are any left, to arrive. I stake out behind some bushes, watching people clamber out of vehicles. Most guests are in formal wear, cocktail dresses and suits. I hold back, hoping someone will appear in something that looks more like uniform. There's a young couple I think might be waitstaff, the boy in a white collared shirt and chinos, the girl not dissimilar. I study them closely as they light a cigarette and pass it between themselves. Trying to catch snippets of their conversation, I edge closer.

The boy looks down at a watch too big for his wrist. 'We're gonna be late,' he says, stamping the cigarette out under his patent leather shoe.

'What a ball ache,' the girl drawls. 'Can't wait to stop serving posh drinks to wankers on my weekends.'

They push off from the rusted Honda Civic they arrived in and as they do, I step out with the brightest smile I can manage.

'Hello!' I say, hoping they don't notice just how much I'm shaking.

The girl takes in my appearance, the tattered dress and dishevelled hair. When neither of them respond, I speak again.

'I wondered if you could help me?'

'Yeah?' the boy asks, cocking a half-shaven eyebrow at me.

'I've had a bit of a tumble, as you can tell!' I attempt a giggle, but already my eyes are starting to sting with tears. These two may be my only hope.

'What do you need?' the girl asks curiously.

'When you get to the barn, do you think you could find my bridesmaids for me? There's three of them, they'll all be wearing the same dress.'

I wait for one of them to say or do anything but they remain deadpan.

'I might need their help cleaning up a bit before the ceremony starts, you see?' I try again.

'We can do that,' the boy says slowly. 'Let's go, Pip.'

I don't hold out much hope, but as I watch them walk away, I call after them. 'Oh, and guys? Please try to keep it subtle. I wouldn't want to worry anyone.'

They nod, saying nothing, and continue on their path to the barn.

If my bridesmaids are in the barn with the other guests, hopefully those two kids can pass them the message. If my bridesmaids aren't in the barn, however, if the James family has done something with them, I'm still completely alone.

Clomping up the steps to the cabin I'm greeted with the warmth inside as I enter.

With my fever spiking and my energy dropping, I need a moment to rest, but I can't let myself fully, not even as I fall to the sofa. Not even as my eyes close, because as I do, Joanna's lifeless body flickers into my mind. It's an image I'll never be able to forget or forgive myself for.

Every muscle in my body feels leaden and tender to touch. I wrap my arms around my bare shoulders and start to rock.

* * *

Footsteps break my daze. Not the urgent clack of three pairs of heels but a heavier, slower pound of boots.

Shooting from the sofa, I open the curtains and peer outside. Someone is at the front door, but I can't tell who it is. Terrified it's Marcel, blocking the only exit to the cabin, I dart to the staircase and start to climb them, tripping over the gown with each step.

There's no way out, but there is a room I can lock myself in, biding time.

As quietly as I can, I click the bathroom door shut and twist the lock. A man could break this door down with one kick. It's only a flimsy thing, but it's my only barrier.

'Ivy?' It's Stephen. 'Ivy, where are you?'

His voice, the voice I've allowed to purr in my ears over the last couple of years, knocks me off-kilter. This is the moment, this is when I must choose whether to put my trust in the man I love or not. Like on one of those sick reality shows I've always loved watching. It's not quite as fun when I'm in the contestants' shoes, though their situations weren't quite life and death.

'Stephen,' I say slowly. 'I need you to listen to me.' I'm pressed up against the door of the bathroom, listening to every move he makes from out in the bedroom.

He steps closer to the bathroom. 'What is it?'

'Your dad,' I start, but falter.

'What about him?' he whispers. 'Has he said something to you? Are you okay?'

He sounds so worried, so like the man I fell in love with. My heart constricts as I try to find the words. Despite everything, every part of me screaming not to trust him, I do. He's my fiancé, and he's been there for me through everything. I love him, and I'm cross with myself for ever doubting him. I just hope he'll understand why I did, and why I was so scared.

'Stephen, he's not the man you think he is,' I say, my hand on the lock, but I don't twist. I stay inside, barricading myself as I continue to speak. 'He kidnapped that girl. I'm sure of it. She's here, Stephen, in that cabin by the lake. We need to leave, to get to the police, now.' I stumble over my words, speaking too fast.

'What're you talking about?' Stephen asks. 'The girl on the news?'

I nod, even though he can't see me. I can hear him sigh, see his shadow creeping closer from beneath the door. He doesn't believe me. I knew he wouldn't — and that only makes me surer of his innocence.

'I'm sorry,' he says, spluttering. 'I don't know why I'm laughing.'

'Because it sounds ridiculous, Stephen. I know it does. But it's not,' I cry, slamming my palm against the door.

'How do you know all this?'

I swallow. 'Because I went inside the cabin. We all did. Me, Kayleigh, Georgie and Rosie.'

'You went inside the cabin down by the lake. When?'

'Yes. Last night, when everyone had gone to bed. We've spoken to her. To Charlotte Walker, I mean.'

'Ivy,' Stephen sighs, clicking his tongue. He seems to rest against the door, breathing heavily.

Breaking into a sudden cold sweat, I feel my legs go weak. I know what I'm about to do is dangerous, stupid even. Looking down at the engagement ring glittering on my finger, I touch it fondly with my thumb. 'I'll show you,' I whisper, and unlock the door separating us.

His eyes widen at the sight of me. At first, I think it's because I'm in the wedding dress, but then I catch myself in the mirror and notice just how bedraggled I look.

He plucks a twig from my hair. 'Your dress?' he mutters, confused.

'It's ruined,' I say, brushing at the dirt embedded into the material.

'You still look beautiful.' He smiles sadly. I think he's starting to understand what I already do: we aren't getting married today.

I want to hold on to this moment, to remember every part of it. Me in my once perfect dress, him in his navy suit looking as handsome as I've ever seen him. I have never loved anyone the way that I love him. My Stephen James. The man who has patiently stood by me through even my darkest of days, who hasn't left my side at the hurdles I've struggled to jump over.

I want to remember the way he's looking at me now, his eyes full of affection. I know after today, he may never look at me that way again.

'I'll show you. Please, let me show you. Then you'll believe me,' I beg.

'Fine. Show me,' he says, humouring me with a smile.

'It's not funny, Stephen. Why are you laughing at me?' My words come out hysterical.

'You've spoken to this woman, you say?' he asks, dropping his hands to his sides.

'Yes. She's in there, tied to a chair!' Mascara runs down my cheeks, landing on the bodice of the dress. I swipe at my face with the back of my hand but only succeed at rubbing makeup further into my eyes, making them burn.

'And there's more, Stephen,' I say.

'Go on,' he says. His eyes have narrowed but he's still smiling. I try to read his expression but can't.

'Joanna. The tarot reader, I — I found her body. She's *dead*, Stephen. In the tack shed.' That's when I watch something shift in Stephen's face. A flicker of darkness casts over his features.

I still, glancing up at him, trembling. This is why I thought twice about unlocking the bathroom door, but it's too late now.

'*You* told me she left Shadowmoor Lodge. You promised me she got safely to town.' I'm pointing a finger at him, quivering.

'I did say that didn't I?'

My blood runs cold as the tone of his voice changes. It's lowered, become darker somehow.

He pinches the bridge of his nose and as his hand pulls away, he's no longer smiling.

CHAPTER 34

The front door bangs open, making us both turn towards the bedroom door. Neither of us speak. I don't think I can speak even if I tried. A scream seems lodged in my throat, and I can't move.

'Stephen?' Marcel's voice booms up the staircase.

Stephen tries to hide a smile, rubbing his hand over his mouth. His expression changes at the sound of another voice.

'Ivy!' Georgie shouts.

There's a scuffle downstairs, making us lock eyes. Rage burns at my insides. I can't allow Marcel to hurt my friends. Pushing my hair back out of my face, I take one last look at Stephen. If I could tell him I love him, I would. But the words die on my lips, because how can I love someone I can't trust?

'I'm sorry,' I breathe, hoping what I'm doing is the right decision. I leap past him and out of the room and as I do I feel him reach for me, hear the rip of my dress and the scatter of crystals as they cascade onto the floorboards.

I carry on going, refusing to stop when I hear him roar my name. I almost trip down the staircase, but I don't stop. Swivelling my head left to right, I spot Georgie at the corner of the hallway. Marcel has her up against the wall, his hand wrapped around her throat. Even from a distance, I can see the veins popping from Georgie's head as she struggles against Marcel.

'Ivy,' she wheezes, making Marcel whip his head around. 'Go!' Her leg flies up and lands in the centre of Marcel's groin. His fragile body buckles.

Stephen thunders down the stairs, stopping as he sees his father sprawled on the floor. Georgie and I look towards him, mouths agape.

'Ivy, go. Now. I've got this.' Georgie nods.

I don't want to leave her. If anyone can protect themselves, it's Georgie, but that still doesn't make me want to leave.

As Stephen descends the stairs, Georgie charges towards him. 'Go!' she screams, knocking him off balance.

They land with a crash and I watch, stunned, as Georgie tries to keep my fiancé down.

'You crazy bitch!' Stephen seethes, flailing beneath Georgie. 'Get off me!'

I know she won't be able to hold him long. I have to run, and hope that Stephen will spare Georgie by running after me instead.

With one last fleeting glance at them, and then to Marcel who still has a hand clutched between his legs, I bolt to the front door.

The snow has turned to sludge and sinks into my sandals as I tear through the woods. I don't know where to go. I don't know if anywhere is really safe, but surely some of the wedding guests will protect me.

As I start to run back in the direction of the barn, I spot two figures cannoning towards me. John and William. Wheeling round, I charge in the opposite direction, towards the tack shed and stables. I try to misdirect them, running in a jagged trail, but my footprints are easily traceable in the snow.

Inside the stables, Shadow's tacked up, the bit in his mouth. His hooves stomp into the ground at the sight of me. I stroke a hand over him, my fingers gliding over the tight braids in his mane. He's been dressed, ready to enter the barn for the wedding ceremony. My jaw clenches, thinking about how differently today could have gone. I'd probably be saying my vows right now in some sort of parallel universe or alternate timeline.

'Don't you look handsome,' I say, trying to soothe him, but his ears are pinned back. He can sense my fear.

The crunching of snow underfoot makes me freeze. They're here. The other horses snort, their tails swishing wildly as they try to back away.

As the doors to the stables bang open, I search for a place to hide. The only place I can think of is in with the horses. I gulp, slipping behind them, my hands shakily trying to still their restless legs. Their bodies are tense, and one buck could very easily finish me off. Their hooves are frighteningly close to my face, but I bunch up behind them as I hear the scuff of shoes against the asphalt. The sound of a ragged breath enters, steps falling gently as someone explores the stables. I want to look, but I'm paralysed, my body and face buried into a stack of hay. If I could, I'd weave myself inside it, but all I can do is breathe in the earthy fragrance and hope no one notices me balled up in the corner behind the horses.

Whoever is inside the barn is still there, taking cautious steps towards the horses, when I spot something that makes me blink rapidly. A gun.

* * *

I stare down at the barrel of the gun at my feet, precariously sitting there next to a weathered box of ammunition. I don't want to think about why these things are in the stables, hidden with the horses.

I wish it didn't have to come to this, but as heavy footsteps get closer, I touch the cold metal of the rifle. My hand quivers, my fingers just grazing the barrel. The door to the barn dances on its hinges, the incessant clanging thundering through my ears.

Just touching the gun is enough to send me spiralling into my memories, to when the muzzle of a gun had been at my temple. Pressing hard, promising to end my life if I didn't do exactly as I was told. Just the reminder is enough to make me convulse, to palpitate like it's happening all over again. I remember that rancid breath hot against my cheek, shouting orders I was too scared to refuse. That sharp, oniony sweat, burning my nostrils. A smell that has never left me, even after all these years, embedding itself into my pores, lingering. Even after all that time practising with guns to take back my power, I never wanted to find myself around a gun again. Not outside of the shooting range, but now I have no choice but to face my biggest fear head on.

'Ivy?'

I hear my name being called through the howling wind, and my heart leaps. It's Stephen's voice. I open my mouth to respond, but stop myself, my voice fizzling out against my lips.

'Ivy, where are you? We're here to help you,' he cries, his voice coming from just outside the shed.

We? Who is he with? Who is already in the stables? Every morsel of my being screams at me to keep quiet. Survival instincts kicking in. Hands bang on the sides of the shed, the disintegrating wood trembling.

'Ivy? Are you in there?' Another voice calls out, more frantic. Marcel's voice.

Terror swoops over me as the storm rumbles fiercely outside.

'Shh!' I hear who I assume to be Stephen hiss. He doesn't want me to know Marcel's with him. That they're searching for me together.

I hoist the gun up, and its heaviness surprises me. I fiddle around for the safety mechanism, hoping to God I've done the right thing. The gun, and everything about it, its power, its dreadfulness, is foreign in my hands.

With the trigger beneath my fingertip, I nestle the gun into my shoulder. I don't know much about guns, I'm no expert, but I do know with one like this I only have a single shot before I need to reload, and reloading isn't something I know how to do.

One of the horses moves, making me completely visible. I see Ben, his hands wrapped around the wooden railing, looking down at me. My fingers grip the gun tighter as he calls to his family. 'Found her. She's here.'

Marcel staggers towards me. His eyes glitter like an evening in Bordeaux, where Stephen and I are supposed to be in just a few hours.

'Ivy,' he purrs, eyes searing right into mine. 'What're you doing?'

'Stop moving,' I bark, thrusting the gun in his direction.

He laughs, a hollow noise that chills me to the bone. Stephen reaches his dad and looks down at me too. I don't even recognise the man looming in front of me, this strange six-foot man with clammy skin, slick with sweat.

'Why are you doing this?' I screech, trying to keep a firm grip on the gun. I point it between them, Ben, Marcel and Stephen.

John and William crash inside, halting at the sight of the gun in my hands.

'Don't panic, boys, she can't shoot. Thing's probably not even loaded,' Marcel sneers.

'Dad,' Stephen says softly. 'She—'

'Shut up, Steve,' Marcel snaps, silencing him. It's the first time I've ever seen Stephen look small, overruled.

'Tell me why?' I ask again, pressing myself as far into the hay as I can while the horses snort and toss their heads around.

'You could've become a James, Ivy,' Marcel says, gesturing around him. 'But you just had to meddle, didn't you?'

I don't know how to respond. I keep my eyes trained on him, the barrel of the gun aiming right in the centre of his chest. If he takes one step towards me, I'll squeeze the trigger. I'm ready.

'I knew you saw me that day I brought Charlotte Walker here. Quite unfortunate, really.' He lets out a breath.

'Why did you take her?' I snarl.

'She was going to get rid of my baby,' Ben says.

'We couldn't allow that,' Marcel says, shaking his head.

'She's not ready to have a child!' I say, a sharpness to my voice.

'And that's why we'll take it from her, once she's had it.' Marcel grins.

'You're sick!' I gasp. 'You'll keep her here for nine months? Then just take the baby from her?'

'You said yourself, she's not ready to have a child.' Ben shrugs.

'And then what? You expect me to believe you'd just let her go?'

Ben and Marcel laugh, a dark chuckle. Stephen stands to the side, staring down at his feet.

'Oh no, Ivy. Charlotte won't be leaving Shadowmoor Lodge again,' Marcel says.

I let out an involuntary shiver. 'You'll kill her,' I whisper.

'She'll have served her purpose.' Marcel looks at me savagely, shifting his weight. His movement makes me tense.

'Why do you want her baby so badly?' I ask, my arms starting to ache from the weight of the gun.

'Ivy, my wife and I have seven sons,' Marcel says, as though this is news to me. 'She wanted a daughter so badly.' He stops a moment, coughing.

I swallow, not liking where this is going.

'We struggled a long time,' he wheezes. 'It almost killed her.'

As I look at him, I'm sure I can see real hurt in his eyes.

'Ingrid developed . . . shall we say, an *obsession*,' he says. 'Her need to grow this family, expand the James bloodline, it consumed her. John's first wife went through similar fertility struggles, didn't she, John?'

John nods solemnly, looking from his dad to me.

'You'd think it would make Ingrid connect with the girl more, wouldn't you?' he laughs.

I stay very still, listening and studying him closely.

'It didn't, though. Ingrid resented her. The *hate*, Ivy . . . the hate was festering in her. I had to stop it.' There's so much passion in him as he speaks, his body seems to vibrate.

'I had to kill her, before Ingrid let that resentment devour her. She was no use to the family, anyway,' Marcel reveals with no semblance of remorse. 'John found a new partner eventually, went on to have a couple of kids. You might've seen them running around here.' His face warms as he says this.

'He murdered your wife?!' I tremble, addressing John directly, but like Stephen his eyes are at his feet. 'Because she couldn't conceive? Are you absolutely insane.'

'No!' Marcel roars, slamming his hand against the stable wall. 'I did what I had to do to make sure my wife, their mother, didn't get sick.'

'You're all sick,' I mutter.

'I couldn't lose her, you see? She'd have gone to the loony bin, and I couldn't have that. I need her. So I did what I had to, to eliminate the problem.'

'Were there others?' I ask, thinking about all those names on the Monopoly board.

'Oh yes,' Marcel says with pride. 'There certainly were. William's wife said she didn't want children, if you ask me, it should've been discussed before they got married. So she had to go, didn't she, Will?'

William says nothing, but his emotionless eyes don't leave the gun.

'So Charlotte wanted an abortion, John's wife couldn't conceive, and William's wife didn't want children, so your plan was to kill them all?'

'When you love someone unconditionally, Ivy, you'll do anything to keep them safe and happy,' Marcel says.

My mouth turns dry, and I turn to Stephen. 'What about you? Your exes?'

Marcel laughs again. 'There's been a few.'

Stephen rakes his eyes up from the ground to meet mine. Instinctively, my free hand closes around my womb.

'Ivy?' Ingrid's voice sounds from outside the stable doors. 'Ivy, I'm here.'

Everyone jerks their heads up as Ingrid rushes in.

'Ingrid,' Marcel says, softening.

'Marcel,' Ingrid grimaces at the sight of him. 'I just heard everything,' she says, tears falling down her face. 'How could you?'

Marcel grapples for something to say. 'I did it for you, darling,' he says slowly.

'It was never me who was sick, Marcel,' she sobs. 'It's always been you.'

'But I saw what it was all doing to you,' he says. 'I was losing you.'

'I would never want to kill a woman for not having a child,' she exclaims. 'Marcel, what've you done? What've you made our boys do?' She turns to me, wet eyes lowering to the gun. 'Ivy, love. Put the gun down please. We're going to get you out of here.'

'I'm afraid that's not possible,' Marcel interjects.

'She's leaving, Marcel,' Ingrid says firmly.

'I can't let that happen. She'll go to the police.'

'And so she should!' she cries, trying to stop him as he starts opening the gate to the horses. He pushes her aside, her brittle body falling into her sons.

I thrust the gun at him in warning.

'Oh, Ivy. We both know you can't shoot,' Marcel says, the corners of his mouth sneaking up into the cruellest smile as he strides towards me.

'I never said I don't know how to shoot,' I spit, pulling the trigger before I really understand what I'm doing. The recoil comes faster than expected. The force of the shot slams the butt of the gun into my chest, throwing me back into the haystack.

The crack pulsates into the woods, a booming, thunderous peal travelling far and wide. Bone fractures, my clavicle shattering as I let out a guttural yowl. I drop the gun, its weight too much for me. 'I just don't like guns,' I finish.

CHAPTER 35

Marcel sprawls on the ground, the sound of the horse's sharp breaths and stamping hooves pulsating around him. Stephen's wails overpower the echoes from the gunshot. We're all motionless while we wait for the blood to start pooling from beneath him, but it doesn't come.

I've missed, my chance hindered without knowing how to open the bolt and insert more ammunition. I look down at the gun, trying to understand the different parts of it, but it's no use. Why couldn't they have left out a typical handgun? A Glock, maybe. I have no idea how many rounds a handgun has in it but I know it's more than one.

'She missed,' Ben exhales, relieved.

Stephen and his brothers look up, still gripping onto Ingrid, holding her back. Very slowly, Marcel starts to move.

'Ivy, get out of here. Go!' Ingrid screams. 'Get to the barn. People there will help you.'

I hope I can trust what Ingrid is saying. I've never heard someone sound so feverish.

'Marcel, stop this madness, right now.' I hear Ingrid shriek in a frenzy, still fighting against her sons.

Stephen has left his mother's side and gone to help Marcel up, and I can't help but stare at him a moment longer, taking in who my fiancé truly is. What he's really capable of.

There's a strange, gritty feeling deep in my collarbone as I get to my feet.

'Go!' Ingrid cries again, and before Marcel is up, I flee from the stables. I twist my head over my shoulder to make sure no one's following me, but they're all surrounding Marcel.

* * *

Guests are starting to spill out of the barn, no doubt curious after hearing the gunshot. I'm running towards them when I see more of Stephen's brothers pacing towards me.

'It's alright!' I hear one say, his hands up in front of the guests in an effort to keep them back. 'Someone's obviously set off a gun accidentally. Please everyone, stand back.'

As the guests start to scatter, trying to catch a better glimpse of the commotion, I limp closer. As I do, one of Stephen's brothers pulls the tip of a handgun from his pocket, just for me to see. Unblinking, he stares at me sharply, a vicious warning in his eyes that if I get closer, he will use the gun. I wouldn't put it past him, not even in front of all of these guests. To protect myself and them, I pivot. As I hurtle into the trees, the brothers follow me. I can hear the rumble of the guests talking amongst themselves. Surely, they'll grab their phones back from the crate and attempt to find a signal, maybe one will even have the foresight to get in their car and drive off to find help. I can only hope as I push deeper into the woodlands, heat flaring, burning through my collarbone and up my neck. I have to stop. To catch my breath and give my body a break.

Flinging myself behind a gnarled tree stump, I clap a hand over my mouth so they won't hear my heavy breathing. They crash through the trees, and I squeeze my eyes tightly shut as they get closer, but they don't stop. They keep going, deeper into the woods, further away from me.

The second I allow myself to move, twigs snap and pop. I try to be as quiet as I can as I get to my knees and scan the trees. When I'm sure I'm alone, I grip the ends of the wedding dress, and grind my teeth together as I rip the dirty hem. The pain is like a knife twisting into me, agonising. The fabric shreds easily, and I continue to tear until I think I have enough for a makeshift sling. Placing my elbow inside the material, I wrap it around my wrist and over my shoulder. I need to keep moving.

If only I hadn't given up my phone, I'd have been able to head in the direction of the signal spot I now know about, but I'm sure that's where Stephen's brothers are headed.

Cradling my arm in the crystal encrusted sling, I start to make my way back to the clearing.

'Hello, Ivy,' I hear a voice wheeze from behind me. My stomach drops.

Slowly, I turn, locking eyes with Marcel. John and William are directly behind him, panting.

'You've really caused quite the scene,' Marcel says in a flat, monotone voice dripping with disappointment. 'The guests are all in a bit of a panic. But no harm done. I'm sure the others are busy calming them as we speak.'

'Are you deluded?!' I spit. 'They can't be calmed. They know something bad is going on here now! They're going to get help!' I think of all those guests, innocent bystanders who came to witness a union of two people, not the crumbling of an entire family.

Marcel's body shakes with laughter. 'I can assure you; no help is coming.'

He's bluffing. He has to be. I try to catch a flicker of doubt or the telltale sign of a lie from him, but his confidence is unwavering. He steps towards me.

'Stay away from me,' I scream, no longer caring about being overheard. If I scream loud enough, some of the guests might come to help.

'Shut her up.' He nods at his sons, both six-foot, stockily built giants.

I won't let them silence me. I scream, my vocal cords turning raw as I cry out into the woods. I try to run, but they're too fast for me, and soon I feel beefy arms wrap around my waist and mouth. I kick and fight, but it's no use against their strength. Together, they carry me through the clearing and up the steps into my cabin.

They throw me to the ground, John locking the door behind him.

'What now?' William asks, his eyes wide.

'I dunno,' John replies, and together they look at Marcel for the answer.

'We're screwed,' William says, panic-stricken.

'We are not *screwed*,' Marcel says firmly. 'I will kill every guest here if I have to, to get away with this. We've worked too long and too hard to have this little leech ruin it all.' He points a wrinkled finger down to me.

'Dad,' John whispers, shaking his head. 'This is crazy. I can't do this anymore.'

Marcel rounds on his son. 'Then get out.'

'You need help, Dad. Mum's right. It's you that's sick,' John's shoulders drop. 'I should've realised that a long time ago.'

'Everything I've done is to keep our family strong,' Marcel snarls.

Sliding his hand into his pocket, John withdraws a gun. It's small, toy looking.

'What're you going to do, shoot me?' Marcel laughs but pauses as John raises the gun up to him.

I watch intently, too terrified to move, remaining pressed into the floorboards, not breathing. Just as I'm wondering where the hell Stephen and Ingrid are, William barges between the two men and grabs for the gun. It explodes, a bullet firing right into wall behind me. It stuns me, my ears ringing.

As a fight breaks out between Marcel, John and William, I scramble back to my feet. I'm about to wrench open the front door when I spot Stephen sprinting up to the cabin through the window. I bolt up the staircase, knowing there's no point in locking myself in the bathroom again, but I see no other option. I have nowhere else to go.

The mounted stag head glares down at me as I get into the bedroom and slam the door shut behind me. Footsteps are already drilling up the staircase. Spinning round, I search the room for something to use to protect myself, but all I can see is the lamp. I'm about to reach for it when I look back up at the stag head, at those twisted, sharp antlers.

When Marcel kicks the bedroom door open, I'm ready. He takes me in, holding the stag head out in front of me. His face contorts into an expression of amusement.

'Heavy?' He smiles as I struggle beneath the weight of the taxidermy animal.

The pain in my shoulder takes my breath away, and my vision starts to cloud.

'What a pity you'll never leave Shadowmoor Lodge, eh?' he says, and I wonder if this is what he says to all the girls before he kills them.

As he starts closing the gap between us, I push the stag head at him. He laughs again, thinking I'm using it as a shield, as a protective barrier between us. But he doesn't know how my brain really works.

'Fuck you,' I roar, hurtling towards him with the mounted stag head held out in front of me at full force.

There's a sickening squelch as the antlers drive beneath his shirt.

CHAPTER 36

'Ivy, no!' Stephen howls, barrelling into the bedroom, but it's too late. This time there is blood. So much blood that Stephen slips in it as he reaches his father.

He's breathing, but barely. The antlers are jutting into his chest and stomach. I step back, watching the horror, the suffering not just in Marcel but in Stephen too. The scene reminds me of some sort of grotesque Francis Bacon or Francisco Goya painting.

My hands are sticky with blood. I hold them out in front of me. My entire body quivers, adrenaline kicking in as I try to make sense of what I've just done.

'Dad?' Stephen's voice cracks as he grabs his father by the shoulders, shaking him.

Marcel doesn't respond. His breathing becomes shallower, his eyes starting to flicker.

'Look after your mother for me,' he whispers and takes one last inhale.

Stephen looks up at me through tear-filled eyes. 'You,' he says shakily. 'You killed him.'

'I-I had to, Stephen!' I say, my bloody hands clenched into tight balls. 'He was going to kill me.'

Stephen drops his father's limp hand and stands. 'But now, I'm going to kill you,' he whispers.

As his footsteps get closer, I close my eyes, steeling myself for a blow that never comes.

'Stephen James, you take one more step towards that woman and I'll disown you,' Ingrid breathes. Such a simple threat, but as I peel my eyes open, I see Stephen has stalled.

Ingrid is in the doorway, makeup running down her face. She's resting against Freya, who is no longer in her ethereal dress. She's in a plain shirt and jeans, the makeup scrubbed clean from her face. It looks as though she's been crying.

I watch their eyes swivel to the body of Marcel, take in the blood so dark it's like ink pooling beneath him. Ingrid's chin trembles, but she keeps her head held high as Freya's hold on her seems to tighten.

'Mum,' Stephen says. 'Dad. He's — he's . . .'

'Dead,' Ingrid finishes for him. 'I see that.'

I turn back to Stephen. I look at him, slowly letting reality sink in: if Ingrid hadn't shown up exactly when she had, if she'd been just five minutes later, Stephen would have killed me. He might still. But I'm starting to see, Stephen's love for his mother runs deeper than I could ever have thought possible. Like the other members of the James family, he'd do anything to make her happy, and right now that is the only thing keeping me safe.

Ingrid faces me, those cold eyes suddenly brimming with emotion. 'You're safe,' she tells me, but her words are hollow. Seeing her family fracture has broken her.

'Mum,' Freya whispers, trying to pull Ingrid to her but she pushes her daughter away.

'No, darling. I've got this.' She licks her lips, once painted a vibrant red, now patchy and pale. 'Ivy, I've been trying to warn you since the moment you arrived.'

'Warn me about what?' I ask, frowning.

'This family, it isn't safe. I didn't want you to be another victim. Stephen's been trying to keep you away from me this entire time!'

she cries. 'Every time I worked up the courage to speak to you Stephen seemed to step in. I never seemed to have the chance.'

'I don't understand.' My mind swirls.

'Neither do I, not fully,' Ingrid says.

Far away, the sound of sirens amplifies. Stephen hears it too, his back straightening.

'I understand,' Freya says softly. 'I know the game they've been playing.' She dips her head to her chest. 'Marcel made this Monopoly board.'

'I've seen it.' I swallow.

'It was like this disgusting role-playing game,' she says through gritted teeth. 'Every woman they took to that cabin went onto this board. I guess it was kind of like his version of saving a souvenir from each kill.'

She tells Ingrid and me again, about Marcel's habit of killing any woman who couldn't or wouldn't deliver the family a baby. Ingrid takes it in, her eyes growing wider with each breath Freya takes.

'It was all for you, Mum,' Stephen croaks as the sirens swell through the trees, getting closer.

Ingrid purses her lips together, shaking her head side to side. 'You're going to hand yourself in,' she says eventually, looking up at her son.

'Mum,' Stephen sobs.

I stare at him in disgust, suddenly so unsure of who he is, of who he ever was. If it weren't for my staring, perhaps I wouldn't have seen the subtle movement of his hand sliding into his pocket.

'Ingrid, look out!' I scream as Stephen rips out the same small gun I'd seen earlier. But he doesn't point it at Ingrid. He points it at me.

'I'm not going to jail for this,' he shouts, his nose running as he cocks the gun. 'You've ruined everything. I should never have brought you here,' he says to me.

'Was any of it ever real, between us?' I find myself asking, my eyes travelling down the tiny barrel of the gun pointed directly between my eyes. If I only have moments left, I'd like clarity on that at least.

'Oh, I loved you,' Stephen says with a mirthless chuckle. 'But then you struggled to fall pregnant.'

I touch my stomach, trying to calm the little life growing inside me. 'But I am pregnant,' I murmur, noticing Ingrid's head jerk in my direction.

'You're pregnant?' Ingrid breathes, and even now, I see the hunger in her eyes for the child in my womb.

'That's what makes doing this so hard,' Stephen says, and pulls the trigger.

CHAPTER 37

I wake in the hospital, entangled in tubes and wires. The very last person I expect to see by my bedside is Freya. But there she is, in the bed next to me, scrolling through her phone. She hasn't noticed that I've opened my eyes yet, and I think about closing them again, but a nurse enters the room and startles us both.

Freya turns from the nurse to me. Her facial expression is hard to read. If I wasn't clearly medicated, I'd almost think she looks relieved.

'Hi there,' she says softly.

I eye her cautiously as the nurse checks us over.

'Your friends will be sad they missed you. They've been here at your bedside waiting for you to wake up,' she says.

'Where did they go?'

Her eyes soften. 'I'm sure they're not far. I'll keep an eye out for them.' She nods reassuringly.

I hear a cough and turn to find Ingrid sitting in a visitor's chair, a Costa coffee in hand.

'Ivy!' she croons. 'How're you feeling?'

'I don't know,' I say truthfully. My mind is foggy, and I'm working hard to try and piece together what happened before I got here.

'Well, I feel like I've been shot,' Freya says, deadpan.

The nurse stifles a laugh. 'You owe this woman your life,' she says to me. 'And your baby's.'

Those last three words still me. My baby is okay. I blink, slowly first, until the tears start to spill. I don't understand, and the look on my face shows that.

'Ivy,' Ingrid says, clearing her throat. 'Freya saved you.'

I look between the two women, struggling to comprehend what they're saying.

'Took a bullet for you,' Freya winces, gasping as the nurse checks a bandaged wound on her shoulder.

'She did.' The nurse nods. 'Her network of nerves are shattered. She's paralysed throughout her left arm. Lucky it hasn't had to be amputated, though!' she says.

'Doctor says it's tissue death, muscle tearing and scarring. Can't bring myself to look.' Freya grimaces, twisting away as the nurse sponges her shoulder.

My mind is working too hard, too fast. 'Stephen?' I choke.

'Stephen is being held under police guard while he's being treated. They're supervising his room at all times, so he can't get to you, Ivy,' Ingrid says with a nod.

Her words are so solid, so final — all I can do is close my eyes and fall back asleep.

EPILOGUE

It was only after I got back to South Africa, reacquainting myself with the humidity of the Western Cape, the beating sunshine and the rattling cackle of the guinea fowl that anomalies under the frozen lake were discovered. The police had contacted me, telling me holes were cut into the ice at Shadowmoor Lodge, and numerous bodies were found beneath the surface of the lake. Rocks had weighed the bodies down, keeping them submerged under the water.

All of the spirits Joanna had sensed when she'd arrived were there, waiting to be found, encased in the ice. It turns out that before Charlotte Walker, there had been a vast number of women Stephen's dad abducted. Charlotte though, would be the last.

* * *

I shiver in the tainted space I'd once shared with Stephen. Although the bruises and scrapes have faded, Stephen's presence lingers, but I'm depositing my belongings into boxes. I'm moving. It's not the first time I've had to start over — but the difference is, this time I know I can do it. For myself, and for the little person growing inside me.

Trusting my gut is something I'm going to start doing more often now. It just goes to show that sometimes the inconvenient chaos life throws at you truly does happen for a reason, because while my own life did ultimately completely collapse, I saved someone else's life. But it's more than that. I won't admit it aloud, but when I pierced Marcel with those antlers, it felt no different than the thrill I feel when I shove a needle through a piece of material. I'd do it again, given the chance. I liked it. It felt like nothing I've ever experienced before. Raw, visceral power.

'Hey, you.' Charlotte smiles, rubbing a towel through her dark curls.

Charlotte's here, staying with me until she figures things out, escaping the crazy media frenzy back in the UK. We're both pregnant, both trying to work out our next chapter. The health care isn't as good here, but we've each heard our babies' heartbeats, that rhythmic gallop that had made us both cry.

'You both ready? Moving van's here,' Georgie calls, lifting one of the stacked boxes up into her arms.

I look around my old cottage, touching the brickwork I'd once fallen hopelessly in love with when I'd first viewed this property with Stephen, and we'd started our lives together.

'You'll be fine,' Rosie says, fingers grazing my shoulder. 'You always are.'

I turn to her and smile. 'Thank you,' I whisper.

I will be fine. I will start over. Maybe one day, I'll even date again, but for the first time, I don't actually want to. I just want to learn to be alone, and that in itself is pretty powerful.

Before I leave the cottage, I step into the bathroom. I stare at my reflection in the two-doored cabinet up against the wall. On the shelf, my engagement ring glints. There's still an indent in my ring finger from where it once lived. I touch the white gold band gently, the diamond scratching along the surface of the cabinet.

My fingers leave the ring, finding their way to my stomach. I slide them across my uterus, my thumb rubbing over the small bump starting to show. I wonder if the baby can feel it, sense it somehow. My love, my protection.

This child might be part James, but she's also part Cohen, and that's the part that matters, as I'm sure any mother with a child from an absent father will find. Everyone has two sides to them, two bloodlines, linking. But I'm severing that.

Perhaps Ingrid does deserve to know her grandchild — but I refuse to open myself back up to that world. Me and my child, a little girl according to the Window to the Womb scan, will never go back to Shadowmoor Lodge.

I do wonder sometimes if Ingrid is okay, if Freya is recovering from the gunshot wound that had saved my life. I think of Natalia, and Debbie, the women forever chained to the James men, who must live with the family secret unravelling on the news day after day. Do they feel ashamed, and wish they could have stopped this all sooner?

Charlotte Walker is always at the forefront of my mind too, and perhaps now she always will be. The woman who changed everything for me. Had I not seen Charlotte Walker in Marcel's car that morning, my life might be entirely different right now. Charlotte Walker caused the butterfly effect in my life.

Charlotte seems to be okay, traumatised certainly, but okay. She's moving forward, slowly. Telling her story to various media channels. There's a rumour it's being turned into some sort of Netflix true crime documentary, hearsay of a book deal, too. Good for her, I think. Every cloud has a silver lining and all that.

Rarely do we speak about what happened in England. Neither of us really need to dredge up those awful memories of the days spent at Shadowmoor Lodge.

I blink at my reflection, my eyes tracing every premature line now etched into my face, each telling a story of a hardship I've faced through the years. But I've overcome each and every one, and that's what each line really symbolises. Not the hardships, but my strength. There will be more, I'm sure of it — for someone like me, life has never come easy and I suspect it never will, especially now with a baby on the way. I'll continue to claw my way through the tough times, the way I always have, for myself, and now, for my daughter . . . my daughter who I will ensure never knows the family secret.

THE END

ACKNOWLEDGEMENTS

First and foremost, my thanks to the entire Joffe team for all that you do. For the work you put in, the belief you have in me and just how generally awesome you are.

To Tara Loder, freelance line-editor for your meticulous attention to detail as always, and Sharon Rutland for her eagle-eyed proofreading.

To Lorella Belli — when I got the news that Audible snapped up *The Wedding Lies* and *The Baby Group*, I actually screamed . . . and then popped the prosecco! What a dream come true!

To my husband for the many car journeys or meals spent deep in discussion about plot twist ideas — you're so supportive and I appreciate the time you give me to write my books, even if you do bank them so you can disappear into the garden for a couple of hours! But in all seriousness, I couldn't do this without you. Thank you, my love.

To my sons, Felix and Chester — you're just the most wonderful boys and generally so very easy, which makes writing my novels more doable, which I'm very grateful for. I'm so lucky to be your mummy.

To the many family and friends who have supported me with the publication of my novels, buying copies, leaving reviews and spreading the word — thank you for being so encouraging.

To The Book Party team, Victoria Hyde, A.J. West and of course the sweetest woman in the book world, Emily — coming to the 2025 summer party in Bristol and seeing my name and picture up with so many other incredible authors was such a surreal moment. I love what you guys do for this community and how you help make everyone feel included and special. Thank you.

To my tutors at The Open University (Tim Reeves, Sheila Moss and Sarah Ralph). Studying an English Literature and Creative Writing degree has been so beneficial for my writing and through your guidance I can see such a growth.

And as always, to my dad who passed too soon. You believed in me more than anyone from a tender age when I was always equipped with a notebook and pen. Thank you to you and to Mum for instilling in me the passion for literature. Miss and love you both. Mum's illness and Dad's death is a wound that can never be cauterised — I'm devastated that you weren't able to be here for all the big things in my life like getting married, having children, getting published . . . I can only hope you're watching from somewhere, and that I'm making you proud.

Lastly, to all of the readers around the world — thank you. None of this would be possible without you.

THE JOFFE BOOKS STORY

We began in 2014 when Jasper agreed to publish his mum's much-rejected romance novel and it became a bestseller.

Since then we've grown into the largest independent publisher in the UK. We're extremely proud to publish some of the very best writers in the world, including Joy Ellis, Faith Martin, Caro Ramsay, Helen Forrester, Simon Brett and Robert Goddard. Everyone at Joffe Books loves reading and we never forget that it all begins with the magic of an author telling a story.

We are proud to publish talented first-time authors, as well as established writers whose books we love introducing to a new generation of readers.

We won Trade Publisher of the Year at the Independent Publishing Awards in 2023 and Best Publisher Award in 2024 at the People's Book Prize. We have been shortlisted for Independent Publisher of the Year at the British Book Awards for the last five years, and were shortlisted for the Diversity and Inclusivity Award at the 2022 Independent Publishing Awards. In 2023 we were shortlisted for Publisher of the Year at the RNA Industry Awards, and in 2024 we were shortlisted at the CWA Daggers for the Best Crime and Mystery Publisher.

We built this company with your help, and we love to hear from you, so please email us about absolutely anything bookish at feedback@joffebooks.com.

If you want to receive free books every Friday and hear about all our new releases, join our mailing list here: www.joffebooks.com/freebooks.

And when you tell your friends about us, just remember: it's pronounced Joffe as in coffee or toffee!

Printed in Dunstable, United Kingdom

79702039R00163